*A Dead Hand*

## Books by Paul Theroux

### FICTION

Waldo

Fong and the Indians

Girls at Play

Murder in Mount Holly

Jungle Lovers

Sinning with Annie

Saint Jack

The Black House

The Family Arsenal

The Consul's File

A Christmas Card

Picture Palace

London Snow

World's End

The Mosquito Coast

The London Embassy

Half Moon Street

Doctor Slaughter

O-Zone

The White Man's Burden

My Secret History

Chicago Loop

Millroy the Magician

The Greenest Island

My Other Life

Kowloon Tong

Hotel Honolulu

The Stranger at the Palazzo d'Oro

Blinding Light

The Elephanta Suite

A Dead Hand

### CRITICISM

V. S. Naipaul

### NON-FICTION

The Great Railway Bazaar

The Old Patagonian Express

The Kingdom by the Sea

Sailing Through China

Sunrise with Seamonsters

The Imperial Way

Riding the Iron Rooster

To the Ends of the Earth

The Happy Isles of Oceania

The Pillars of Hercules

Sir Vidia's Shadow

Fresh Air Fiend

Nurse Wolf and Dr Sacks

Dark Star Safari

Ghost Train to the Eastern Star

# A Dead Hand

## A Crime in Calcutta

PAUL THEROUX

HAMISH HAMILTON
*an imprint of*
PENGUIN BOOKS

HAMISH HAMILTON

Published by the Penguin Group
Penguin Books Ltd, 80 Strand, London WC2R 0RL, England
Penguin Group (USA) Inc., 375 Hudson Street, New York, New York 10014, USA
Penguin Group (Canada), 90 Eglinton Avenue East, Suite 700, Toronto, Ontario, Canada M4P 2Y3
(a division of Pearson Penguin Canada Inc.)
Penguin Ireland, 25 St Stephen's Green, Dublin 2, Ireland (a division of Penguin Books Ltd)
Penguin Group (Australia), 250 Camberwell Road, Camberwell, Victoria 3124, Australia
(a division of Pearson Australia Group Pty Ltd)
Penguin Books India Pvt Ltd, 11 Community Centre, Panchsheel Park, New Delhi – 110 017, India
Penguin Group (NZ), 67 Apollo Drive, Rosedale, North Shore 0632, New Zealand
(a division of Pearson New Zealand Ltd)
Penguin Books (South Africa) (Pty) Ltd, 24 Sturdee Avenue,
Rosebank, Johannesburg 2196, South Africa

Penguin Books Ltd, Registered Offices: 80 Strand, London WC2R 0RL, England

www.penguin.com

First published 2009
1

Copyright © Paul Theroux, 2009

The moral right of the author has been asserted

The author is grateful for permission to reprint lines from the
poetry of Tishani Doshi, copyright © Tishani Doshi, 2006.

Set in Monotype Dante
Typeset by Rowland Phototypesetting Ltd, Bury St Edmunds, Suffolk
Printed in Great Britain by Clays Ltd, St Ives plc

A CIP catalogue record for this book is available from the British Library

HARDBACK ISBN: 978–0–241–14463–3
TRADE PAPERBACK ISBN: 978–0–241–14474–9

greenpenguin.co.uk

Penguin Books is committed to a sustainable future
for our business, our readers and our planet.
The book in your hands is made from paper
certified by the Forest Stewardship Council.

# Part One

# I

The envelope had no stamp and only my name underlined on the front; it had somehow found me in Calcutta. But this was India, where big pink foreigners were so obvious we didn't need addresses. Indians saw us even if we didn't see them. People talked grandly of the huge cities and the complexity, but India in its sprawl seemed to me less a country than a bloated village, a village of a billion, with village pieties and village pleasures and village peculiarities and village crimes.

A letter from a stranger can be an irritation or a drama. This one was on classy Indian handmade stationery, flecks of oatmeal in its weave and reddish threads like blood spatter, with assertive handwriting in purple ink. So I dramatized it, weighed it in my hand and knifed it open slowly, as though I were being watched. In populous Calcutta, city of deformities, my being watched was highly likely. But how did anyone know I was at the Hotel Hastings, east of Chowringhee, in an obscure lane off Sudder Street, in every sense buried alive?

I happened to be looking for a story, but Calcutta had started to creep on my skin, and I had even begun to describe how the feel of this city in its exhalations of decay in the months before the monsoon was like the itch you experience when you empty an overfull vacuum cleaner's dirt bag, packed with hot grit and dead hair and dust bunnies and dander, and you gag and scratch at the irritation and try to claw the tickle and stink off your face – one of my arresting openings.

As I was rereading the letter to see if it was authentic, a wasp began to swing in short arcs and butt the windowpane, seeing only daylight. I opened the window to release it, but instead of flying out it drowsed to another window and butted it – stupid! – then settled on my damp arm. I flicked at it. It made an orbit around my head and finally, though I'd tried to save it, did not fly out of the window but seemed to vanish somewhere in my room, where it would buzz and sting me in the night.

I remembered how my friend Howard at the American consulate had asked me the day before if I'd ever been married. I said, 'No, and I'm at that stage in my life when I no longer see a woman and say to myself, "Maybe she's the one for me."'

Pretty good answer, I thought. I was surprised at my own honesty. For years I had told plausible lies, saying that I was too busy with work, the travel pieces I wrote. I used to enjoy musing, 'Maybe she's the one.' But travel had absorbed me. It was so easy for a writer like me to put off the big decision – not a travel writer but a travelling writer, always on the move, always promising a book. I had disappointed two women back in the States and after I left I became one of those calculated enigmas, self-invented, pretending to be spiritual but ruthlessly worldly, full of bonhomie and travel advice, then giving people the slip when they got to know me too well or wanted more than I was willing to give. I no longer regretted the missed marriage, though I had a notion that I should have fathered a child. Now, too late, I was another evasive on-the-roader who spread himself thin, liking the temporary, the easy excuses, always protesting and moving on. *I have to be in Bangkok on Monday!* As if the matter was urgent and difficult. But Bangkok was a lovely hotel, beers with other complacent narcissists like me and a massage parlour, the best sex – hygienic and happy and anonymous, blameless relief.

*You're a nomad*, people said to me. It was partly true – if you know anything about nomads, you know they're not aimless. They are planners and savers, entirely predictable, keeping to well-established routes. I also had a nomad's sometimes startling receptivity to omens.

The day of the letter, for example, was eventful – strange portents, I thought. First the wasp, then the sight of a twisted paralytic child on Chowringhee creeping on hands and knees like a wounded animal, a new species of devolving human, reverting to all fours. And that afternoon my dancer friend, the willowy Parvati, revealing for the first time that she was adept in a kind of Indian martial art called *kalaripayatu* and 'I could break your arm, but I could also set it, because if one knows how to injure one must also know how to heal.' Parvati wrote sensual poems, she played the tabla, she wanted to write a novel, she wasn't married – and I was happy knowing her because I never asked, 'Maybe she's the one for me.'

That same day, my friend Howard at the American consulate told me about the children disappearing from the streets, kidnapped to work in brothels or sweatshops, or sold to strangers.

'And get this –' He knew an expat couple with a young child who could never find their amah at home. The amah explained, 'We walk in park.' The child was very calm when he was with the nanny and the nanny was upscale: gold bangles, an iPod, always presents for the kid. 'I saving money.' But one day on their way home at an odd hour in a distant neighbourhood the couple saw their nanny panhandling in traffic, another *bhikhiri* at an intersection, holding their infant son – a classic Bengali beggar, pathetic in her tenacity. And the child, who was drooling and dazed, was drugged with opium.

'Maybe you can use it,' Howard said, as people do with writers. Oddly enough, I just did, but it was the letter that changed everything. The letter was obviously from a woman, obviously wealthy.

Rich people never listen and that was why I preferred the woman's letter in my hand rather than having her bray into my face, one of those maddening and entrapping monologues: 'Wait. Let me finish!' I could read the letter in peace. Something about it told me that if the woman who wrote it had been with me, she would talk nonstop. And given the nature of the facts in the letter – a dead body in a cheap hotel room, a frightened guest, his fleeing, the mystery – I needed a clear head and silence and time to think. She was asking a favour. I could reach a wiser decision if I made my judgement on the basis of facts alone – the form of her appeal, her handwriting, the whole tone of the letter, rather than being attracted or repelled by the guilefulness of the woman herself, believing that the written word is more revealing than a face.

I knew she was rich from the gold-embossed Hindu symbol on the letterhead and the expensive paper. I knew she was an older woman from her handwriting alone – a younger person would have scribbled or sent me an email. Wealth was evident in her presumptuous and casual tone, even her slipshod grammar, the well-formed loops in her excellent penmanship. The envelope had been hand-delivered to me at my hotel.

'Post for you, sir,' Ramesh Datta, the desk clerk, said, handing it over. He too was impressed by the plumpness of the thing: a long letter, a big document, a sheaf of words, as though it represented witchery or wealth, an old-fashioned proposition.

Amazing most of all to be holding an actual three-page letter, written in purple ink on thick paper, like an artefact, and even the subject and the peripheral details were old-fashioned: a wealthy woman's wish, a corpse, a shocked hotel guest in Calcutta just after the Durga Puja festival.

*Dear Friend*, it began.

*I heard your marvelous talk last night at the American cultural center and wanted to come up afterwards to speak to you, but you were surrounded by admirers. Just as well. It's better to put this in writing, it's serious, and I'm not sure how you can help, but I've read your travel articles, so I know that you know quite a bit about the world and especially about India, which is my problem.*

You see what I mean about the grammar and the presumption?

*My son loves your writing and in a way you're responsible for his coming to India. I think he's read everything you've written. He has learned a lot from you and so have I. I have to admit I get a little jealous when he talks about you, but the truth is that the written word is so persuasive he feels as if he knows you, and I guess I do too. Consider yourself one of the family. We have read many of your travel pieces and shared them with our globe-trotting friends.*

6

*A little bit about me. I am an entrepreneur, with homes in New York and Palm Beach, and my hobby for many years was interior decoration – doing it for my friends. They encouraged me to start my business. Doing something you love is always a good way of being successful and I think it happened to me. My son joined me in the business. By the way, I have always felt that it would be a wonderful challenge to decorate a writer's studio – I'd love to do yours.*

*I come to India to oversee my charity, which is to do with children's welfare, and also to look for fabrics – linens, silks, fine cottons, floor coverings and textiles of all kinds, old and new. I often do walls in fabric, cover them with a lovely silk. It's become a signature with me. I am buying at the moment. I could show you some really exquisite pieces.*

*Now comes the hard part. First I need your utmost discretion. I am asking you to respect my confidence. I am writing to you because, based on your close relationship with the US consulate, I feel you can be trusted. It is also incredible luck that we are both in Calcutta at the same time, as though somehow preordained, our paths crossing like this. If it turns out that you have no interest in what I have to say next, please destroy this letter and do nothing more and – regretfully – I will never communicate with you again.*

*But I am counting on you to help me. Given your wide experience as a traveler, I don't think there is anyone else who could be as effective as you in this sensitive matter.*

*Here is the problem. My son's dearest friend, who is an Indian, believes he is in serious trouble. He normally stays with us, but because we were traveling and buying after Durga Puja he was staying at a guesthouse near Chowringhee, not a very nice place but you know what fleapits these little Indian hotels can be. He was there for a few days and then, like a scene from one of your stories, he woke up one night and found a corpse in his room – a dead boy on the floor. He was frantic. He had no idea how it had gotten there. He didn't know what to do. If he told the hotel they would accuse him of murder. How could he explain the presence of this dead body?*

*He then did a very silly thing, or at least he said he did. He packed his things and left without checking out, and he hid. Calcutta as you can imagine is not a hard place to hide in. I have spoken to him about this* but the fact is that he is terribly afraid of what will happen to him if he is found and somehow connected with that dead body.

Of course, I am also worried that my son will be associated with this business and my worst nightmare would be for my son to end up in an Indian jail.

We are planning to leave India at the monsoon, but first I want to make sure that my son's friend is safe. I could not live with myself if I abandoned this poor boy. I know I have the resources to help him and it would be criminal if I did not do so.

I have given you no names or dates or helpful facts. This is deliberate. I must use discretion. If you think you can help and want to know more, please get in touch with me at my cell phone number above and perhaps we can have a chat. Perhaps at the Oberoi Grand? Given the parameters of my problem, I would not blame you if you just tore up this letter and went your merry way. If that is so, thank you for reading this far. Bottom line, whatever you decide, my son and I will continue to read you.

Warmly,

Merrill Unger (Mrs)

# 2

Should I have burned the letter? I didn't. I kept it. I reread it. I was, as jokers say about wines, amused by its presumption.

Even with the boasting, the bad grammar, the clichés and that awful word 'parameters', I was flattered. The handmade paper, the letterhead, the handwriting, it all fascinated me. Had it been a man's letter, I might have tossed it aside. But it was from an American woman, with the lovely name Merrill, in Calcutta like me, offering me a story. And I was far from home with time on my hands, needing a story. My lectures were done: 'Your time is your own from now on,' Howard, the public affairs officer, said. It seemed like a hint that I should pursue Parvati. She was lovely and gifted, but her whole life lay ahead of her and mine was mainly in the past.

Yet it seemed that a little vacation had opened up, with the uncertainty and emptiness – and, I felt, pointlessness – of holidays, which in foreign places always left me at a loose end. Because the consulate had sponsored my talks at Calcutta schools and colleges, I had been looked after up until now. I didn't like the thought of having to fill my days with occasions. Why not have a drink with this Mrs Unger?

I was not persuaded by the letter; it seemed too colourful not to be a set-up. But I was curious. I had nothing else to do. This was a blank period in my trip and in my life. My hand had gone dead too; after that arresting opening about the atmosphere having the tickle and itch of a bulging vacuum cleaner bag, I could not continue. I'd thought I had something to write. I'd never had a dead hand before. I assumed that any day now the mood would strike me, but so far my head was empty. I endured the racket of the city from my cheap hotel and fantasized about places like the Oberoi Grand, and I smiled and didn't write and felt mind-blind.

At my age, after all that hack work, it was possible that my condition was permanent. The young feel an affliction but always assume they'll overcome it: a young person encounters an obstacle or a block yet never believes it can last, in fact cannot even imagine extinction or utter failure. I had felt that, but no longer felt the warmth of this hope. Now I knew that the climacteric occurs and there is no going back, you're losing it, it's downhill all the way. Your poor eyesight does not improve, there is no hope of your ever matching your earlier stride and you won't regrow that hair. For the writer I was, there was a chance that the barren period would continue, that I was written out, that I had nothing more, and worse, because the work I had done was not much good, I'd never have a chance to redeem myself. It was probably over.

This sense of diminishing hopes had been with me ever since I'd come to India, when Howard had asked, 'What are you working on?' I hadn't the heart to say 'Nothing.' I said, 'I've got an idea,' and that brought me low – my lying always made me sad and self-pitying. Why was I telling him a lie? Because the truth would have shamed me. Obviously having an idea mattered to me or else I wouldn't have concocted a lie. I was not fatally wounded; it was simpler and a lot less dramatic than that: I had nothing to say, or if I did have something, I had no way of saying it. 'Dead hand' was a devastating expression for writer's block, but in my case it seemed a true description of what I was facing, a limpness akin to an amputation.

One of my writer friends, a real writer, a writer of good novels, knew Nelson Algren, the great chronicler of Chicago. No one talks about him now, but his books were celebrated once, and electrifying to me. Just the sonorous titles – *The Man with the Golden Arm, A Walk on the Wild Side* – I heard these titles and thought he had to be a writer to his fingertips. Algren was a Chicagoan himself. He'd had an early and voluptuous success. He'd had an affair with Simone de Beauvoir, in effect making Jean-Paul Sartre a cuckold. He was a great gambler. He was a lone wolf. He'd had an enviable career. He lived simply in a small apartment, but even so he invited my friend and his wife to stay with him on their visit to Chicago.

On the first morning, seeing Algren sitting alone at his kitchen table having a cup of coffee, reading the newspaper, the wife said, 'Are you one of these writers who gets up early and does all his work before breakfast?'

Algren smiled sadly and said, 'Nope. I'm one of these writers who doesn't write any more.'

I dialled the number of Mrs Merrill Unger's cell phone.

'Mrs Unger's line.' A young man's voice, not Indian, but a bit put-on and over-formal, making me feel like a petitioner. 'Who is calling?'

I told him. He seemed even less interested and did not reply with a word, merely grunted.

'It's for you, Ma,' I heard him say.

'Good. You got my letter. When can we meet?'

Her first words – no greeting, all business, a bossy-sounding woman with a deep, ensnaring voice.

I said, 'I'm staying at the Hastings.'

'I have no idea where that is. Why don't you come over to the Oberoi Grand tonight? We can have a drink and go on from there.'

This was all too urgent and stern for me, much too insistent. I also felt – like a kind of echo – that she had an audience, some people listening to her auntyness, and that her tone was meant to impress them as much as to dominate me, taking charge and making me do all the work. The Hastings was a comfortable enough hotel; it was just snobbish posturing on her part to dismiss it.

Though I had nothing to do, I said, 'I'm pretty busy. Tonight's out of the question.'

'Tomorrow, then.' That same bossy, over-confident tone.

I almost said *Forget it*. 'I'll check my diary.'

'What are you waiting for? Check it, then.'

I didn't trust myself to say anything except 'I'm looking.'

'He's checking his diary,' I heard her say to her listeners, with a note (so I felt) of satire.

My diary was blank. I smiled as I looked at the empty pages and said, 'I'm not free until five,' and thinking she might be an even bigger bore than she sounded, I added, 'I might have something to do later.'

'Five, then. We'll be on the upstairs verandah.'

She hung up before I did, leaving me angry with myself for having weakened and called her. Looking again at the letter, I found it irritating, and I was further irritated by my own curiosity. I was sure I was wasting my time with this bossy old woman. She was not the first person who'd said to me, *I have a story for you.* In every case I replied, *This is a story you must write yourself. I can't help you. I'm sure you can do it justice.*

So I was breaking one of my own rules, giving in to this temptation. I told myself that her letter justified my interest. It didn't have the insubstantial scrappiness of an email. It was written in purple ink on heavy paper; it was old-fashioned and portentous. And I had nothing else to do.

Before I told them who I was and why I'd come, the staff at the Oberoi Grand seemed to know me: the saluting Sikh doorman, the flunky in a frock coat ushering me across the lobby to the colonnade lined with palms in big terracotta pots and more wel-comers – the smiling waitress in a blue sari, the man in white gloves holding a tray under his arm, who bowed and swept his arm aside in an indicating gesture, his glove pointed towards the far table where a woman sat like a queen on a wicker throne, a courtier on either side of her.

I was relieved that she was pretty and slim. I had thought she'd be big and plain, mannish and mocking and assertive. One of the young men was an Indian and for a moment I thought the woman was an Indian too – she wore a sari, her hair was dark and thick. But when I came closer and she greeted me, looking happy, I realized I was wrong. She was an attractive woman, younger than I'd imagined, much prettier than I'd expected, much better natured than she'd sounded in her letter or on the phone.

'At last,' the woman said. 'It's so wonderful to meet you. I'm thrilled. I'm so glad you came.'

She sounded as if she meant it. I thought, *She's nice*, and was reassured: it might be bearable.

And at that moment, as she smiled and held my hand and improved the drape of her sari by flinging a swag of it over her shoulder with her free hand, as Indian women did, I realized that she was not just attractive but extremely beautiful – queenly, motherly, even sexual, with a slowness and elasticity in her manner and movements, a kind of strength and grace. I did not feel this in my brain but rather in my body, as a tingling in my flesh.

'Please sit down. I thought you might not come. Oh, what a treat! What will you have to drink?'

The waiter was hovering.

'Beer. A Kingfisher,' I said.

'One more of these,' one of the young men said.

'I'm fine,' the other said – the Indian.

'My son, Chalmers.'

'Charlie,' he said. 'And this is my friend Rajat.'

'Should I have another drink?' Mrs Unger asked. 'I never know what I ought to do. Tell me.' She winked at me. 'They're in charge. I just take orders.'

'Go on, Ma,' Charlie said.

'It's only *jal*, water with a little cucumber juice,' she said. 'One more.' The waiter bowed. 'This is Sathya. He is far from home. He knows that I am far from home. Maybe that's why he's so kind to me. *Onek dhonnobad.*'

'*Dhonnobad, dhonnobad.* Kindness is yours, madam,' Sathya said. He was a gnome-like figure in a blue cummerbund, and round-shouldered with deference. He bowed again, then hurried off sideways, as though out of exaggerated respect.

'Ma babies him,' Charlie said. I was still turning 'Chalmers' over in my mind. 'He loves it.'

'I'm the one who's infantilized,' Mrs Unger said. 'That was the great mistake the British made in India. They thought they had the whip hand here. They were waited on hand and foot. They didn't notice that the servants were in charge. It took a while for

13

the servants to realize they had the power. And then the flunkeys simply revolted against these helpless sahibs.'

Rajat said, 'Our love–hate relationship with the British.'

'Why on earth would you love these second-rate people?'

'Institutions,' Rajat said. 'Education. Judiciary. Commerce.'

'India had those institutions when the British were running around naked on their muddy little island.'

'Road and rail system,' Rajat said, but ducking a little. He was a small, slightly built man in his twenties with fine bones and a compact way of sitting. 'Communications.'

'Self-serving, so they could keep India under their thumb,' Mrs Unger said. Seeing Sathya returning with a tray of drinks, she said, 'Ah!'

Sathya set down her glass of juice and our beer.

Charlie said, 'They make their own whisky. That's a great British institution.'

'When Morarji Desai was PM he closed down the breweries and distilleries. They turned to bottling spring water,' Rajat said.

'Desai had his own preferred drink,' Charlie said. 'A cup of his own piss every morning.' He stared at me. 'Did you know that, doll?'

'Chalmers is trying to shock you,' Mrs Unger said.

Rajat said, 'Some people think it has medicinal properties.'

'I am one of those people,' Mrs Unger said. 'I'm surprised Chalmers doesn't know that.'

'Ma is a true Ayurvedic. You won't believe the things she eats and drinks.'

'But I draw the line at tinkle, efficacious though it may be. I don't quite think my body is crying out for it.'

'Ma has healing hands.'

'Magic fingers for Ma,' Rajat said.

'I try,' Mrs Unger said. She lifted her slender hands and gazed at them in wonderment, as though seeing them for the first time.

She told me about her earliest visits to India, recalling cities and experiences, but because she didn't drop any dates I could not work out her age. Charlie was in his mid-twenties. I took her to be in her late forties – younger than me but forceful, assertive, more confident and worldly, so she seemed older. Charlie did not look like her at all. He was pale, beaky, floppy-haired, languid, his lopsided mouth set in a sneer.

She talked about her business – textiles and fabrics, being funny about how she was overcharged, lied to, and always having to bribe customs officials – while I looked closely at her and at her attentive son and his Indian friend.

Her opinionated humour and energy made her seem generous. She had a lovely creamy complexion, not just the smoothness of her skin but the shine, a glow of good health that was also an effect of the warm Calcutta evening, a stillness and humidity on the hotel verandah. That slight dampness and light in her face from the heat I found attractive, the way she patted her cheek with a lace hanky, the dampness at her lips, the suggestion of moist curls adhering to her forehead, the dew on her upper lip that she licked with one wipe of her tongue.

'I don't mind the heat,' she said. She seemed to know what I was thinking. 'In fact, I like it. I feel alive. Saris are made for this weather.'

She wore the sari well, the way it draped lightly – her bare arms, her bare belly, her thick hair in a bun. She had kicked off her sandals and I noticed that one of her bare feet was tattooed in henna with an elaborate floral pattern of dots.

She was a beautiful woman. I was happy to be sitting with her, flattered – as men often are – that a lovely woman was taking notice. The very fact of such a woman being pleasant and friendly made it seem she was bestowing a favour.

That was how I felt: favoured. I was relieved too. I had come here because of her urgent letter and now there was no urgency, just this radiant woman and the two young men.

Charlie said something about shipping a container to San Francisco.

'I don't want to think about shipping,' she said. 'Fill the whole container and then we'll talk about shipping.'

The Indian had gone silent, so I said, 'Do you live here?'

'For my sins, yes,' Rajat said. 'I live in Tollygunge. I'm good for about two weeks in America and then I start to freak out.'

'Poor Rajat, you're such a love.' Mrs Unger extended her arm as he was speaking and touched his shoulder, letting her hand slide to his arm, his side, her fingertips grazing his thigh, a gesture of grateful affection. And she smiled, more light on her face, the glow in her eyes too.

'I could spend the rest of my life in India,' Charlie said.

'But Calcutta is a powder keg,' Rajat said.

Mrs Unger said, 'Don't you love it when Indians use those words?'

'The city is toxic.' And I heard Mrs Unger murmur the word as *doxic*. 'When I was young,' Rajat went on, 'I had terrible skin. It was the sweat and dirt of Bengal. I'm from Burdwan, about two hours from here. My face was a mess. My father got a job teaching in Calcutta and as soon as I got here my skin cleared up.'

'You were going through adolescence.'

'I was ten!' he shrieked. 'I hate dirt. The last time I was in America my skin broke out.'

'What you needed was a salt scrub and some pure food. Your mother should have known better. I'll take care of you.'

'My poor mother,' Rajat said. 'All she did was fuss around my father and try to please him. He was a typical spoiled Indian man who couldn't do anything.'

'And you're not?'

'Obviously I am living my own life in my own fashion,' Rajat said. He spoke a bit too loudly in a broad accent, too assertively, and then in his echo in a broader accent.

Merrill Unger said, 'I never had that problem with Ralph Unger.'

'Ma had him killed,' Charlie said.

Mrs Unger smiled and said, 'It was not of my doing. He simply popped off. There is justice in all events.'

'But he thought Ma was poisoning him.'

'He had a rich imagination,' Mrs Unger said. 'His great fault was that he was an Anglophile. That's why he hated India. But he couldn't live in England either – Anglophiles never can. He sat around complaining that the empire was finished.'

'I think I might have liked him,' Rajat said.

'You are a deluded and perverse young man,' Mrs Unger said with a smile, and I noticed that sarcasm always brought out her brightest smile. 'Ralph's other fault was his diet. Know-it-alls and bullies eat so badly. He was a big carnivorous lout, a rather sad man really, if you looked at him objectively, something I never did. I watched him eat himself to death. Is that insensitive? He never listened to me. He thought I was frivolous and faddish. He didn't realize that he could have saved himself.' She leaned over to look at my eyes, my whole face. 'Most people don't realize it.'

'I try to be a vegetarian here,' I said, feeling that a reply was expected of me.

'It's way beyond that. Have you seen an Ayurvedic doctor and had a thorough check-up?'

'I've been pretty busy.'

'I keep forgetting you're a celebrated writer.'

'Just articles. I keep meaning to write a book.'

'You need creative energy for that. Have you done anything about your *kundalini*?'

Charlie said, 'Isn't Mother a doll?'

Rajat shook himself in his chair like a shivering girl, seeming to giggle with his body, and said, 'I'm one of those people who does all his reading on the Internet. But I've seen your magazine articles all over Charlie's flat.'

'You don't know what you're missing,' Mrs Unger said to Rajat, so firmly as to sound like a reprimand. She turned to me. 'I've learned so much from you. I'm so grateful.'

'Very kind of you to say so.'

She said, 'If only I could give something back to you. I'd be so happy.'

'This is enough,' I said. 'Sitting and talking like this. If I hadn't met you, I'd probably have just stayed in my room, read a little and gone to bed early.'

They stared at me as though I were being insincere and my

statement hanging in this silence began to droop the way exaggerations do.

'But I thought there was another reason for my being here,' I said.

As I spoke, Mrs Unger seemed to swell – to straighten, anyway – and Rajat to shrink. In growing smaller he became darker, more distinct and brittle and conspicuous. All the while a kind of suppressed and silent hilarity trembled through the three of them, a tension, as just before someone breaks out laughing in intense and mirthless embarrassment. As Rajat's face tightened, his knees together, the shrinking man twisting his hands, Charlie looked bored and slack. He stuck his legs out so they touched the table and jarred the pot of flowers and a carafe of water.

'Do you want to tell him,' Mrs Unger said, 'or shall I?'

Rajat twitched a little, as if at a spectral buzzing around his head, then said in a thin voice, 'Go ahead.'

'Rajat believes he has a little problem,' she said in a soothing tone.

'Not so little,' Rajat said in a whisper, clutching his knees.

'May I continue?' Mrs Unger said, smiling her severe smile. She went on in a breathy, actressy way that was just short of satire. 'Rajat had an unfortunate experience and as a result he did a very silly thing. Am I right?'

He nodded and looked at his hands, his fingers crooked around his bony knees. Charlie reached over to pat his shoulder, as Mrs Unger had done earlier.

'What was the unfortunate experience?' I asked, though I remembered some details from the letter and the words *dead boy on the floor*.

'He found something in his room, didn't you, love?'

'Found it?'

'It turned up in the night,' he said.

'You woke up and there it was?'

He rotated his head in the Indian way, meaning yes, biting his lip, looking fearful.

'Tell him what it was,' Mrs Unger said.

Rajat moistened his lips and said, 'Body.'

The word *bhodee* spoken by this Indian sounded sacred and awesome in its density, like a slab of terrifying meat.

'What was the silly thing you did?' I asked.

'He ran away,' Mrs Unger said and then quickly, in a practical voice, 'I don't blame him. I would have done the same myself. And I would have found myself in the same position Rajat is in right now.' She smiled at him. 'In a pickle.'

Rajat covered his face with his hands, his skinny fingers over his eyes.

'Where did this happen?'

'Right here. Calcutta. In a hotel. A very cheap hotel, I'm afraid,' Mrs Unger said.

'It's clean, anyway,' Rajat said.

'Except for the corpses that now and then turn up.'

'Ma, please,' Charlie said.

Rajat clasped his cheeks and looked as if he might cry.

'I'm stating a fact.'

'Did you report it to the police?' I asked.

'We don't trust the police,' Mrs Unger said. 'Can you imagine how one would be compromised? I mean, if the story were true.'

'I could tell you stories, doll,' Charlie said to me.

'Look at him, poor boy,' Mrs Unger said. 'He doesn't know what to do.'

Anxious and compact in his misery, Rajat sat looking glassy-eyed, almost tearful.

'Was it anyone you knew?' I asked, not knowing where to go with this.

'I never thought to ask that question,' Mrs Unger said. 'You see? I knew you'd be a shrewd judge of this business.'

But it seemed the wrong question. Rajat began to stifle a sob and then he let go, covering his face again and weeping into his hands.

The show of emotion, his red eyes brimming with tears in this public place, unnerved me. I said, 'How can I help?'

'You see? I felt sure he'd be willing,' Mrs Unger said.

'I have no idea what to do,' I said.

'Take an interest, as you would a situation in one of your marvellous stories,' she said. 'The important thing is that this must not be linked to poor Rajat.'

'Don't you think the best thing would be simply to let the whole matter go away? I mean, just forget it ever happened?'

She smiled again and I realized that the only times she smiled were when she was being sarcastic or disagreed with something that was said. Her smile threw me at first, since it indicated the opposite of what she was saying; but as soon as I got used to it I was charmed. She had a beautiful smile.

'Someone knows,' she said. 'More than one person, most likely. They have something on poor Rajat. He is open to blackmail. He has already suffered crank telephone calls.'

'What did they say?' I asked her, but she inclined towards Rajat.

'Nothing,' he said. He swallowed, his eyes widening. 'Just rang off.'

'Maybe wrong numbers.'

Mrs Unger beamed one of her brightest, most contrary smiles.

'I wouldn't know where to begin,' I said.

'Let's drop it,' she said. 'You're being honest. That means a lot to me. We shouldn't burden you with this sordid business.'

'I wish I could help.'

'You've listened. Your sympathy is an enormous reassurance. And I think it helps that we've been able to talk about it.'

I said, 'It might be better if you didn't say anything.'

She smiled her disagreeing smile and said, 'Shall we drop it?'

Sathya the waiter stepped into that silence. 'Fresh drinks?'

As so often happens, the waiter's appearance to take an order became the occasion for Rajat and Charlie to get up and say they had to go.

Mrs Unger just watched them with her pale, indifferent eyes. She didn't (as I expected her to) urge them to stay. She said, 'Please do be careful, Chalmers.'

'He is knowing his way around,' Rajat said.

She smiled at that and as soon as they were gone, her manner became more relaxed, less formal, less motherly, less queenly – all

20

the qualities I now recognized because they were absent. People can seem a bit deflated when they're grateful and frank – she did. She said, 'I really mean it. I've learned so much from your writing. I'd love somehow to be able to pay you back for all the pleasure you've given me.'

I almost said, *I've come to Calcutta to write a story but I have nothing to write. Give me something.* But I said, 'Don't even think about it.'

'But you see, I have something specific in mind.'

I said nothing, merely tried to imitate the indifferent glance she had given her son and Rajat.

'Does Chalmers look healthy to you?'

'In the pink,' I said. It was true – he was tall, not thin but slender, with a blushy unsunned face and long light hair swept back, and even his languid way of sitting suggested contentment and good health. Although he did not physically resemble his mother, his disposition matched hers: all-seeing, finding a severe humour in the strain of India.

'In the pink because Ma knows best,' she said. 'Let me take you to dinner. It's not healthy to eat late. I know just the place. It will be the first step.'

I said yes. I was glad that Charlie and Rajat were gone. Now I could give all my attention to Mrs Unger. I liked the sudden change in her, from motherly to mildly flirtatious, while still making all the moves.

'Don't be shocked,' she said in the taxi. 'Foreigners are always being shocked in India for the wrong reasons. Of course it's dirty here. Of course people are poor and the traffic is atrocious. And of course the restaurant we're going to is very humble. But the food is pure.'

I had been all over India and I knew Calcutta a little, but even so I might have been shocked at the restaurant if she had not said that in the taxi. I did not recognize it as a restaurant. It was a ground-level room, with a verandah open to the street and the crowd, just above a storm drain. Four bare tables, no other people. A man in a gauzy white dhoti with the caste marks of a priest raised his arms and clasped his hands in welcome – some obscure tattoos on his wrists.

'Madam, madam.' He showed respect without servility as Mrs Unger swept past him and sat at one of the tables, as though she were entering the Four Seasons rather than this room filled with the noise and the smells of the Calcutta back street.

'I hope we're not too late.'

'Never too late.'

'This is my friend. He's a famous writer.'

'Welcome, sir.'

I sat opposite Mrs Unger. A barefoot boy in shorts and a white shirt approached carrying a basin and a pitcher. Mrs Unger washed her hands in the basin, the boy pouring water over them, and following her example, I did the same.

'There's no menu,' she said. 'This is really a private home. We'll have whatever his wife prepares. But I assure you it will be good for you.'

Very soon, the old priestly-looking man in the dhoti stood near our table as a girl set down a tray of dishes and arranged them before us: bowls of lentils and mushy peas, bowls of cooked gluey okra and deep-green spinach-like leaves, a stainless steel tureen of thin soup with a fragrant aroma, a mound of brown rice on a plate. Glasses of *nimbu pani*, lime water. That was all. The old man gestured over it and then scuffed away.

'This is what you need. Clean food.'

I spooned some of the okra and spinach and rice on to my plate and tasted. Its bland and earthen hum lingered in my nose. I wondered how much of it I'd be able to force myself to eat.

'I'm surprised. No spices.'

'Ayurvedic. Most Indians eat far too many spices. Too much garlic and onion, tons of salt, way too much ghee butter and oil. They love sweets – they're like children. Did you see that man? He does two hours of yoga every morning. But most Indians get no exercise at all. Probably the unhealthiest people in the world.'

I was staring, because she was eating delicately but with gusto and because she seemed so sure of herself.

'Really?'

'Yes. They have all the answers, but they just ignore them. This is an Indian meal, yet how many Indians eat it regularly? They eat junk and rich food, or else they're starving and hardly eat at all. Have you ever seen people so unhealthy? I don't mean poor Indians. The poor eat better than the rich ones. Poor Indians eat lentils and roti and rice and green vegetables. The rich eat butter and sweets. Look at the shapes of Indians – the rich man's belly, the rich woman's butt. They get no exercise, they play no sports.'

'Cricket,' I said.

'That's not a sport. It's a game that hardly requires fitness. Apart from the man that throws the ball, it's mostly standing around. You never see an Indian kicking a ball or running. Punjabis are tall. But where are the basketball players? Where are the marathoners? Over a billion people and they can't win an Olympic medal.'

'I did a story on this once. They average about one medal in each Olympics.'

'One!' she screamed. 'In what sport?'

'Shooting an air rifle.'

'That's my point! You can be a fat air-rifle shooter!' This fact delighted her. 'They are weirdly shaped, either stuffed or skinny. Is it sexual? I sometimes think so. Of course, Indian girls can look heart-breakingly beautiful, but the women look fat and frustrated, the men look angry, the boys look wretched and onanistic. The eternal question for an Indian traveller is "Where will we eat?"'

'Americans say the same thing.'

'I know. Americans are fat too, not from frustration but from excess. The poor are fat in America. The rich are thin. It's the awful food there. Not like this.'

She was chewing as she spoke, as though to prove her point. 'This is so pure. I can see by your slightly puffy eyes that you don't have good kidney function. But after you get a thorough check-up, establish your body type and your chakras, you'll be on the right path.'

'You're taking me by the hand, I see.'

'It'll do you good. Each of these dishes has value and balance.'

I swallowed, trying to convince myself, and said, 'I see.'

'It's almost sacramental, eating like this. Think of your body.'

Her saying that made me conscious of her lovely body, her hand dipping into the rice, making a ball of it, dipping it into the lentils. Thomas Metcalfe, of the Governor General's office, could not bear to see a woman eat cheese. I guessed it was not disgust, but probably aroused something within him. Sitting with Mrs Unger I realized I loved to watch a pretty woman eat, especially messy food, her trying to be dainty over it and failing, the flecks of food on her lips, the chewing, the neck sinews tightening with a swallow. I could see more: Mrs Unger's stomach muscles framed by the bodice of her sari and her wraparound. The pleasure of her eating was also the pleasure I took in admiring her good health. She sat upright with strength and grace, using her fingertips on the rice, the dripping okra, the mushy peas. And I was aroused by the small splash of food on her lower lip, her lapping at it like a cat, making the lip gleam.

'I assure you that tonight you'll sleep like a baby.'

The old man came over to make sure we had everything we wanted. He chatted cosily but with respect to Mrs Unger. He directed the girl to refill our glasses of lime water. I struggled to eat a believable portion; the tang of soil lingered on the unsalted, spiceless food.

When the old man had gone, she said, 'Do you get regular massages?'

'I wish I did.'

'That's what you need.'

All this time I had feared that she would ask me again about what she mentioned in her letter, the body in the hotel room, Rajat's worry, the danger for him. But she said nothing more about the letter, which when I had received it seemed so urgent.

'You should have a massage. I know just the place.'

She fluttered her fingers in a bowl of water and, as she did so, the Indian girl appeared behind her with a towel. After drying her hands, Mrs Unger took a pen and pad out of her bag and wrote down a name. The purple ink and her loopy handwriting reminded me of her letter.

'Morning is best. Have a light breakfast. Be at this place at ten.'

As she gave me the piece of paper, I laughed, because she was bossy in such an appealing way, mothering me with concern and care.

She said, 'I hope your friends won't mind my taking charge of you.'

This seemed to me an odd remark, at once full of confidence, presuming on me. Yet her assurance made me wary. Confident-seeming women often made encumbering statements like this when deep down they were uncertain, the sort of over-familiar bluster that was easily punctured by a sharp reply.

Instead of embarrassing her by game-playing, I said, as politely as I could, 'I wish I knew which friends you mean.'

I wasn't offended. I was in Calcutta, living by my wits. I was seriously interested in which people she might mean. But even my polite response made her shy, as though I'd been blunt.

'The folks on Ho Chi Minh Sarani, maybe.'

That made no sense to me and I couldn't help smiling. Yet she was smiling back at me in a kind of challenging suggestion that she knew more than I'd guessed.

'Where's that?'

'The American consulate.'

'Is that the name of that blocked-off street?'

'You must have been there many times, you're so popular.'

'Yes, but someone else was doing the driving,' I said.

'That's the mixed blessing of being in Calcutta. Someone else is always doing the driving.'

The ambiguity of this made me pause. I didn't have a reply to it, though I knew I'd remember it. I said, 'So that's how you knew where to find me with your letter.'

I felt obvious and fooled with the conceit that I'd attributed it to my high visibility as a big pink *ferringhi*. But she dodged that – this had become a fencing match – and said, 'I don't have much to do with those people. But I know how greatly they value you.'

'Really?' I said, mildly surprised because I'd never been convinced that Howard took me seriously as a writer. He liked my availability and that I was willing to give pep talks at colleges at short notice, a volunteer speaker, glad for the *per diem*, who was not terrified by Calcutta, helping him do his job.

'Oh, yes,' Mrs Unger said. 'They're big fans. You know that Indians are very suspicious of the Americans that come out here, especially the ones sponsored by the US government. They have a long history of being patronized. The consulate regards you as a friend who won't let them down.'

'And what do they think of you?'

'I don't exist for them. But I'm glad you do. I'm glad your writing means something to them.'

Once again I wanted to say: I have no writing, I have a dead hand, I am out of stories, I have stopped believing. And maybe it will never happen. I didn't have much to write about at the best of times, and now it's done. But I had also thought, when I'd reflected on my dead hand: a writer without an idea, without the will or the energy to write, is someone in need of a friend.

Nelson Algren had had friends, cronies, gambling pals, drinking buddies, and though he wrote nothing in his last years, he'd had companions. William Styron did not write anything in the last fifteen years of his life. His dead hand hadn't hastened his death; it had made him immensely gloomy, paranoid and impatient, long-ing to write yet incapable of it. But he had been surrounded by a doting family and a loving wife. I had no writing, I had no one, I was alone with my dead hand.

So I said, 'I'll be there.' Then I said, 'Shall I call you Merrill?'

'Call me Ma.' And she looked closely at me. 'Everyone does.'

It was a word that had always made me uncomfortable, so I resisted saying it, yet I allowed myself to be swept up. And it was all unexpected, which was why it was so pleasant: the drink, the meal and now this appointment for a massage.

I wondered if I looked idle to agree to so much at short notice. I hoped she understood that I was interested in her, even if I was bewildered by the story of the corpse in the hotel room. I was glad to have found her and it seemed – I was sure of this – I was making her happy too. She had praised my work; she knew I had friends at the consulate. She seemed glad I had come. You go away to be anonymous, but sometimes the opposite happens: you excite interest, even in big, villagey India, in the stew of Calcutta.

# 3

Over breakfast the next morning on the verandah of my hotel, the Hastings, conscious that I was eating what she'd instructed me to order – a little yogurt, green tea, a slice of mango, a handful of unsalted almonds – I mentally reviewed the meeting with Mrs Unger, or Ma, as I now thought of her. I was grateful to her for giving me something to do in Calcutta, to take my mind off my writing failure and my idleness. I had dreaded being stumped, having to sit in the heat over a blank page. I could not force out a story and the few words I had written rang false.

Trivial as it was, the appointment she'd made for me had given me a purpose, a destination for the day. I could have called Howard at the consulate, but he had a real job and obligations. I could have met Parvati for tea, providing she was in the company of some of her friends; it was considered indecent for a man like me to meet a virginal Hindu like her alone. She was gifted, her whole life ahead of her as a dancer, a poet, a practitioner of Indian martial arts. I wished her well, but I knew that not much would change in my life. Old age was not an accumulation of thought and experience but rather the reverse: by writing of my most vivid experiences I had disposed of them. Old age for me was an emptying of the mind.

Old age for me was also a narrowing of possibilities and maybe (as I was beginning to think) a slow dying, parts of the body becoming useless – my empty head, my dead hand. What body part next?

Calcutta was the perfect place to feel like a physical wreck or a failure. Virtually everyone else was much worse off than I was. Maybe that was why I had lingered after my work was done, though I hadn't made anything of my experience in the city. Had I not met Ma the day before, I would have spent the day walking as though in a hot-weather stupor, window-shopping, museum-going or heading to Howrah station and considering the outbound trains. I had thought of leaving but, having met Ma, I was curious and sentimental and dog-like, sniffing at the memory of meeting her and hoping to see her again.

And sitting on the Hastings verandah, the sun dazzling in the slats of the shutters, I remembered more of what she had said at the Oberoi – more than what I have already written. The talk of the British Empire and her Anglophile late husband had led her to talk about the English in general and the royal family in particular.

'They love royalty here too. The British spend half their time lying to themselves about their dysfunctional country. The Indians do the same. I'm not surprised they find common ground. "We love pageantry," the British say as they hide behind the flags and the funny-looking hats. And Queenie's the head of the Church, the Defender of the Faith – it says so on the money. But look at her. Have you ever heard anything so ridiculous? She's a gilded crock, a posturing old dear who regards Britain as her personal property. Imagine finding spirituality in this little old lady. It's like finding spirituality in a skinny cow, which Indians do.'

'If you want to be worshipped, go to India and moo. Isn't that what they say?'

But she wasn't listening. She was saying, 'I think the Indians easily came to admire Queen Victoria because she was the super-queen, the Rajmata. Indians believe in hierarchies and the British model came ready-made, as a big unifying social contraption.'

She was speaking slowly but intensely, with the kind of fluency that made me think she'd recited this denunciation many times before, because it was a speech rather than a conversation, and whatever I said was an interruption.

'India's dirty little secret is that they dislike each other and are untrusting. The British are the same – English especially. Can't bear each other. Never talk. Don't even say hello. That's why they're so happy in America, because we believe this fictional version of themselves. They hate their lives. They can only be happy by promoting the myth of the terribly British and that's only possible overseas, in faraway places like India. Indians have bamboozled Americans too. "We don't eat animals." Most of them do! "We are spiritual, madam." They worship money!'

'It's true,' Rajat had said. 'We are so materialistical.'

'I suppose it's a commonplace to regard the British royal family as social upstarts.'

'I never heard that before,' Rajat had said.

'The royal family is bourgeois – if anything, they're lower-middle class but with insane pretensions. Prince Philip used to complain to newspaper reporters that he had no money, that he couldn't afford to keep polo ponies, that Buckingham Palace got horrible aircraft noise. That's typically shabby. "We just don't have the money!" "We're stuck here in this rackety house!"'

And then: 'They get all sorts of freebies, you know. They ask for them. The Duchess of Whimsy goes to New York and stays free at a hotel with her whole parasitical entourage. She does the same in India and it's even worse because the Raj still exists in the mind of the British royal family. Before any of these royals leaves London, she has her lady-in-waiting send a memo detailing how many rooms she'll need, usually four or five suites, how many other people have to be accommodated, all the meals she'll want and the pick-up times at the airport for the hotel limos. A list of demands, you see. At the end of her freebie she agrees to appear at a cocktail party and to have her picture taken. No money changes hands. It's all grace and favour.'

I had not known this. I was impressed and slightly shocked by her version of a royal visit. I took out my almost blank notebook and wrote down what Ma had said.

'Hotels in New York compete to host the British royals and take tea with them. It makes me ashamed to be an American. My late mother-in-law was English. She adored the royals, the Queen especially, that perfectly hideous woman. Isn't it ghastly?'

The *Isn't it ghastly?* I found especially interesting. Whenever Americans denounced the British they always did it with a mimicky British turn of phrase: *Take tea with them, Perfectly hideous, Quite disgusting* or the one word, *ghastly*.

'It's even worse in India. Faded maharajahs and scruffy English aristocrats slobbering over each other and lamenting the loss of the Raj. It's absolutely frightful.'

Charlie had said to me, 'You shouldn't have gotten Ma on this subject.'

But I hadn't. I had only listened and nodded, and she still went on snapping away at it.

'What a pathetic family – and it's all there in full view, the whole sorry lot of them. You think less of the British just looking at them.'

'But they are beneficial for tourism,' Rajat said. 'Like our maharajahs, faded though they may be.'

'Have you ever seen anything that was good for tourism that wasn't a complete blight for everyone else? Here, I think of those superfluous maharajahs, chain-smoking and drinking whisky,' Ma said. 'In America it's Disneyland. Golf courses. Gambling casinos. Strip clubs. Nothing artistic. The monarchy – all monarchies – are a confidence trick. All they do is diminish people. Yes, I agree, probably good for tourism, like a freak show. But if Queenie was really a freak I'd probably like her a little. She's not. People make excuses for her. "She works jolly hard." You know who works jolly hard? Not the greedy Queen, not you or me, but those sweepers out there in Chowringhee. The real aristocrats of the world are the native peoples, the so-called tribals in India, the Mizos, the Nagas in Assam.'

'Tell him your vow, Ma,' Charlie said.

Ma straightened and said, 'I refuse to read about the royals. If there's a story about Queenie's dogs or her children's foolish marriages – have you ever seen so many divorces in a holy family? – anything related to the royals, I turn the page. The headline "Prince Charles in Skiing Accident" has me thrusting the paper aside. I change channels when they're on the telly.'

What was strange about this was that Ma had the vaguely provincial English accent that well-educated Americans sometimes have and, as I mentioned, a put-on English turn of phrase. The words 'thrusting' and 'telly', and 'artistic', which she'd pronounced *autistic*.

'They are a decaying family,' she said. 'You can see it in their

faces. Inbred, lifeless people without a point or purpose. I understand why royals are never jailed, why – when the time comes
– they are lined up and shot.'

'Mother upsets her London friends,' Charlie said, his face
gleaming in admiration.

'Because I speak the truth. I daresay, most of the British royal
family are Germans.'

While I smiled at 'I daresay', Rajat laughed. He shrieked,
'Germans!' Then he said, 'Indians are just as false. Sonia Gandhi is
Italian.'

I pushed my breakfast aside and continued to write this down,
delighted to have something for my notebook, glad to have something to do today. And when I was done I took the envelope that
I had tucked into the pages. I opened the letter again and glanced
through it. *I come to India to oversee my charity*. What did that mean?
And what of the rest, the intrigue at the hotel? I tried to recall
whether she had mentioned it over dinner. I remembered more
of her rant about the royal family (a detail related to their TV
watching), but very little about the letter, which was the reason I'd
gone there in the first place. I wrote all that I remembered: *Shall we
drop it?* She tended to the theatrical, but I loved her confidence, a
certainty that enhanced her beauty.

I was glad to be relieved of the obligation to solve the crime.
And the simple breakfast gave me a feeling of well-being. I lingered
on the verandah reading the *Statesman*, with my feet on a hassock.
The tang of spices from the shop next door to the Hastings, the
rattle and beep of cars jostling with pedicabs on the back lanes,
the babble of human voices, mostly hawkers; the sense of life
being lived outdoors, the city exposed. Ma had said she'd come to
Calcutta for Durga Puja, but that had been months before, and this
midwinter weather was perfect – warm days, chilly nights, an
aroma of woodsmoke and burning charcoal in the city.

I resisted writing what I could barely put into words, that I'd met
someone I liked, who seemed to know my mind, whom I'd hoped
to go on knowing. A rare feeling in life, that one has made a friend.
I am not thinking of a love affair, although that is the extreme

example of such a feeling. I mean the desire to see a person again, the curiosity, the sense most of all that the person is a generous and vitalizing force – that I will be happier and stronger because of this friendship.

She had made me no promises. She'd said only, 'Go to this spa' – had she said 'spa'? – 'you'll be glad you did.' And I concluded that if I did it, obeying her, she would be pleased and want to see me again. She'd want to know how I liked it. She'd want to say, 'See? I was right. You're glad you went.'

She wanted to be right. I wanted to report to her that she'd been right. I wanted to obey her. And, as on previous occasions in my life, I thought, not in words but in rising wavelets of feeling, like promises of health: *If I don't see her again I'll be very disappointed.* This eagerness, like a schoolboy crush, made me feel young and happy and a little silly. Out of the chaos and noise of Calcutta, the rejection, the indifference of the Indian mob, I'd found a purpose and someone to like.

I had made up my mind that she was exceptional – generous, motherly, flirtatious, kind, out of the ordinary. She seemed to know me. She seemed to care for me. And she was attractive. Ever since leaving her at the little restaurant – we left separately in taxis – I had begun to miss her.

All this was out of character for me. I am by nature suspicious and solitary, an eavesdropper not a buttonholer. The rich don't interest me, and for the rich, usually, people without money are of little account. I hate the way the rich cut corners. I can't stand their timidity. I hate their whining about the high cost of living or how little money they have, for the indirection of the rich is their incessant howl that they're poor.

But the new emotions in me, a nostalgia for attachment, made me feel better. I had the sense of unfamiliar sentiments being uncovered in me, like discovering a taste for a certain wine or a forgiveness for an old slight. I was thrilled to feel something new. It was knowledge, a surprise, and I was grateful because it came with a distinct optimism. Something new might be something to write about, another reason not to feel old.

33

'Your car is here, sir.'

I looked up and saw the desk clerk, Ramesh Datta. What car? I hadn't ordered a car. I was reminded of the suddenness of the letter he'd brought me. I looked beyond the verandah and there it was, a black Ambassador with yellow curtains, an Indian in a white uniform standing next to it, awaiting orders. I hurried downstairs.

'You're looking for me?'

The man in uniform made a wing-flap of his arm and gave me a little salute. 'Transport to Lodge, sir.'

Another surprise, more pleasure, life becoming easier, the sort of thing one hopes for in India, usually in vain.

'My appointment's not until ten.'

'I will wait, sir, and proceed at your pleasure.'

'I appreciate that.'

'Therefore I will bide my time,' he said. 'Cool heels.'

That was another thing about India: the huge number of people whose job it was to stand and wait for those few who kept them waiting. Most were drivers, idle beside the car until the owner flashed into view and made an impatient gesture. But they were also door openers, secretaries, personal assistants, cooks, reception-ists, every conceivable job description reduced to the level of flunkey.

In my month of giving lectures in and around Calcutta I'd had to wait for people to show up – the sponsor, the audience, the person introducing me. And now I was someone for whom a flunkey waited. This role did not suit me; it made me feel conspicuous and anxious, but I told myself that I had not asked for the car and driver.

'Who sent you?'

'Ma.'

In all Indian legends, in every ancient narrative, the god or goddess has a vehicle. For Durga it is a lion, for Vishnu the eagle Garuda, for Shiva the bull. In this odd-looking pantheon Ganesh, the elephant god, rides on a mouse, Kali on a demon corpse. Ma had an Ambassador Nova with stringy curtains.

Chauffeur-driven cars rarely arrived at the Hotel Hastings, and when they did, they never lingered. For the first time since checking in I became an object of interest, not whispers but earnest glances. The staff seemed relieved. If I happened to be someone of substance, I might be a tipper. The ability to provide *baksheesh* was the principal determiner of a person's worth in India.

That chimed with the feeling within me that had surfaced this morning – that I was someone else today, not perhaps a whole new person but an aspect that had been slumbering inside me had been awakened, someone new to me. This smiling creature was sitting up and wagging his tail, open-mouthed and eager.

Still with a twitch of obligation, a sense that I wanted to please Ma, I put down my newspaper and went out to the car that was parked in the lane next to the hotel.

'You know where we're going?'

'Lodge, sir.'

'What's your name?'

'Balraj, sir. Thank you, sir.'

He swung open the door for me, then took his place at the wheel, jamming his peaked cap more firmly on his head. We were soon lost in traffic. I had not recognized the name of the spa. I'd planned to show it to a taxi driver. I had a general idea of the main streets, but Balraj took side streets, back lanes and alleys, jostling with bicycles, auto-rickshaws and now and then hand-pulled rickshaws – as though wheeled off the pages of a Victorian print of old Calcutta, every detail intact. Barrows too, the ancient kind: I saw hairy legs and thick wooden spokes in wooden wheels. When the car slowed down, people peered in the window at me, their faces pressed against the glass.

'Not far, sir.'

I had not said a word. Balraj had the driver's instinct for a passenger's anxiety, but I presumed that his reassurance was also his way of bucking for a tip.

The lanes were becoming narrower, the car slowing to fit through them, but at the point where I expected Balraj to speed up and pull away from a high wall of cracked stucco, he swung the car sharply and, as he did, an iron gate with rusty spikes suddenly opened and Balraj drove between a pair of flaking whitewashed pillars. A man rushed forward to open my door.

'Where are we?'

'Lodge, sir.'

An old three-storey plaster and brick villa, modified mock-Georgian, Indian-style, with porches, fluted columns, a high portico, slatted blinds and a date at the base of a plinth, 1892. It could have been a school or a rotting hospital, but probably – this being Calcutta – it had once been the residence of a tycoon, a jute merchant or tea magnate. A fountain in the courtyard, its centre-piece a nymph in the act of emptying a water jar, was dry and the nymph was missing one arm. Two rusted urns held geraniums. A fresher eye than mine, someone new to Calcutta, would have seen the villa as derelict; but I knew that it was a usable antique: it was clean and orderly, the courtyard swept, the flowers watered – all of them deep red lilies. To one side was a gateway with a garden of shade trees visible beyond it. This was one of those Indian time warps that I had stepped into many times but without surrendering to it, because I was the travelling writer who always had to leave early the next morning for a new place. I kicked off my shoes and mounted the steps.

A man in a white smock and leggings stood barefoot at the doorway, a woman beside him in a white sari. She held the usual tray with a flame, passed it under my chin and applied a red thumbprint to my forehead.

'Welcome to the Lodge, sir.'

'Lovely place.'

'Your home, sir,' the man said.

I followed them inside and through a high-ceilinged lobby, across a marble floor. The ruinous outside was not repeated here: the interior was whole and cool, with painted murals of classical European landscapes on the walls of the lobby – Palladian villas set amid tall poplars, deer and birds in a pastoral scene, a great sweep of bay, perhaps Naples, all of these faded paintings blurred with an overlay of dust.

I had seen a few spas in India; this was not like any of them. The ruin on the outside did not suggest anything hygienic and the lobby here was more suited to stuffed shirts and evening gowns. In this newer incarnation I would have said it was a school – for the odours alone, with the whiff of chalk dust in the air, the tang of varnished desks and mildewed books, the battered woodwork, the baseboards looking kicked and bumped. I imagined children jostling here. And I could hear voices: the singsong of children's laughter, the sounds of their playing, reciting, the shrieky rat-a-tat of childish taunts. And more, the tapping of feet – the peculiar dry scuff and thump of bare soles; the fleeting shapes – faces at door cracks, faces at the spindles in the upper galleries, the contending screeches of small boys, the imploring voices of little girls. Because I could not see any of them clearly, they seemed to be especially numerous, a whole mansion of murmuring children, interrupted from time to time by the odd dull nag of an older woman.

The unseen but vibrant presence of life, an intimation of children, made me uncomfortable. I felt I'd entered by the wrong door, somewhere I didn't belong.

I looked at the man who was leading me through the cool, odorous – smell of damp mop on old tile – corridors, and I hoped to be reassured. I wanted him to say *Never mind them*, or to explain what the voices were.

He didn't say anything, not even his name. He didn't smile, or, if he did, I could not see it beneath his moustache. He had the face-forward and rather resigned and glazed expression of an Indian menial doing his duty. That is, both submissive and slightly haughty.

We turned into another corridor – fleeting shapes of children – and then went through a latched door to an annexe of the old building. A woman waiting at the door handed me a parcel, like a delivery of hotel laundry, and the man said, 'You can change in there. Wear robe only and cloth slippers. Valuables will be deposited in this container' – he indicated a basket on a shelf – 'for containing only. No one will disturb.'

When I stepped into the changing room, he left and so did the woman. I shut the door and changed quickly, took off my watch

37

and put it with my wallet into the basket. Just then, a knock at the door: he seemed to know that I was done.

'This way, sir.'

'Where to?'

'To vault.'

What he said was *walt*, and the word thrilled me. He led me deeper into the Lodge, past adjoining rooms and narrowing corridors to a heavy door. Behind this door was a room with a long wooden table in the centre, a shower in one corner, a stool in another corner. The tiny smoke trail rising from a taper in a dish must have accounted for the fragrant and dizzying aroma.

Two young men in the room bowed to me, their hands clasped in a gesture of *namaste*. The taller of the two motioned me to the stool where the other had already begun to crouch.

This second man washed my feet with lukewarm water, massaging my toes, rubbing them gently, cupping my heels. It was more than mere pouring water and soaping; it was not an empty ritual but rather an act of purification, a slow and thorough cleansing of the flesh of my feet, making them live – reminding me that I had two feet.

'Table, sir.'

These laconic directions were all I got. I could not tell whether they knew a whole English sentence. But it didn't matter. They had removed my robe and my wrap, and I lay face-down on the table, feeling exposed. My first thought, the fearful one, was that I was to be killed: I was in the helpless posture of an animal on a slab. I lay like a human sacrifice, blind to my captors, my ass in the air.

One of them hosed me with a fine spray while the other scrubbed me with a mild abrasive – salt, I realized. Each of them wore cloth mitts, and they worked the salt over my body the way you scour a pot. This went on for a while, their rocking me with scrubbing motions.

I was possessed by a strange sensation, as though I were not human at all but an enormous vegetable or a dumb animal being cleaned. I gave myself up to it and was amazed at their conscientious scrubbing, the chafing of their mitts. Then they sprayed all the salt off me and I heard the gulp of the excess water in the drains.

When all the salt had been removed from my body and the table, one of them gave me a towel and helped me to a sitting position.

'Take time, sir.'

He knew I was dizzy from their pummelling. Was this what Ma had meant when she'd said, *You'll be a new man*? I dried myself and stood up on the wooden slats of the floor. One of the men draped a robe over my shoulders, the other tied the cords in front.

'This way, sir.'

Down the hall to a new room, a dry table as sacrificial-seeming as the last but with a more pungent odour, like sesame oil, and a burning smell too. An oil lamp, a sacred statue in a shrine garlanded with marigolds.

I lay on the table, again face-down, but I saw one of them take a brass pot from a squat, stove-like heater, and he poured hot oil on my back and buttocks and calves, and he worked it into my muscles. He dripped it into my hair, massaged my scalp and proceeded from there to my feet. I felt like a piece of meat being marinaded for the pot.

Some minutes of this, then, 'Thank you, sir,' and they left me alone in the warm room that was thick with the scent of oil.

# 4

Naked in this strange interior room in an old, ripe-smelling mansion in a district of Calcutta, I began to mock myself, thinking: *This is what happens when you surrender.* I didn't really know where I was. Somehow curiosity and vanity had led me here, and a sentiment I thought I had outgrown, the greed for experience, agreeing to the suggestions of a beautiful stranger. That willingness had served me before when I needed something to write about.

I did not know what would happen next. Mine was an act of faith or stupidity – I was a credulous fool. The car had been sent, like a vehicle in a ghost story or an Indian myth, and I had got in and allowed myself to be transported here. Now I lay, literally with my dick in my hand, in the posture of submission, alone and bare-assed, like a big buttered man on an altar.

Yet I was not alarmed. The hot oil had calmed me. Prone, coated in it, I was warmed and relaxed, the lamp flickering in the aroma of sesame and ghee. The only light came from the flame wagging on the wick in the oil lamp. The last identifiable sound I'd heard was the door's decisive click as the masseurs had departed. I wasn't sorry: I didn't like being touched by a man. But I wasn't surprised. In puritanical caste-crazed India it was unusual for a woman in a spa to attend to male clients.

I must have dozed. The whole business had been soporific. With my face on a folded towel, I was dimly aware – perhaps in shallow dreams, or in adjacent rooms – of the murmur of life nearby, like a children's chorus, vaguely taunting and competing as children's voices seem to do. My body was penetrated by the vibrations of busy lives, the shuffle of small feet, the competing cries of kids, the whole huge house pulsing around this small room, the vault.

And I thought, or dreamed: *This is not like any spa I've ever seen, in India or anywhere else.* The muted life, the deliberate pauses, the silences of a spa were unavailable here. This was like being in a household – a large one – or a schoolhouse or (the thought occurred to me as a grotesquerie) a big throbbing body. I had the absurd thought that I'd been swallowed whole by a monstrous creature and that I was in the belly of this monster. But it was an Indian beast, accommodating and warm, its blood pounding in my ears, and still the shrieks and calls of children echoing in the walls.

When I woke, Mrs Unger was beside me.

She seemed to inhabit a vapour, a fragrant cloud filled with the aroma of flowers and also of Indian spices, mingled oils and perfumes. She was warmth and softness and a kind of light too. This sounds hyperbolic. I supposed I was overreacting to her because I was so relieved to see her. She brushed my shoulder, the caress of warm skin or silk against my side. I lifted my head a little and saw she was wearing a purple sari. She was moving her hands, palms downward, paddling the air over my body as though warming them like fingers over a fire, and in another motion lifting them in a gesture of levitation, and then making a flourish with them as though she was earnestly searching, my body the object of her dowsing motions.

'Just breathe normally,' she said, and that was all she said for a while.

Still I lay naked, slick with oil, imagining that I could feel her fluttering hands. I was glad she was there, not just relieved that she was not an Indian masseur but delighted to see her again. Since the previous day I'd been thinking about her – involuntarily, she shimmered in my memory – and I'd even had a vivid dream of her in which she smiled at me, then turned around and was someone else, a demon version of her bewitching side. The everyday horrors on an Indian street or in an average temple make this sort of nightmare a common occurrence. Without speaking, but (in the manner of dreams) knowing what I wanted, I tried to get her to turn again so I could behold that sensual side of her.

'Trying to see where you need work,' she was saying with banal practicality over my feverish memories. Her hands were still active

41

in the air, hovering as if receiving signals with her fingers and palms.

'Where did you come from?'

She didn't answer. With a frown in her voice, she said, 'Yes, you do need work. Upper trapezius muscles. Very tight.'

Hearing that pleased me. I wanted her to stay. I wanted her attention.

'Now I'm going to ask you to turn over.'

I skidded slightly as I rolled on to my back. Then I felt the warmth and weight of a towel over my pelvic area; she tucked the ends under my buttocks, so I was decent. A moment later she placed a damp cloth over my eyes. In the darkness I became more aware of the music in the room – a sitar, a warbling flute and, in bursts, the *pok-pok* of tabla drums.

Now I felt her confident fingers on me. She was holding my toes, one by one, explaining softly, 'This is your shoulder' – the small toes – 'very tense,' and working her way from toe to toe, 'your neck, your ears,' and gripping my big toe, 'your head.' She dug her nails into the sole of each foot and lifted it, applying pressure. After a minute or so, the same refrain, 'You need work.'

The very pressure of her fingers relaxed me. She took my right arm and kneaded it from the shoulder downward, my biceps, my forearm, my wrist, my palm, each finger, being thorough, squeezing hard at times, just this side of pain; and then the other arm. She worked my head, my ears, my neck, my face, sometimes caressing me, more often probing, finding a muscle, twisting hard to awaken it and leaving it vibrant with heat.

She said little more, though I could sense her breathing, both as a sighing softness in the air and a pressure against me, the swelling of her midsection of bare skin between the sari and the bodice.

All she said was, 'Don't help me – relax,' as she went lower, lifting my legs, bending each one, stretching and flexing them, my feet, my ankles. She pinched all the muscles from my ankles upward, tracing them and working her knuckles against them, to my thigh; then gripping my inner thigh and making it a bundle of muscle meat, twisting it, and as she did so brushing my penis with the backs of her hands, though (this thought burning like a hot circuit in my mind) giving the thing no direct attention.

That was the thickening query, stirring under the towel, the dumb 'What now?' that made it so awkward to be a man, the dog-like obviousness of it. But if she noticed, she didn't say so, intent upon warming my thighs and, muscle by muscle, taking possession of every part of my body.

An hour or more of this, though I had lost track of time – it could have been two hours. I was keenly aware that she knew what she was doing. Her touch was sure; she knew each muscle and every connector and bit of gristle in me. And she knew – how could she not? – what effect she was having on me. But apart from her incidental brushings and touches, she did not take hold of my penis, which was not erect but swelling.

All her massaging with her querying fingers had been working towards my centre, seeming to push energy into my groin. I wanted to say *Touch me there*, but there was something delicious in the delay. Of course I wanted more. I supposed that much was visible, but I was also eager to see what would come next, for as she massaged me, and as I became more relaxed and grateful, I had the impression of her as a person of immense power and authority.

*Healing hands*, her son had said. *Magic fingers*, Rajat had said. She hadn't denied it. She had lifted her hands and admired them. I had smiled then, but I wasn't smiling now. She was inflicting pain on me, at the periphery of my groin, pushing hard, and as she did, her hair must have come undone, because I could sense the cool sweep of her loose tresses on my aching muscles.

After a while, in a stupor of ecstasy, I did not feel her hands on me. I seemed to be floating. Her arms were extended above my body and she was paddling with her hands again, palms-down.

'Better,' she said, leaning over me. 'But I can still feel tightness here and here.'

'Good.'

'Not good,' she said.

'So I'll have to come back.'

'If you want to.'

'I want to.'

'Are you sure?'

This testing was a little like the massage – a questioning pressure, a tentative flirting, a deeper return, that teased me and gave me pleasure.

'Please.'

When had I ever pleaded before? But I meant it. Nothing else seemed to matter. Her silence was also a form of pressure.

'This place is magic,' I said, to encourage her to speak to me.

Her muted laugh, more like the contraction of a muscle, made me wary, almost fearful of what she'd say next.

'You don't even know where you are,' she said with the energy of that same suppressed laughter. 'And you don't know me.'

'I want to know. I want to come back.' I must have sounded like an over-eager child. I lay naked and oily on the table.

'I know exactly what you want,' she said. I did not see her move, though she must have because the flame of the oil lamp had begun to shimmy.

She put a robe over my shoulders and I slipped off the table, stood unsteadily and tied the cords. She, who had loomed over me and had seemed so powerful, now stepped aside, looking almost fragile.

I wanted to convince her of my sincerity and my worth, but I was out of ideas. I knew I was in subterranean Calcutta, but above ground the chaos in the city echoed the chaos in my mind. Perhaps that was why I wanted to come back to this vault. I yearned to see her again. This need gave me a vague sense of obligation, as though I owed her for her good will, the close attention of her hands. She had touched me. I wanted somehow to repay her so that I could return.

'What's the name of the hotel?'

'The hotel?'

'Where Rajat had the problem.'

'Where Rajat claims he had a problem,' she said, correcting me and putting her hand on my arm, a mother's caress of consolation. She went on, 'Never mind that. It's Rajat's affair. I'm sure you have plenty of more important things to do.'

'I have some spare time.' I wanted to say more, that I had nothing but time, that I was grateful for her attention precisely because I had failed to make anything of my visit, that I had nothing to write about, nothing in my head, and only the slightest desire to make notes. Looking at the hotel would help me kill one of my vacant hours.

She saw the earnest, perhaps pathetic willingness on my face and looked almost pityingly at me.

'You'd be doing Rajat an enormous favour,' she said.

'I want to do you a favour, too.'

'We're a happy little constellation,' she said. 'You could be part of it.'

'I'd like that.'

'It's, um, a shabby little hotel called the Ananda, behind New Market – the Hogg Market.'

'The corpse just turned up in the room?'

'I have no idea. Rajat was hysterical. He'd been traumatized. All I know is that is what he told me, that he saw the dead person and he ran.'

'When did this happen?'

'It was three weeks ago. Charlie and I were out of Calcutta then. That's why Rajat was in the hotel. He was waiting for us to come back.'

'So you don't know more than that?'

Her obstinate smile of disapproval had never looked brighter.

'Don't you see?' She was beaming at my stupidity, pushing the door open to take me back to the lobby of the mansion and the waiting car. 'That's why we were counting on you.'

All this kindness and consideration – the car, the driver, the masseurs, Mrs Unger's surprise appearance, the massage, the teasing conversation about the hotel, then the car again, the driver again – seemed so generous and helpful, anticipating my desires.

But when it was over and I was back on my verandah with (at Mrs Unger's suggestion) a glass of mango juice, I realized that I'd been manipulated. Every move had been planned and I had allowed myself to be exposed – manipulated in every sense, exposed in every sense.

When you're alone in a distant city, floating as foreigners do, and someone is kind, the kindness is magnified and so is your gratitude. If you're a man and that kind person is a woman, you might feel you've been touched by an angel.

A first-time traveller might have been smitten. I was not. I had been travelling too long not to be suspicious of such attention. I had not forgotten that this had all come about because Mrs Unger had asked me a favour. She had been specific at first, but had got me to the Lodge and into her hands by a deft series of moves, the way someone might try to sell you something expensive – in the very manner an Indian might sell you a carpet. 'Have a cup of tea, sir. No need to buy, just look . . .'

I was almost persuaded. But some people are so smooth, their very persuasiveness is suspect, again like the Indian in the carpet emporium who marshals so many arguments in favour of the value of the thing he's trying to sell you, you are convinced it's a fake.

It was hard for me in the midst of this to see Mrs Unger as an American. The finely draped sari and the meticulous henna tattoos on her feet impressed me, but I'd seen other Americans with that studied appearance. Her haughtiness and her decisive manner made me listen, but something else bothered me – her presumption. She wanted me to do her a favour; she, like her Indian counterpart, wouldn't take no for an answer. And there was the sequence of events, from the drink at the Oberoi Grand to today, her hands on me. She had planned everything, as an angel might, as someone diabolical too, and she'd thought I hadn't noticed her calculation.

The very skill of the manipulation made me doubtful, the way the sweetest words can make you shrink in fear. *I won't hurt you* can sound terrifying. I did not want to fall too fast. Mrs Unger seemed to know a lot about me. *Your friends at the consulate.* She knew my work and where I lived, and she probably knew that I was living hand-to-mouth. But what she didn't know, because wealthy people never seemed to know this, was that I had all the time in the world. I didn't want to be possessed by her.

I did not hear from her after that. Not a word. After the imploring letter, the pleasant meeting, the magic fingers – nothing. She had occupied two full days of my time in Calcutta and now I spent a day waiting, feeling uncomfortable, in suspense and sensing rejection.

She had teased me, made me feel helpless, invited me to the inner room of her strange mansion, which I now thought of as Mrs Unger's vault; and now she was inaccessible. *I know what you want* was a tease, but truthful. It put me all the more in her power, because she knew, because she denied me.

That night I made some notes, something to the effect that the first infatuation of a love affair is a delusion of possession. Nothing else matters. And about how I enjoyed the feeling for its making me youthful. But I also knew that it made me obvious and foolish, even ridiculous, because I was middle-aged and out of ideas.

With time on my hands, I decided to investigate her request by paying a visit to the Hotel Ananda.

The Ananda was one of many narrow, decaying four-storey hotels on a side street off New Market. A persistent beggar, a woman with a baby, pleaded with me, dogging me for a whole block, moving as quickly in bare feet as I did in sturdy shoes. I was reminded of Howard's story of the nanny who used her boss's child for begging. I got rid of her with five rupees and, seeing my money, a tout shouldered me aside, chanting, 'Shawls, pashminas, scarves for you, sir, shahtoosh,' while another tout with a skinny, sweaty face howled, 'What you want, sir? Anything!'

What I wanted was to get a clear view of the Ananda as I dodged oncoming traffic and the march of pedestrians. Approaching the hotel, I was spotted by a man sitting in front of the Taj Palace, another flophouse, who said, 'Try here, sir. Best price.'

But I kept going, up the stairs and into the incense stink and gloom of the Ananda, its lobby no more than an entryway with a window like that in a ticket office. A calendar, a blotter, a bell. I rang the bell.

A thin, small woman appeared, and instead of a sari she wore a faded pink dress with a white collar, her hair plaited into one thick braid which lay on her back.

'Good afternoon, sir.'

'Do you have any vacant rooms?'

'Yes, sir. Single. Double. Garden view. Family suite. Which, sir?'

'I'm not sure. Can I see some?'

Without replying she plucked some keys from hooks on a board just inside the ticket window. Following her up the stairs – no elevator – I asked her her name.

'Mina, sir.'

'Christian?'

'Indeed, sir.'

'What's your family name?'

'Jagtap, sir.'

'Thanks for helping me, Mina.'

'Pleasure, sir.'

The first room was small and stifling. She showed me the bathroom, the plastic shower stall, the closet, the cot.

'Double is next door.'

The double was only a little bigger, with two cots separated by a low table, on which a vase held two extravagant plastic blooms. I found these rooms depressing and almost frightening in their rankness, with the tang of mice and roaches, airless and entrapping.

'This hotel was mentioned by someone I know.'

'Thank you, sir.'

'He had a little problem when he was here.' I had looked at the calendar. Three weeks ago, Mrs Unger had said. That was the weekend of the seventh. I said, 'Around the seventh or so. Did anything unusual happen then?'

'No, sir.'

'It might help if I knew what room he was in.'

'Nothing unusual, sir. Not on premises.'

'Let's go downstairs, Mina.'

At the ticket window she replaced the keys on the hooks. 'Which room do you wish to book, sir?'

'I'm not sure. It's not for tonight. Some other time.' She shrugged and turned away. I said, 'Mina, I need to see your guest register.'

The big, old-fashioned, clothbound ledger lay out of reach on a shelf, just inside the window.

'Cannot, sir. Register contains confidential information.'

What annoyed me was the efficient way she dismissed my request, with a perfectly formulated phrase in good English. It was an Indian rebuff, articulate and final.

But I said, 'Do you have a brother, Mina?'

'Three, sir.'

'What if one of them was missing? What if your mother was desperate to know his whereabouts? Wouldn't you want someone to help you?'

'Sir' – and she looked anguished – 'register cannot be shown to general public for examination without manager's permission.'

'Mina, I don't want to examine it. I only want to look at one page.' I could see her weaken, a slackening in her shoulders, a tilt of her head. 'Please. Just the page showing the weekend of the seventh.'

Without speaking, she slid the ledger on to the counter under the grille. She opened it, wet her thumb and whittled away at the corners of the pages, and when she found the right page she glanced behind her in the direction of the manager's office and propped the book open before me.

Five days were shown. This was not a busy hotel. I was looking for Rajat's name. I wanted to find his room, the rate, any information under *Remarks*, his home address, anything. All the names I saw were Indian. His name was not there. I turned the page.

'You said weekend seventh.'

'I may have been mistaken.'

But there was no Rajat on that page either. I turned back to the week before the seventh.

'Please, sir.'

I was running my finger under each name, seeing 'Rajat' nowhere, when Mina snatched the register away. At that moment, the front door opened and a man in a white kurta glared at me with blazing eyes, his calculations as obvious as the tremor on his face and his fierce discoloured teeth. His sudden anger convulsed him and gave him a neuralgic gait.

'He demanded to see, sir.' Mina was breathless with panic.

In one limping movement the man stepped behind the counter and with a furious uppercut slapped the register shut. He shoved it on to a high shelf and pushed Mina aside – bumped her with his arm – his eyes wide, his lower lip jutting beneath his nose.

'I was checking the rates,' I said.

'Rates are not there. Rates are here,' he said, tapping the glass of the counter with a yellow fingernail. Under the glass was a small card with columns, headed *Room Rates – Daily – Weekly – Monthly*. 'Register is strictly confidential.' He spoke as though in stereo, in two directions, to Mina and me.

I thanked him, but as I was leaving I heard him shout – a bawling in Bengali, the sort of rage I'd heard before in India, uninhibited indignation, pure fury, always a man screaming at a woman.

That night, back at the Hastings, I called Howard on his cell phone. He said he was working late at the consulate.

'You still here?' he asked.

I knew he was teasing me, but I was bothered by the seriousness that lay beneath his teasing, because I could not easily explain why I had lingered in Calcutta. I had given him the idea that I was going to make my way south and then eventually west to Mumbai, where I'd be catching a direct flight back to the States.

'Doing a little work,' I said. This much was true. I'd written those lines about the air in Calcutta reminding me of the times I'd emptied a vacuum cleaner bag; I'd made those notes about Mrs Unger's opinions; I'd started a journal that might form the basis of a story, one of those idle, meandering, time-filling and self-important diaries that love-struck people keep when they have no one to console them. *Calcutta Diary* I'd written on the lozenge-shaped front label, hoping it would enliven my dead hand.

Howard said, 'Parvati was asking about you.'

The gifted Parvati, another inaccessible woman, whose very presence was a reminder that I was old and pale and out of ideas.

'How is she?' I asked, hoping I sounded interested.

'Why don't you ask her?'

Just hearing her name, and talking to Howard, I realized how much I had to conceal. In the four days since seeing Howard and Parvati, a great deal had happened: the letter from Mrs Unger, the meeting with her and her son and Rajat at the Oberoi Grand, the massage at the Lodge, the rebuff at the Ananda, and my gloom caused by (I guessed) thwarted desire.

'Anyway, it's nice to hear from you,' he said.

'I had a question.'

'Shoot.'

I said (the big lie I had rehearsed), 'I had an email from someone in the States saying that I should look up a certain American in Calcutta. I was wondering if you'd heard of her.'

'Try me.'

'Mrs Unger. I think her name is Merrill.'

'Philanthropist,' Howard said. 'With all that that implies.'

'Please don't be enigmatic.'

'I am being enigmatic, I am indulging in ambiguity. And you notice I am using the historical present, Bengali style.'

'So do you know her?'

'Only heard about her. Bossy, wealthy, motherly, famous for her saris. I had the idea that she came here originally to work with the Missionaries of Charity, Mother Teresa's outfit. But that might be wrong. I know she has her own outfit, mainly humanitarian. She works with street kids, orphans. She relates to Indians – that's the secret of her success. Other people find her unapproachable.'

'So she's well known.'

'Well known for her independence. She avoids us.'

'Why would that be?'

'Low profile. It's not odd for Americans in India. Lots of them come here to connect, or to indulge themselves for all sorts of reasons. A lot of them are looking for outsourcing, joint partnerships, high-tech ventures, cheap labour. And some are looking for spirituality, even sainthood. Maybe a few are looking for both.'

'I thought you had to keep tabs on Americans here.'

'Mrs Unger is entirely self-funded. Famous for not asking for donations. She doesn't have to file a financial statement because she isn't accountable to anyone. So we have no idea how extensive her foundation is. That's one way of keeping secrets – pay for the whole thing yourself. It's also one way of being a saint.'

I had begun to scribble some of this on to a piece of paper, thinking I'd add it to my diary, and I'd become so preoccupied, I'd fallen silent.

'Are you there?' Howard asked. 'How long are you going to be around? Maybe we could get together.'

'Not sure. I'll let you know,' I said, and I knew I sounded as squirmy and evasive as I felt.

I hung up, regretting that I'd told him anything. To my shame, I now knew how desperate I was, how badly I needed to talk to someone, just to reassure myself that I wasn't dreaming.

Infatuated, needy, helpless: I was a middle-aged fool, but I didn't know how to rid myself of the feeling except by seeing Mrs Unger again. I'd even begun to think of her as Ma. From what Howard had said, she seemed almost unknowable, deliberately secretive; but that was part of her attraction for me. A woman with secrets suited me and seemed to represent a kind of sensuality I craved. Perhaps I was one of her secrets. She certainly was one of mine.

All these speculations were time killers. Another full day went by without my hearing a word from her. A full day in Calcutta in a cheap hotel, with nothing to do, was like a week anywhere else. I stewed and, interrupting my reverie, Parvati called.

'Howard said you were still in Calcutta.'

'I have a little work to do.' The same lie, sounding lamer.

'You were asking about Mrs Unger, he said.'

Now I really hated myself for having called him.

'Someone in the States was enquiring about her. I was just passing on the message.' Blah-blah.

'She's rather controversial.'

'Oh?' But this was not what I wanted to hear.

'Some people think she's practically a saint.'

'Really.'

'And some don't.'

'I'm sure the answer lies somewhere in between.'

Parvati laughed. 'This is Calcutta. Both could be true. What say we meet?'

I hesitated. I said, 'I've got this work . . .'

She became intensely self-conscious, as though I'd rebuffed her – and I suppose I had.

'I shouldn't have been so forward. You're busy, I understand. It's an unwarranted intrusion on your time. I'm so sorry. Believe me, I know all about filling the unforgiving minute.'

One of the aspects of Indians I loved most was that they had the language for every occasion. It was still possible to be subtle, even sinuous, in a conversation, probably as a result of the weirdly Victorian verbosity, using politeness and amplification and elaborate excuses and courtesies.

I was sure of this when, unable to stand the silence any longer, I went to the Oberoi and prowled around, hoping to see Mrs Unger. I would have gone to the Lodge, except that I had no idea where it was: I'd gone in her car, been driven there through the maze of streets and been driven back. I didn't recognize any landmarks and so the location of her villa was yet another of her secrets.

As I crossed the lobby on my way out, I glanced at the arm-chairs on the verandah and saw Rajat sitting alone over a drink. He recognized me but hardly reacted.

'I was looking for –' I didn't know how to finish. I stammered at saying her name. I said, 'The *grande dame*.'

'Ma.'

He looked small and miserable. I wanted to see Mrs Unger, but I could also tell Rajat about my visit to the Ananda. Feeling lucky from my encounters with Mrs Unger, I was disposed to help him, out of superstition, for my luck to continue.

In his bewilderment, Rajat reminded me of how I had felt on the day I'd received the letter from Mrs Unger, when I'd had nothing in my head – no ideas, no desire, just a vacancy of spirit. I wasn't sad; I was too insubstantial to be possessed even of sadness. I didn't matter, I'd felt invisible, and everything I'd done in my life had seemed pointless. I had kept myself from making any kind of commitment because of my writing, and now I had no writing. I'd sacrificed for nothing. Mrs Unger had rescued me. I could return the favour by doing something for Rajat.

I knew that bewilderment and sense of being lost. By a series of deliberate choices and a horrible accident – if the corpse story was true – he'd arrived nowhere and saw nothing ahead of him but emptiness. It was like a grim parable of recognition, the time in your life when you feel there's a corpse in your room – and it's you. With my sense of having a dead hand, this morbidity suited my mood.

'I've been to the Ananda,' I said.

He hung his head. 'I know what you must think – a terrible place.'

It was exactly what I'd thought. A dump, just the sort of hotel where you'd find something shocking in your room. He saw the acknowledgement on my face.

'It's not as bad as it looks,' he said. 'Charlie recommended it to me. He was on a buying trip with Ma and he suggested I stay there while they were away. He doesn't like me to stay at his flat at the Lodge.'

'You stay there?'

'Now and again. When Ma's away.'

I did not ask the obvious question: *When Ma's away?* I sat down.

'He seems a nice guy.'

'He's fantastic.'

I did not pursue that either. A waiter approached. I waved him away. I said, 'Rajat, tell me exactly what happened at the hotel.'

He looked at his shoes and did not speak for a full minute, one of those silences you take to be obstinate and pathological, or perhaps tactical. A minute is a long time. I was on the point of saying 'Look, forget it' when he took a deep breath and began to speak.

'I put off checking in as long as I could, because I really didn't want to stay there alone. That New Market area is colourful if you're with someone, but when you're on your own it's scary – noisy, full of boisterous people, heavy traffic. I finally checked in around five thirty.'

'What day was this?'

'The eighth. It was a Saturday. The manager looked darkly at me. He was glowering.'

'Any idea why?'

'Probably because I had no luggage. Just a little shoulder bag with hardly anything in it. He asked how long I was going to stay. I said, "I'm not sure," because Ma hadn't given a return date.'

'Did you register under your own name?'

He didn't reply at once. Another of those silences that seemed stagy until he began to speak and sounded tormented.

'It's a little complicated. We never use our names when on foundation business. It's Ma's idea. So many people want to pry into her affairs. They're jealous of her humanitarianism and good works.'

'What name did you use?'

'My usual one. Krishnaji.'

I tried to recall if I'd seen such a name on the register. 'What room were you in?'

'I honestly don't remember.'

'How many flights up?'

'One, I think. The first floor. A good-sized room, facing the rear of the building. It was noisy and the stifling air kept me awake for a long time.'

'So you managed to fall asleep?'

'Yes. I don't know for how long. It was still dark when I woke up. I opened my cell phone to see the time. It was four something.'

'You saw that on your phone?'

'Phone gives day and time. And that was when – see, cell phone is also like torch. It's adequately bright. I sensed something in the room. Something strange. I shone the phone around, walked a bit and tripped over a bundle, or so I thought.'

Reliving the moment made him pause.

'And?'

'And I shone the light down and saw the body.'

'Describe it.'

'Small, pale, naked – a boy of about ten or eleven. It was terrifying. His eyes open, his mouth open.'

'You knew he was dead?'

'No question. Limp. Lifeless. Looking like clay, a bluish colour. Or that colour may have been an effect of my light.'

'Any blood?'

'None that I could see.'

'Did you turn on the light?'

'No, I was too scared. I had my phone as torch, as I said.'

'What did you do next?'

'Gathered up my things from the bathroom, put them in my little bag and went downstairs. No one at the desk, just a *chowkidar* at the door. I slipped out and went to the market, where some people were setting up their stalls for the day ahead. It was still dark.'

'Did anyone see you?'

He shook his head and said, 'As far as I know.' But he had become ashen. 'You can't imagine what it's like to find yourself in the same room as a dead person. I was so terrified I called Charlie. He was with Ma in Uttar Pradesh. He was wonderful. Ma too. They came back to Calcutta that same day.'

'But you didn't tell the police.'

'It would have been much worse if we had. We didn't tell anyone. I had no idea that you knew until you showed up that night here. To be honest, I was a little surprised that Ma told you.'

I didn't say so, but I was surprised myself. Why *had* she told me? I was a writer who sat at home inventing crimes, not someone who goes into the wider world encountering them.

56

And then Rajat smiled. But he was not smiling at me. He was looking past me. I turned and saw Charlie walking towards us. He greeted Rajat by bending towards him and giggling, and then he glanced at me and said hello, just that one word.

'I was asking Rajat about the hotel.'

'The drama,' Charlie said in a disbelieving tone. 'You have no idea, doll. Shall we go?'

Rajat got up from his chair, but I stayed seated. It was clear that they had business elsewhere and that I was superfluous.

'How's your mother?' I asked.

'Fabulous, as always.'

I wanted to ask him more, but his tone indicated that he had no interest in me – perhaps guessed that I was desperate. But here I was, trying to help his friend Rajat with a problem his mother had suggested I solve. Why didn't they ask me to join them? They had been so friendly when I'd been with them with Mrs Unger present. But she had been different too.

Sitting there in this awkwardness while they stood over me, I felt perversely that Charlie did not in the least resemble his mother. He was dark, she was light; his hair was curly, hers was straight. Though she was slight and small-boned, she gave the impression of power; he was tall, yet he seemed weak and tricky to me. I resented him, especially this offhandedness. The social inferiority that I'd felt as a child in New York resurfaced in India, with all its snobbish inversions and semi-polite rebuffs. I began to hate these two young men looming over me – Rajat too, for the way he had brightened on seeing Charlie. To me he had shown only his bewildered gloom, and I had been fool enough to care about him.

'Ma is probably at the Lodge,' Rajat said.

But of course I had no idea where it was, and I was too insulted to ask them directions.

'Thanks for your help,' I said, meaning *Up yours*.

I guessed Charlie was being competitive, resenting my interest – another of Mother's friends trying to monopolize her time, maybe interested in her money. He had behaved like a rival with barely disguised aggression. So I watched them walk out of the verandah and through the lobby. And I thought, as I had many times in my life: *What am I doing here?*

Humiliated, I decided to leave Calcutta. This was all a horrible mistake. I had been misled and was feeling like a fool. I'd been away too long, I'd begun to drift, I needed to either put myself to work or accept the fact that some travel yields nothing but unrewarding repetition. I had overstayed my visit and in the unreality of being in such an odd place I had become a little sentimental and susceptible. This was often the case – go far enough and something happens, a transformation, the traveller's pleasure and dilemma, an effect of solitude and strangeness. You begin to turn into someone else.

# 5

And the cities change too – or, rather, after a time they reveal themselves. Calcutta, I came to understand, was a city that anyone could see had been made by human hands. Other cities are well cemented and engineered, all seamless surfaces. Calcutta was roughly plastered and painted; the Corinthian columns, the Ionic capitals, the rounded balusters and porticos, and much else that seemed like marble was really whitewashed wood. It was not beautiful but its handmade look gave it a human face, which is also a look of impermanence, if not frailty. The handiwork was evident in its patches, its irregular bricks, the botched painting, the clumsy flourishes in the carpentry, like the sad lacy panels on some house fronts, the lopsided designs, the mismatched joints, the tottering staircases. Nothing was square, nothing was plumb. Peering closely at this bulging and buckling city, I saw the hasty joinery, the hardened putty, the rusty nails, and I thought: *A barefoot man did that with an old hammer in his skinny hand.*

There was one other thing I had not seen at first, something that had slowly come into focus over this spell of living at the Hastings. It was a revelation I'd never had at the five-star hotels where I usually stayed free in return for writing about them. Nothing was new in Calcutta, at least nothing looked new, because every structure in this huge handmade city looked skeletal. Nothing new that worked: no new buildings, no new roads, even the street signs on the renamed roads looked ancient – Free School Street was Mirza Ghalib Road, Wellesley Street was Rafi Ahmed Kidwai. The city went on growing, yet it still looked rickety and ruinous, and in areas of faded elegance and dramatic misery a bad smell lingered, haunted and human.

I wondered whether I should leave, to be myself again. In order to ponder this, to think clearly, I took long walks down the side streets and alleys, zigzagging to the river by Eden Gardens, or making my way northwards in the maze that lay to the east of Chowringhee, the motley neighbourhood called Taltala. I had the pleasure, rare in the world, of strolling in a baroque antiquity. But more than strolling: enveloped by a kind of revisitation that I had known only in dreams, of living in India's past, part Raj, part ruin, which was the present in this unreconstructed city.

Solitary, looking for companionship, or simply to sit among like-minded drinkers, I stepped into bars. Indian bars, usually all male and dark, could be depressing, and the rattle of the air conditioners lowered my spirits further. But I circulated and found some that cheered me up. The Oly Pub on Park Street I liked for being scruffy, and its seediness matched my mood. I indulged myself in that most un-Indian of activities, something that would have shocked Mrs Unger, eating the Oly's famous beefsteak. It pleased me to watch the way they poured me a whisky by measuring it in large or small jiggers, the *barra peg* or *chota peg*. Upstairs among the younger clientele there were sometimes women drinkers, which would have been unheard of in New Delhi or Madras but not in the Calcutta I had begun to find congenial. Now and then I would see a rat in the Oly, and one night I saw two huge rats crossing from one side of the room to the other, showing no more hurry than any of the drifters or drinkers there.

On the first floor of the Roxy Cinema, behind the Oberoi Grand, where I'd first met Mrs Unger, was the Roxy Bar, where there was no chance of meeting her and where in the evenings I listened to live music from Bollywood films. The drinkers here, a step down from the Oly's, were mainly lowly clerks and drudges, people with little education but with enough extra money for a bottle or two of beer. The waiters in bow ties and white shirts were the only formal aspect of the Roxy. In my self-dramatizing way, I fantasized that it would be a good place for someone like me to have a secret rendezvous.

As a change from the Hastings's food, I occasionally went to the New Cathay, on Chowringhee, an old-style Calcutta Chinese eatery with a high ceiling hung with fans that cooled a loyal clientele. I wondered what Mrs Unger would say of me hunched over a plate of chilli chicken and rice. It was another place where I knew I would never bump into another foreigner, where the food and beer were cheap and I could convince myself, as I often did in Calcutta, that I was living inaccessibly in the city's past.

I discovered what residents knew, that all life is there: the hawkers, the touts, the prostitutes, the Anglo-Christian enclaves, the shopkeepers, the vegetable sellers, the families, the running boys, the shouting men. The women and pretty girls tiptoed past the piles of debris; some in saris picked through the rubbish heaps in lanes, and one of these was European Asylum Lane. To locals it was an open-air theatre of activity; they didn't notice the decrepitude, the stinks, the sewers. And so I learned a lesson, that I should do the same, and count my blessings.

Now and then, from deep within the glowering façade of a house or issuing from high up on a tenement balcony draped with drying laundry, I heard the loud voices of adults and the protesting squawks of children. I knew instinctively that parents were in an unstoppable fit of scolding, growing hotter. I never heard these voices in public, but often these angry howls were the voice-overs of my evening walks, people quarrelling indoors in the heat. I was reminded of my own childhood, of being humiliated by my puritanical mother for something I'd said or done thoughtlessly – her raging at me. I felt no rancour; I smiled for my good luck in having met Mrs Unger.

These walks gave me more confidence. I wondered how much this was due to my having known the now unapproachable Ma. I suspected a great deal. I admired anyone, especially an American, who could live for a long time in this disorderly place and not complain or make a drama out of it. On the contrary, Mrs Unger had nothing but praise for the city.

The old splintered and pitted buildings matched my frame of mind; they looked eaten away and incomplete, yet I saw glimpses of their former glory. I was in my element; I was past it. I was decayed and aging. The cracks showing through the peeling paint, the dirty shutters, the windows opaque with dust, the dead bulbs, the flickering neon, the wobbling rickshaws and beat-up taxis, all like a dream of failure, reflected just how I felt about myself.

One day on my way to the Roxy Bar, my walk through New Market took me near the Hotel Ananda. It had been more than a week since my last, unsatisfactory visit, and as I approached I saw the manager on the wide upper step, sitting in the characteristic Bengali way, all his weight on his left hip and left hand, with his left leg drawn up and his right foot planted on the step, his dhoti draped.

I stopped and greeted him. If he had smiled and waved I might have walked on. But he glowered at me, with the dark, beaky scowl that Indian men assume in displeasure and defiance – as though they're imitating a crow-like demon face they've seen in a temple. The man's look of contempt made me pause, reminding me of how unhelpful, even obstructive, he'd been before. I remembered his rudeness.

As I walked up the steps he tipped back slightly, still eyeing me with malice.

'Remember me?'

Instead of replying, he sharpened his look of malevolence, and this he managed by narrowing his eyes and defying me with a twitch of his hooked nose.

'I was hoping to have another look at your guest register.'

'Not available.'

'Just one particular page. To examine it for a singular notation.' One of the consequences of being among Bengalis was that I'd begun to talk this way, hoping to be understood.

'Not possible.'

As he said it, and before I could mount the top step and tower over him, he gathered his dhoti around his legs and got to his feet. He began to withdraw into the narrow lobby of the Ananda, his arms folded. He had hairy ears, and when he opened his mouth to spit a red gob against his own wall I saw that his teeth had been reddened and eroded from betel chewing. His face and his teeth resembled the rotted façade of his hotel.

I saw a glass-fronted refrigerator just off the lobby. 'And I'll have a Thums Up, please.'

'Twelve rupees.'

I gave him the ragged bills and helped myself to a bottle, opening it – because he made no gesture to help – with the church key hanging on a string. Now, with the bottle, I had a pretext to linger.

But he had gone behind the counter with the grille that looked to me like a ticket window.

'So you can't show me the register?'

'Confidential,' he muttered.

I saw just beneath the counter a gleaming head of hair, with a parting that revealed a pale scalp.

'Is that you, Mina?' I asked.

The hair moved and a young woman raised her face to me, squirmed slightly and said, 'Mina not here.'

'What happened to Mina?' I asked the manager.

'No longer employed. Now you must go.'

'I haven't finished this,' I said, sloshing the liquid in the bottle of Thums Up.

'Finish outside.'

'What if I want a room?'

'If you want to book room, provide passport details and money in advance. If not, you can go.'

'May I ask your name?'

'I am manager, Bibhuti Biswas.'

'Mr Biswas, what happened to Mina?'

His mouth went square. His teeth were discoloured pegs, black and red. His ears were not just hairy at the edges but with twists of hair bristling from the ear holes. He had the dark, squashed, beaky face of a crow.

'Get out.'

'Why should I?'

This rude back and forth in the small hot space at the ticket window made the young woman crouching behind the counter visibly nervous. Her boss was agitated. The afternoon sun streaming through the dirty windows half blinded me.

As much to her as to him I said, 'Can you tell me where Mina lives?'

Banging down a wooden yardstick on his desk with a slap, the manager rounded the counter in three strides, almost crow-hopping, and began to bark, showing his teeth again.

'I must ask you to kindly vacate premises.'

'What's the problem?' I tried to keep calm, but I had seen Indians like him go berserk in a matter of seconds, so I was ready to jump.

'I shall call constable forthwith.'

'Listen, this is in a good cause.'

'Bosh,' he said, pressing one knuckle into his nose, but I noticed that in his other hand he still held the yardstick, hiding it in the folds of his dhoti.

'Never mind.'

I walked back to my hotel, liking the city less, believing my amateur sleuthing to be futile and planning my departure – mentally moving out of India. I went to the front desk to look at the railway timetable and, seeing me, Ramesh Datta, the clerk, began to smile. But he was smiling at something or someone behind me.

'Your car, sir.'

I turned and, standing near a pillar as if to take up less room and not intrude, Balraj, the driver, doffed his peaked cap and bowed.

This time on the way to the Lodge I looked for landmarks. I wanted to remember the way. When we were stopped in heavy traffic, beggars pressed their faces against the window and made eating gestures, anxiously motioning to their mouths, patting their bellies, pleading. Turning away, I missed the landmarks, yet even when I could concentrate I doubted that I'd be able to find the route again. We went from lane to lane, squeezed through alleys, and though each of them had its name in Bengali and English on an enamel plate bolted to the walls of corner buildings, I was not able to see any of them clearly. Calcutta was another Indian city where, as soon as I was away from a main thoroughfare, I was lost. And not just lost but transported, seeming to negotiate an alternate, sunken city, a Calcutta underworld from which there was no clear pattern and no escape, another level of the city existing in ghastly light diffused by risen dust.

At the edge of a traffic-choked intersection was the big decaying mansion, the courtyard with the cracked fountain, the broken wall, the wide split-bamboo blinds, the flight of steps, the fluted columns.

In her purple and gold sari, Mrs Unger stood almost regally at the top of the stairs, hands together.

'Welcome.'

The sari shimmered as she straightened. Her hair was pulled back, she wore gold bangles at her wrists and her face was very pale among the Indians who flanked her like retainers.

'Thanks for sending the car.'

'I was told you were enquiring after me.'

*Enquiring after me* was one of her Anglicisms, and an understatement. I was not desperate for her attention, but I'd been curious to know what she really felt about me. I was afraid of falling deeper, becoming so smitten that I risked getting lost in her big, billowing personality, so swaddled in her affections that I'd be blinded and stifled. If I were to be stifled – I was tempted – I had to know that she was the real thing.

'I wonder if you'd like a tour of the Lodge.'

'I'd love it.' It frightened me to think that to know her better I would have agreed to anything she suggested.

She turned to re-enter the mansion and, as she did, she beckoned to a child standing shyly by the carved stone balustrade of the wide porch. He hurried to her, a skinny boy in blue shorts and a grey shirt, and she took his hand.

'This is Jyoti,' she said.

'Hello, Jyoti. How are you?'

'I am well, uncle. Thank you.'

He had a soft but certain voice and he stood very straight, his head erect, his arms at his sides in a posture of obedience. From his shallow breathing and the shutter-blink of his eyelashes I could see that he was nervous, yet he had been so schooled in manners that he knew how to stand his ground. He was poised as a dutiful underling is poised. He knew better than to slouch; he was alert, polite, watchful without seeming worried. And somehow his anxiety only enhanced these traits, because for all his frailty he showed courage. Though he might have been older and he seemed serious, even careworn, he didn't look more than ten or eleven – a small, unswerving soldier. And I liked being called uncle.

'How long have you been here?'

'Eight months, uncle.'

'Do you like living at the Lodge?'

'I am flourishing, uncle. Thanks be to her goodness. Ma is our mainstay.'

I could have said the same.

Mrs Unger said, 'I'd love to take credit for Jyoti's success, but you see he's done it all himself. I can only give these children the tools. They have to learn how to use them. It's all up to them. And Jyoti is a senior boy now, one of the prefects. Aren't you, Jyoti?'

'Yes, Ma.'

'Jyoti is one of the cleverest boys in the Lodge. He came to us as a street child. He was living in a cardboard box in a *bustee* at Sonagachi.'

I knew the place. I had put it on one of my evening walks, the red-light district near Sealdah railway station, where whores painted like clowns leered sadly from two-storey windows. So a little colour for me had been pure misery for Jyoti, whose mother might have lived and worked behind one of those windows.

'I could see he had great promise. Think of the horrors he's seen in his short life.'

I couldn't imagine the life of a child in the streets of that debauched district of Calcutta – the drinking, the fights, the shouting, the contending men. Somehow this child had retained his humanity. But his pained eyes were those of a much older person, wounded and weary. He might have been a bit uneasy as he stood facing me, but his early years had made him unshockable.

'I'd love to help him in some way,' I said.

'Don't you see? He doesn't need help. Do you, Jyoti?'

'No, Ma.'

'He has everything he needs.'

'Yes, Ma,' he said and smiled, and I saw only a little flicker of doubt on his lips, as you get when sad people smile.

'Isn't he a big boy?'

Maybe in Calcutta. He seemed to me undersized and skinny, his legs like sticks, his skin dusty and dry from poor nutrition.

'A street child,' Mrs Unger said. 'We're nursing him back to health. He'll be fine.'

'How long have you been running this orphanage?'

'We never use that word.' She was stern and seemed offended. 'This is a home, a household. We live together as a family.'

The child Jyoti stood slightly apart. He had a mouse face, bat-like ears, a tiny head and narrow shoulders, and he was barefoot in his shorts.

'How many children do you have here?'

'We can accommodate sixty or more, but they have to be separate, boys and girls. They grow, they move on, we bring others into the family.'

We passed a classroom where small girls in white dresses were working at tables, drawing pictures on sheets of paper in coloured crayon.

'I emphasize the arts and language skills. Most of these children were rejected by their mothers, who couldn't look after them for one reason or another. Some were orphaned or abducted or from poor parents who left them here because they know the reputation of my foundation. They might die otherwise. Here is the kitchen.'

Two women in white cotton smocks and white caps were stirring tureens of dhal, another woman was slapping chapattis and frying them on a smooth stovetop. At another table a woman was sorting chickpeas, looking for pebbles.

'Nutritious food, that's the secret,' Mrs Unger said. 'We are entirely Ayurvedic here. All vegetarian. We have an Ayurvedic doctor on the staff.'

We came to a circular staircase. She called to a young boy dressed in blue shorts and a grey shirt, the same sort of school uniform as Jyoti, who ran to him. Then she started up the stairs.

'This was the mansion of one of the great English families,' Mrs Unger said as she got to the landing and we looked down at the large room. 'It was a total wreck when I found it seven years ago, but we're slowly bringing it back. Charlie and Rajat are helping in the restoration. Look at those teak handrails and spindles and that wood panelling. It's very early and well worth preserving.'

'More rehab,' I said.

'That's the word. I want to be a lifesaver.' She pointed left and right as we walked. 'Bedrooms, dorms, showers.'

The big upper rooms were partitioned, and along the walls were bunk beds, in the centre rows of little cots. The ceilings were twelve feet high in some rooms, with fans hanging from vertical pipes.

'Boys here and' – she was still walking along the corridor – 'over here, girls.'

'What sort of ages are they?' I asked.

'We take them young. We encourage them. We train them and then they enter the great world.'

I was impressed by the orderliness of the place, the way Mrs Unger ran it like a kindly headmistress; but when I praised her she dismissed it, as if out of modesty. Yet I babbled and praised her more. I wanted to please her, and though I intended to exaggerate her generosity, I realized that I didn't have to. What she was engaged in was a powerful example of philanthropy, using her own money, not soliciting funds, to create a safe place for lost children.

I told her that.

'Thank you,' she said. 'I like that – "lost children". I'd like to work that into my brochure. Sometimes when they come here they're angry, nearly uncontrollable. The world has been cruel to them. But we try to reassure them. We feed them and give them clean conditions and make them feel secure.'

'How do you do that?'

'By loving them,' she said simply. 'Sometimes I just hold them, wrap my arms around them. I can feel all the tension go away.'

I wanted to be held like that. Here I was, alone in India; I could

relate to the lost children, bewildered in the city. I could understand a child being soothed in Mrs Unger's arms. I had been held by
her – the magic fingers – and I wanted more.

'Call it a safe haven,' she said.

It was serene and orderly and swept clean. The place actually
worked.

We had arrived at the back of the mansion, a room I remembered that gave on to the garden. From here and around the rear
courtyard I recognized the spa area – the massage room I'd been in,
the steam room, the showers and plunge baths, and on an upper
balcony some lounge chairs where, after the exertions of a massage
or a scrubbing or a sauna, a person could lie down and snooze.

Two men lay sleeping there, their faces covered with towels,
their legs stretched out. They were as still as corpses.

'Charlie and Rajat,' Mrs Unger said. 'I love to see them together.'

That first evening I'd met her, she'd said, 'I never know what I
ought to do,' and 'They're in charge.' And I'd seen her as the uncertain mother, being gently bossed by her son and his friend. Now
I knew better, but I was more than ever touched by her kindness.

Here as elsewhere in the mansion were men in white pyjamas
standing like orderlies, or like sentries. They greeted Mrs Unger
with a show of respect, not looking her in the eye but, in a habit of
esteem, half bowing – and I would not have been surprised to see
them drop to their knees and abase themselves, touch the hem of
her sari and bleat in submission. I thought this because one of them
actually made as if to do it, startling me as he knelt and rolled his
whole body forward at her feet in genuflection.

'The garden,' she said, stepping past the servant, extending her
arm, indicating palms and bushes and red lilies and thick, pale tree
roots surrounding a pool of glittering water.

'The massage rooms are down there, aren't they?'

'That's right. Bottom of the stairs.'

'I really enjoyed the experience,' I said.

She smiled, but vaguely. Had I interrupted her train of thought?
She said without much emotion, 'I'm so glad.'

'I kind of thought we were headed there.'

'All in good time,' she said.

Was she teasing me? It was hard to tell. It was not as though this tour was frivolous. The more I saw, the more I was convinced that this was a large project – the size of the house, the number of children, the order of it, both as a school and a refuge, entirely self-sufficient, with a clinic and a spa.

She had said *I want you to know me*. At the time her words seemed like procrastination. But now I'd seen enough to know that she was someone of real substance. She was an idealist and she was kind; she was motherly, yet she had the efficiency and command of a businesswoman – all the qualities of a nurturer.

We had arrived at a downstairs lobby that fronted on to the garden. The moss-covered statuary, the damp bricks on the paved path, the pool with its fountain – a marble cow's head spewing water from the pipe at its rounded mouth, a gurgling that seemed to cool the garden.

'Tea?' Mrs Unger said.

'Perfect.' But I would have said that to anything she suggested.

'It's herbal. One of our own blends. Mint and neem paste.'

'I'd love some. Maybe with ice.'

'We never use ice.'

'Oh?'

'Think what ice would do to your system,' she said and, before I could reply, she went on, 'Traumatize it.' A man in white pyjamas was hovering. 'Two pots of tea.'

'Yes, madam.'

'You run the whole place alone?'

'Charlie and Rajat are an enormous help.'

'I'm amazed that you have no outside funding.'

'I could use more funding, but I don't want the strings. It would mean interference. This place runs smoothly because I'm alone.'

She talked about the running of the house, the staffing of the clinic, the spa, the school; but always I was distracted by her beauty, her fresh face, her full lips, the way her eye-teeth bulged against them, her thick dark hair drawn back and held in a braid, the dangly gold hoops attached to the lobes of her tightly rolled ears, her long neck, her breasts that were defined even in the mass of the twisted silk of her sari and shawl. Her hands – the arousing hands that had brought me to a pitch of delirium. Her words had never meant as much to me as her hands; her words were so abstract or esoteric as to be meaningless. But her hands had been all over me, every bit of my body, inside me. She had remade me with her hands, made me her own.

I was listening to her describe the work she did as a philanthropist, and I marvelled, but I could not erase from my mind the pleasure she had given me as I'd lain naked under her hands. Yet she had not alluded to the episode. She'd given me no relief, only filled me with a kind of desire I'd thought was unattainable.

'I've never met anyone like you,' I said.

'That could mean anything.'

'I'm trying to compliment you.'

'Thank you. It may seem an odd thing for me to say, but I don't think anyone is really able to know another person completely. We try, but – maybe it's best that way.'

'You said you wanted me to know you. You wanted to know me.'

'Know me better. Know you better. Not know completely. That's hopeless.'

'What's the point?'

'Isn't it fun trying?'

'Frustrating,' I said.

The tea had come; the servant had been noiseless. Mrs Unger didn't say anything more. She allowed the man to pour us each a cup of the fragrant tea.

Forming in my head was the line *I was looking forward to your healing hands – your magic fingers*. It sounded pathetic and corny as I silently rehearsed it. But it was what I felt. I wanted more. Sitting there in dumb yearning for her, I felt like a monkey, with a monkey's hunger.

But I said, 'You sent me a letter, remember? It was about a dead body in a hotel – very dramatic. I thought you wanted me to help you.'

71

I couldn't tell her that I'd talked to Rajat, that I had paid two visits to the Hotel Ananda: I had no results. Next to this accomplished woman I felt inept and I had no news.

'I was wondering if you remembered the letter.'

'How could I forget it? I still have it – an actual letter, not an email. Purple ink on handmade paper. Are you sorry you sent it to me?'

'Not at all.' She spoke with utter certainty.

'Then what do you want me to do?'

'Ask no questions.'

'Then what?'

She stared at me, looking triumphant, as though she'd trapped me. And of course she had.

'No more questions,' I said.

'I was wondering if you were planning to stay in Calcutta.'

No questions. I said, 'I'll do whatever you want me to do.'

'Nothing more today,' she said and, with a gesture, she signalled for Balraj to drive me back to the Hastings.

You might think – I certainly thought – her cool smile and distant manner would put me off and perhaps rebuff me to the point where I'd develop another social circle in Calcutta, or (as I had briefly planned) leave the city altogether. The opposite was the case. At the outset, she'd said that she knew I was close to the consulate. Though she didn't know Howard, she probably believed I was another consulate party-goer. She imagined that I mattered to those people.

Yet I'd seen them less and less because of her, and her days of remoteness had made me more dependent on her. Her not mentioning the letter made me memorize it; her distance had kept me in suspense. I had longed for her to call me. I had not been able to call her, nor could I lurk near her Lodge, because I had no idea where it was in this city of lanes and back alleys. I had desired her, she had been inaccessible and I had been helpless – a pathetic way for a grown man to behave, and something new to me.

I had told myself that I didn't want her love, that I saw no future

72

for us, that I thought her son and his friend were a little odd and off-putting. What did I want, then?

I was lying in bed that night, tuning my shortwave radio, trying to get the news from the wider world. I surprised myself by speaking out loud.

'More,' I said.

Alone, I became inward and analytical, taking altogether too much notice of my dreams, as solitary people do, hoping for good omens, hoping for hope. Lately I was dreaming of narrow escapes, of making my way across the ramparts of very high walls and having to descend the narrowest and steepest staircases with no handrail, a great emptiness on either side, tiptoeing, dizzy and fearful. Yet I never fell, in all the variations of this vertigo. The clack of the ceiling fan, the rattle of the blinds, the voices in the street and the bright morning sun only added to the tormenting effects in the dream.

I never suspected Mrs Unger of being a tormentor. She was busy. I was not busy at all. There was not a day I spent in Calcutta in my moping that I did not think how virtuous she was, working every day to improve the lives of those children, and how selfishly I spent my time, helping no one. I thought often of the bat-eared boy Jyoti: how much she had done for him, how she had saved him – the sort of street child I saw every day in Calcutta and simply hurried past, not wanting to think of his fate. I did not regard myself as worthy enough for her to care. I deserved to wait. *Ask no questions* was a conundrum, but it was an order I deserved. My patient waiting was the proof of my loyalty. I was not in love, but something deeper took hold of me, a peculiar form of devotion, a need for her to protect me. And I knew that others must have felt the same – the lost children, for example.

Maybe I was one of them?

One of the sunnier remarks of a gloomy German philosopher was that the only way of knowing a person is to love them without hope.

The other effect of my solitude was that the diary I had started had become the repository of all these thoughts, even a kind of narrative. Keeping a diary is often an unmistakable sign of desperation. It was a log of my feelings, a chronology of incidents (including the ones I have described here) and an account of time passing. It served its purpose: I had nothing else to write; it kept me busy at night and it reminded me of my pain.

*I go for walks,* I wrote. *I look for the man I once was. I believe that by wandering I might find him wandering here. I need to soothe myself in this uncertainty. I want something to write about. Walking in the big, decaying yet eternal-seeming ruin of the city helps me meditate on the past and gives me the hope that I might find the man I had once been – confident in a strange country, so anonymous as to be invisible, living the muffled and spectral existence of a traveller, ghosting from street to street in the endless decrepitude, unseen. I expect to come face to face with myself.*

What a shock, then, in this mournful scribbling, in my mood of anonymity, one afternoon to be touched physically in the street. It was not the sleeve-tug of the beggar or the tout but a hard pinch, skin to skin, by the pincers of a skinny person's fingers. I pulled my hand away.

'Take, sir.'

'No.'

'Please, sir.'

A thin-faced girl in a shawl was urging me to accept a piece of folded paper from her. I imagined she was selling something or that she was trying to distract me so that my pocket could be picked. This was why, when she touched me, I shoved my hands into my pockets and clutched my wallet and keys, pressing my arms to my sides. Or I'd take the paper and she would say, 'No mother, no father. Please, you give me, sir.'

But she said, 'Mobile number, sir.'

'I don't want it.'

'Mina, sir.'

That stopped me. And now I recognized this nervous girl in the shawl as the new clerk from the Ananda, the head of gleaming hair that had bobbed beneath the counter.

I accepted the paper. Without a pause, she drew her shawl

tighter and darted away, dodging oncoming pedestrians, slipping past a man with a barrow piled with coconuts and children's sandals.

It always amazed me to see an Indian run – sprint in this traffic, through the crowds, into the heat. Yet they often ran, and the poorer and more ragged they were, the faster they went, knees pumping, feet slapping. Foreigners never ran in India.

I unfolded the paper. I walked a bit, then stepped into a doorway, dialled the number and cupped my hand over the phone. I heard ringing, then gabble. I could not understand a word. I said into the din, 'Mina?'

'Yes, here.'

'Someone just gave me your number.'

'My friend. I am knowing.'

'What do you want?'

'Pass information.'

'OK. Let's meet.'

'Tomorrow, teatime.'

'My hotel. The Hastings.'

'Cannot hotel, sir.'

'What about the Roxy or the Oly Pub?'

'Cannot Roxy. Go to Eden Teashop. Middleton Row at Park Street. Teatime.'

I had to ask her to repeat this several times.

Finally she said, 'Taxi will know.'

'Will I recognize you?'

'I will find you, sir.'

Of course, the big pink *ferringhi* would be obvious.

As Mina had predicted, the taxi driver knew the precise place, a small bakery and café with some trays of Indian sweets in the window and more in a glass case under a counter inside. I had last seen Mina wearing a pink dress, so I was confused when I went in at the appointed time – I took it to be four – and didn't see a woman who resembled her. No dresses, only saris.

Seating myself in the corner, with a good view of the door, I ordered tea from a waiter and cautiously looked around. Three tables were occupied. My tea was served. I sipped it. I read a section of the *Statesman* that was lying on a nearby chair, and when after thirty minutes or more I did not see Mina, I paid the bill and left. I wondered what had gone wrong. I turned into Park Street and kept walking.

The heat, the stink, the diesel fumes, the noise, all combined to thicken the steamy air and burden me. How could people run in this air? I had stepped briskly on to the pavement but slowed my pace, with the heat on my shoulders, my head ringing from the smells. It was exhausting to be in the middle of so much human activity – so much futility, so it seemed – the people pressed against me and stepping on my feet. It wearied me to be touched and jostled at every step.

I was bumped. I turned to object and saw a woman wrapped in a sari hovering at my side.

'Mina?'

'Indeed, sir.'

'I waited for you at the teashop.'

'I could not enter in. I saw a relation of Mr Bibhuti Biswas inside. I waited nearby, at the godown.'

'So where shall we go?'

'Continue footpath this side to cemetery.'

The Park Street Cemetery – I'd been there before on one of my reflective strolls. We walked, Mina and I, without speaking, she keeping slightly ahead of me. When we got to the cemetery gates she moved quickly on to one of the gravel paths at the side and vanished among the tombstones. I did not hurry. I had lost her, but I counted on her to find me. I plodded like a tourist. Deeper into the cemetery, where the tombs were like obelisks and pyramids, the vaults like little villas and classical bungalows, I saw her sitting on a mourner's bench near a big broken tomb – Doric columns, a marble wreath, a winged angel and bold croaking ravens in the trees and hopping on the ground.

'Mina.'

'Yes, sir. Here, sir. Thank you.'

'Thank you for getting in touch.'

'Sorry for the hue and cry, sir. I could not reveal myself.'

'You're wearing a sari. I was expecting you in a dress.'

I took a seat beside her and now, as she adjusted her shawl to speak, I could see her face. One whole side was swollen and bruised. Her left eye was rimmed with dark skin, the eye itself reddened, the white of the eye blood-drenched.

'What happened to you?'

'Mr Bibhuti Biswas administered a beating, sir.'

She slipped her shawl off her forearm and I saw bruises there, welts, red and crusted, black broken patches on her dark skin.

'I breaking the rules, sir. He beat me with a lathi, sir. He calling me *kangali*. *Bhikhiri*. Other bad names. Then he say, *"Tumi kono kajer na – tumi ekdom bekar!"'*

This outpouring of Bengali left me glassy-eyed and I was stunned into staring at her.

'"You totally useless. Totally worthless." Then he sack me.'

'That's awful.'

'Very bad. What I can do? But I knowing why you come to Hotel Ananda. I knowing about your friend.'

'That there was a dead body in his room?'

'Dead boy, sir. Rolled in carpet, sir. Like tumbaco in beedee.'

'You saw it?'

'When they taking it away, we all knowing. Mr Bibhuti Biswas say *Chup karo*. Not say anything! But it is human child, sir. One of God's children.'

'What could have happened to him?'

'I cannot know how he dead.'

'No. I mean, how did they dispose of him?'

'Disposing in pieces, sir. So horrible. I was witness. They used very sharp *dah*.'

'I mean, in the carpet?'

'Not carpet afterwards. Crate, sir. Steamer trunk, so to say. Maybe in the river. Or in municipal dustcart.'

'We'll never find him.'

'So many people die in Calcutta, sir.'

'Some of them are right here.'

In the stillness of the cemetery, behind the thick perimeter walls, among the high monuments and the ornate inscriptions, the fluted columns and the statuary.

'But I am liking to come here.'

'For the tombstones?'

'For the angels, sir. See them.'

Angels kneeling at prayer, angels on plinths in repose. Angels with their wings spread – some of the wings clipped, other angels beheaded – angels sounding trumpets. They were cracked and battered, some of them carved in stone, others in marble, and in this city of peeling paint most of them were mottled or moss-grown, but they were angels nonetheless. The angels put me in mind of the dead boy in the room.

'But how did he get there?' I asked. Mina was staring at me, her good eye registering concern. 'The boy. In the hotel. In the room.'

'I duty manager.'

'At the desk?'

'Yes. It was a parcel delivery.'

I smiled at the explanation, as I had smiled at *duty manager*. 'They delivered a dead body?'

'A carpet, sir. I sign for it, sir. The carpet was dispatched to room of your friend.'

'What room?'

'Fifteen. Garden view.'

'Where was the body?'

'Carpet was parcelled. Body was inside.'

Now I saw it: the skinny child rolled in the carpet and brought upstairs, perhaps in the darkness, lugged into the room and un-rolled. Rajat had woken and seen it, the corpse on the floor, and had fled.

'So my friend wasn't imagining it?'

'You not tell Mr Bibhuti Biswas, sir, that you speak to me. He be so angry.'

'He's not your boss any more.'

'He be terrible to me again, beating me. He knowing my residence in *bustee* in Tollygunge. I have new job.'

'What doing?'

'Sweeper, sir.'

This tore at my heart – the bruised face, the skinny fingers tugging at her shawl. Helpless and ashamed, I gave her two five-hundred rupee notes.

'God bless you, sir.'

She reached into the folds of her shawl and took out a small cloth shoulder bag and set it on her lap. She plucked open the knots on the flap and slid out a plastic pouch that was taped shut.

'Not be fearful, sir, please.'

'Why should I be fearful?' I had started to smile, but her bruised face sobered me.

'It be so strange to you. You must not cry out. It is very important. It is all that is left. The only thing.' She spoke slowly, annoyingly so. She was nodding as she put the plastic pouch into my hand. 'You will be knowing what to do.'

'Shall I open it now?'

'After I gone, sir. I can't bear look it again. It is terrible thing indeed.'

She flung her shawl around her face, pinched it at her chin so that only her eyes showed, then she bowed, said 'Bless you, sir' again and slipped between the gravestones and the many angels and was gone.

I held the soft pouch. I was sceptical: Indians loved drama; their natural element was hyperbole. They lived in words – words were kinder and more habitable than the *bustees*. Mrs Unger was like that too. So I picked at the lightly taped parcel with the feeling that I was being trifled with in the Indian way: *It be so strange to you. You must not cry out.*

I did not cry out at once. I thought: *A piece of meat, how odd in vegetarian India.*

But then I saw the small fingers, the tiny fingernails, almost reptilian, the lined palm, the severed wrist bone, the ragged flesh bound by a piece of string. A human hand – a dead hand, stiff and grey. And I let out a cry, as though someone had stabbed me and twisted the knife.

With this thing in my possession I knew I could not leave Calcutta.

Had I been in a house, I would have hidden the dead hand in a distant room, or in a box in the basement, or in an attic trunk. There was something creepy about carrying this horrible thing back with me to my bedroom in the Hotel Hastings. I kept thinking of the yellow fingernails, the neatly severed wrist tied with string. Wherever I put it in my room, I would never be more than six feet away from it. I could not put it in a drawer or in the closet – the cleaning woman would find it. So I locked it in the side pocket of my duffel bag, using my little padlock. Because the pocket was small I could see where it swelled, could almost make out the contour of the dead knuckles – my eye was constantly drawn to the bulge.

Who was it? Someone who had only worked, who had never laughed, who was forgotten, someone perhaps more useful dead than alive; a sad soul. My memory of the thing woke me in the night. I imagined it flexing to be free, trying to claw out of the side pocket. Even liberated, saved from cremation, it was no more than a stiffened hand, a little paw that had been detached from a body.

Severed, in its discoloured plastic bag, it was pathetic, needing attention. I felt a severe sense of obligation. In spite of being so small it imposed a great weight, holding me here in Calcutta, pleading to be identified. It was my secret and my responsibility. I had been entrusted with it. Mina knew how valuable it was, but she could not have known how much it mattered to me – how it reproached me. I wished I had never seen it, because I knew now that it obligated me. I had seen hands like this many times in Calcutta – just like this, stuck into my face as I sat in traffic, or imploring me as I walked around the city, the cupped hand of a beggar.

At my lowest points at night, studying the bulge in my duffel bag, I knew who this sad neglected figure was who'd been bundled up and brought to the room. It was me. I knew whose this dead hand was. It was mine.

★

80

Mrs Unger had said early on that she needed to see me. Now she seemed to be ignoring me. That paradox wounded me, but what could I do about it? Only obey. Ask no questions.

I called Howard at the consulate, hoping that he would help me identify the dead hand, as I assumed Mina wished me to do.

'I need a favour.'

'This is why I'm here, to grant favours to itinerant Americans.'

'It's serious. I want you to put me in touch with a forensics expert. I have an item that needs examining, in confidence.'

'Tell me what you've got and I'll let you know.'

'A dead hand.' I had said it so softly I had to repeat it three times before he understood.

'Is this a figure of speech?'

'A human hand. Rather small. No joke. I need to know more about it.'

When he realized I was serious, he became solemn and a bit chastened. He swallowed hard and said, 'You want to see my friend Dr Mooly Mukherjee at police HQ. I'll call him and tell him you're coming.'

The next day, following directions to Bazar Street, near Dalhousie Square, I presented myself at the main police station and, after a long wait, was brought upstairs by a *chowkidar* to meet Dr Mooly Mukherjee. He was big-bellied with a full moustache and the brisk, confident manner of a medical man.

'Howard is a great friend,' he said. 'He left me a message on my voice mail. I hope I haven't kept you waiting.'

He must have known he had. I'd been downstairs for almost half an hour.

'I want you to look at this,' I said, and was glad to see, as I spoke, that he stepped behind me to shut his office door.

He hardly reacted when he opened the pouch. Then he frowned and stroked his moustache. He did not remove the dead hand, as I had done. He looked at it closely through the clear plastic wrapper.

'I will not ask you how this body part has come to be in your possession. I shall assume that you came by it honestly, or happened upon it. Hooghly is teeming with body parts of incomplete cremations. My good wife and I encountered a human leg one day at Tolly's Nullah.'

'So you understand.'

'I shall log it in as DNA rather than evidence. What is it you require?'

'I want to know the age. The sex. Most of all, the fingerprints. I'd like to identify who it is.'

After he had agreed and I had left the office, walking to calm myself, I thought: *And who am I? Please tell me who I am and what I'm doing.*

Then all that changed.

# 6

The smoky half-dark room, Mrs Unger's vault, was arranged as though for a Black Mass. The only light was the flame of one fragrant candle, near a stick of incense burning in a dish before a fierce-faced goddess. The air was ripe with the gummy odour of hot oil. Saturated with this same oil, I lay face-down on the table of heavy wood, which was shaped like ancient altars I had seen in the Middle East – in Syria and Jordan – at which animals were slaughtered and offered as sacrifices. This one was also scooped out at the end and gouged with grooves, so that blood could drain from the beheaded animal. I was surrendering, I was offering myself up. I was happy.

I was calm because – how can I describe this without sounding mawkish? – I was convinced of Mrs Unger's goodness, her pure intentions, her great works among the poor and the innocent in Calcutta. And yet I was also invigorated by her passion. I wanted her to know how I felt. She had been testing me – in a way, everything she did or said was a test of my sincerity. She had sent me a letter, she had introduced me to her son and his friend, she had taken me for a meal, she had massaged me with her healing hands. And then she had made me wait, tormented me, met me again, said, 'Ask no questions,' and finally she'd shown me the interior of her mansion, the house of lost children.

I had cooperated. I could not have refused. I was smitten with her, half in love but also afraid, because in my life (and she seemed to know this) I had not loved anyone without having been wounded. Love was power and possession, love caused pain: you were never more exposed than when you were in love, never more wounded; possession was an enslavement, something stifling.

Then Mrs Unger had summoned me to her vault, and I felt at last that she needed me, perhaps not as much as I desired her, but desire was never equal. Maybe that accounted for its intensity, the tantalizing difference making me eager, while her holding back a little, or at least her not matching my passion, made me overstate mine and want more from her.

This sounds like a power struggle, and I suppose most passion amounts to that, but it is of an overwhelming kind in which both parties are satisfied. It just wasn't possible to be an equal in desire, nor to play the same role: there was always a giver and a receiver. I mentioned earlier the paradoxes and contradictions of the wealthy. Mrs Unger embodied some of those contradictions and reminded me of all the conflict I felt when faced with a rich person. I looked at one of these people and knew I did not matter. I did not feel there was anything I could give her, and then I realized that my gift to her was my submission. It is the ultimate gift to any powerful person. Over the course of this semi-courtship she had managed to strip me of the last traces of my resistance, all my hesitation, all my questions.

She had asked me if I planned to stay in Calcutta.

*I'll do whatever you want me to do,* I'd said.

That was the posture she required: unconditional surrender.

It took no effort on my part. I wanted her to do whatever she wished with me; I wanted her to use me. She was virtuous and I was not, and to prove it, here I was on the sacrificial altar, flat on my face, stark naked.

I didn't hear her enter the vault. I heard the door latch being lifted like a nail scratch, the bolt thrown decisively. Then I became aware of a powerful odour of flowers filling the room, a perfume that hovered at my face and heated my scalp, a sweetness that was like an anaesthetic, the aroma humming and thickening in the air that half stifled me and made me dizzy. And being in the vault was like being inside her body.

The silken sari lapped against my arm and slipped against my shoulder and brushed my cheek. I wanted to eat it. I felt a light touch, her fingers on my head as though anointing it, and fingertips on my naked back, tracing my spine. I had started to raise my head when I felt the pressure of her hand. But I was too dazed by the strong perfume to do much except lie there on the altar-like table and receive her touch.

She did not say a word, yet her hands on me spoke, prodding me with her thumbs, pressing her knuckles into my backbone, interrogating my flesh with her fingers. She held my head, lifted and twisted it until my neck seemed to swivel on crusted grains of sugar. She pinched my neck the way a cook flutes pastry and even in my drugged state it hurt. She massaged my ears, beginning with the rims and working slowly towards the lobes. Head, neck, shoulders, spine – she clasped me and seemed to penetrate my body, digging to the attachments of my muscles.

All this time I lay flat and face-down on the hot oiled wood of the sacrificial table.

She gently lifted my right arm, dug her fingers into the muscles starting at my shoulder and pressed so hard she could have been using pliers, inching downward to my wrist. The pressure was painful, perhaps the more so because I could hear her breathing as she made an effort. And when she slipped to my hand and held it and pushed the meat and muscle of my palm apart, using her thumb on the bones, I was almost overcome by a feeling I could not tell was pleasure or pain.

I worked with this hand. My right hand was the instrument of action and creation – holding a pen, making love. It contained the soul of my handshake, it was a weapon, it fed me and consoled me when I stroked my cheek or clasped my chin or rubbed my eyes: my life was scored in its lines, my labour in its calluses. This hand was my writing instrument.

She seemed to know how important this hand was to me as she separated each muscle in my palm and used her fingertips to find the small bones beneath, finally cracking the joints finger by finger.

*I give you my hand*, lovers say at a betrothal. It was exactly what I felt. She had picked up my hand, massaged it, pulled it apart, heated it with her own hand and made it her own.

She lifted my other arm and did the same, breaking down the

muscle, disconnecting the bones, taking me to pieces muscle by muscle, a ritual of separation and connection, a kind of bloodless surgery.

I had not realized how strong she was. In the dark, feeling the sharpness of her touch, I was like a child in the hands of a giantess – small, not weak but overwhelmed. She shifted to stand at the end of the table and placed the crown of my head just above her knees and clasped it, thrusting as she worked on my back.

Naked under her hands, I could easily have been a child; not just a young boy but an infant, lying there receiving a mother's attentions. But instead of an innocent caress, I wanted something explicit, dominant and sensual. I had yearned to be touched. I loved her hands and the way heat radiated from the soft skin of her silks, and I longed to be touched more, harder, with more assertion. She lingered on the small of my back, caressed me, and finally made an elaborate business of finding the muscles in my buttocks, pouring hot oil on them and plucking at them and grinding her fists into them, using both hands until my body was flattened against the table.

She briefly let up. My skin chafed, tingling and short of breath I was aware of her movement in the room, a disturbance of the perfume, little wisps and eddies of the warm odour at my ears.

Inhaling through her nose, she gripped my shoulders and with a sudden upsweep of her sari got on to the table, straddled me, her knees at my sides. Then she lay lengthwise against me, fitting herself to my back and legs, her chin resting lightly on the nape of my neck, her silks like flesh, the warm weight of her slender body holding me captive.

Like a mother, like a lover, she lay there for a long time, pressing closer, using her arms and elbows, squeezing the breath out of me, imprinting herself on my body. She slowly insinuated herself against me, preventing me from making the slightest movement. I could sense her breathing, her hot mouth open on my neck. I loved her soft body on me, her knees against the backs of my legs. She pressed so hard it was as if she were forcing the life out of me, displacing me, inhabiting me.

86

I was helpless the whole time. I had done nothing but receive her attention. She was maternal, but more than that: she entered that intimate zone of mothering that is also erotic. Still she lay on top of my naked body, subtly stroking it, using her whole body, confining me until I was overcome with the heat of her breath and the heavy perfume and her flesh vibrant on me with the pulsing of her blood, massaging me with her heartbeat. I did not sleep. Instead I died. No dreams.

I came to life lying face-up, blinking in the light of candle flames. She was holding my head. I was groggy, I couldn't speak. She touched my face, my lips, my eyes.

'You're mine.'

She could tell from her fingertips against my head that I was too happy to reply.

'That was amazing.'

'*Bhoga*,' she said, and then, 'There's something I want you to see. But not now.'

I knew better than to ask when.

She led me through the shadowy corridors of the mansion and, as always, I heard the sound of children's voices, the slap and scuff of their feet, the scrape of chair legs, the clink of cabinet doors and the deeper voices of women, nagging, warning and drawling reprimands.

The car was parked near the broken fountain, Balraj beside it in the same squatting posture as I'd last seen him. He stood and opened the door for me.

'Don't take a bath,' she said from the top of the stairs. 'It would wash off all the fragrances and oils. Just rest and drink water. You'll need to rehydrate.'

'Traffic,' Balraj said as we sat becalmed among hundreds of honking cars and trucks and auto-rickshaws.

Too tired to reply, I nodded at his eyes in the rear-view mirror. Later, after he dropped me at the Hastings, I drank a pitcher of water and slept for ten hours. She had imprinted herself so intimately on me that the whole night I felt her flesh against me, her spirit within me, the touch of her hands, her breath on my neck, her weight and the cool liquid silkiness of her sari, her skin on my skin, her bones against my bones.

I was not sleeping alone: she was still with me, her odour, her warmth, her womanhood on me, the throb of her blood. I could feel her so distinctly that when I finally awoke I was surprised to find myself alone.

Yet she existed within me. She had insinuated herself there, her spirit lived inside me, I could still feel the pressure of her body. She was palpable, I could taste and smell her, she had left an impression on every part of me, as a physical presence, as a mental image that glowed like a dark flame in my mind. I understood this lightness of soul as something exquisite that strengthened me. I thought: *This justifies everything*. But I was too superstitious to give it a name.

# Part Two

# 7

Slashes of daylight as white-hot stripes dazzled at the slats of my blinds. I had always regarded this light as a reminder that I was in Calcutta; now this brightness was like an apparition of Mrs Unger. She was warmth and light to me, she was my reason for being in the city, she was life to me – my first thought as I drew a breath that morning, feeling her fingers on my hands. I yawned and sat on the edge of my bed, limp but rested after the deep sleep.

The telephone rang. I guessed who it might be. I fumbled with the receiver as though I'd just settled to earth. The room phones at the Hastings were heavy black Bakelite specimens with stiff, twisted cords, phones that had been junked as obsolete everywhere else in the world, but in Calcutta nothing was obsolete. Before I could say anything, I was jarred by a man's voice.

'Dr Mukherjee here, speaking from police headquarters.'

'Yes. Do you have any news about the, um, item?'

'Just a preliminary report regarding fingerprints.'

'What did you find?'

'Better question – what did we not find?' he said, pleased with himself for being paradoxical. 'I have some issues to address. I will need to see you in person.'

'Any time.'

'I am booked up. Next week is better than this,' he said. 'Do you know occupation of the deceased?'

'I have no idea.'

'Could it have been masonry? Tilery? Bricklaying? I have some general notions. Ironmongery?'

I smiled at the old word 'ironmongery' in the old crusty voice on the old bulky telephone. It was the Indian illusion, as though I were speaking to someone on an antique line that stretched to the distant past.

'But Dr Mukherjee, this was a child.'

His voice rising in protest, he said, 'Child can be manual labourer. Why not, sir?'

'In India.'

'India and elsewhere.'

I considered this. 'Is that all you can tell me?'

'We are proceeding with further tests, as scheduled. Please come next week for consultation.'

I was bewildered by his call. To restore my mood, the lightness I'd felt on waking, I worked on my diary after breakfast and for most of the day, writing a description of the massage Mrs Unger had given me. But it was more than a massage: it was an act of possession. All my hesitation left me when I wrote about it, and it seemed as I reconstructed the episode that I had not only regained my ability but in the writing began to understand what had happened to me, the transformation. And I thought how she had made that day important, and she had given me this day too, a day of writing. So, as she had done for me, in her work in Calcutta she gave her lost children time and hope.

I found I could sit quietly now. I felt no urgency to leave Calcutta nor even to leave the hotel. I was content; she had calmed me. I understood her better as a humanitarian – a mother figure – giving reassurance. It was not a matter of money but rather of a depth of feeling. It amazed me that she was hardly known.

The following morning, another blazing day, the phone rang again, this time before I was fully awake. I took it to be Dr Mooly Mukherjee with an update, but it was Mrs Unger.

'I'm downstairs in the lobby. Don't be too long – we need to be somewhere fairly soon. And we've got a big day ahead of us. Have you been sleeping well?'

I made an appreciative sound. She was a glow at the other end of the line. I could not clearly recall her face.

'I knew you would.'

Another surprise: after that bewitchment she was all business. But she was full of surprises.

Feeling hot and damp from the long sleep, I took a shower,

dressed and hurried downstairs, eating a banana on the way.

'You shouldn't eat bananas,' she said. 'Not with your body type.'

'What's my body type?'

'*Pitta*. Fire and water.'

'What should I eat?'

'Figs.' She was smiling. She assumed a dancer's posture. 'Melons.'

I heard the words as I stared at her body. And I was thinking how lucky I was to have this woman in my life, appearing in the lobby of my hotel on this sunny morning. She was dressed in a white sari, her shawl over her head instead of draped on her shoulder. She was arrayed like a Madonna, her face framed by the folds of her shawl; but even so, as a figure of holiness she had an aura of sensuality, something about the way she stood, then the slope and glide of her walk, her short, swift steps, a way of moving her hands, her slender, beckoning fingers. She touched me softly as I passed and when I paused to savour the moment I saw the curve of her hips, a rotation, slipping beneath her sari.

I did not ask her where we were going. I obeyed the rule.

'Madam?' Balraj was steering into the flow of honking cars.

'Kalighat.'

As we moved slowly along Chowringhee, I glanced at my watch. It was not yet seven thirty. That accounted for my drowsiness and I had the slight hangover I often got when I worked late writing. But this feeling was welcome. I had actually written six pages. In this dense traffic, crawling through the heat – and it would be stinking hot in a few hours – I realized she must have woken me at seven or a little before. I had been so eager to see her I hadn't minded the early hour.

'I know that name, Kalighat.'

'One of the sacred places,' she said. 'We have something important to do there.'

I loved her for saying 'we'. I was elated and reassured, because that's how I wanted her to think of me, as a friend, as an ally. More than that, as a partner.

'That's wonderful,' I said, meaning everything. 'What does *bhoga* mean?'

'Tantric term. Intense physical desire.'

I had to turn away from her. I looked out of the window. We passed Mehboob Panwallah and Eatery, the name assuming an irrelevant importance because I was glancing at the signboard as she spoke.

'What do you do when you're on your own?'

She asked big questions bluntly. I could have told her about Parvati and her poems, that empty flirtation. Or about Howard and his consular stories ('you could use that'), the shuttling life I lived between jobs and cities and magazine pieces, the occasional radio item, my ill-fated TV travel show, my life of procrastination – the opposite of her life of action and commitment. But all that had stopped.

'Not much,' I said. I wondered if I dared to tell her, because in telling her I was exposed; I'd have no more secrets. Yet she would know if I were lying and she was so truthful herself it seemed unworthy to try to deceive her. I wanted her to trust me. I had wooed enough women in the past to know that only a woman's trust – and hope – led to sex.

Mrs Unger was staring at me with her pale eyes, which were dark in a dark room, greenish in candlelight, grey in daylight like this; and I could see from the cast of her lips, the set of her jaw, the way her eye-teeth bulked against her lips, that she expected me to say more.

'I think of you when I'm on my own,' I said. I had told women this many times without meaning it, but I meant it now, in a desperate way. 'That's all I think about – how long it will be before I see you again. And I wonder what you're doing. Please don't laugh.'

She touched my hand. 'That's so tender.'

'It's a little pathetic too.'

She laughed and held on.

'Because I think of myself as a big strong man,' I said in a joking tone, but I meant what I said. I hardly recognized the man I'd become. I'd been planning to leave Calcutta around now, and here I was, in suspense at my hotel, making notes, avoiding friends, waiting to be summoned by Mrs Unger, reduced to a needy boy.

'That means a lot to me,' she said.

I hoped that she'd say that that was how she felt too when she was on her own, thinking of me. But I wanted her to be truthful. I could not phrase it as a question.

I said, 'I'd be happy if you thought of me now and then.'

'I think of you always.' She was a little too prompt, as though observing a form of politeness. Yet she wasn't lying: I could feel her sincerity in her fingers, the way she held my hand. 'I think we have a special bond.'

A person's hand can be like a lie detector. In hers I felt no tremble of deception, only a *but*, something unspoken at the end of her statement.

As though answering a question I hadn't asked, she went on, 'I need you to know everything.'

'That's what I want.'

'It'll take time,' she said. 'If you're patient –' she paused, looked out of the window, the Calcutta Zoo on the right, the viceroy's mansion, another of Calcutta's decayed wedding cakes, now the National Library up ahead on the right behind a big white sign – 'you'll see.'

'I often think about that letter you sent me.'

'My invitation.'

'It was more than that. You wanted me to help you save Rajat from being implicated in that business. The corpse in his hotel room.'

Her face became paler and less animated with thought. She said, 'I still want you to help. Poor Rajat must not be compromised. It would destroy him.'

If I'd had anything to report I would have told her then – that I'd visited the hotel twice, been rebuffed the second time and discovered that the girl who'd helped me had been assaulted and fired; that I'd met her in the Park Street Cemetery and she'd given me a severed hand. But I had no positive news, only these inconclusive events.

'I want to do everything I can to protect him,' she said. 'I think the world of him.'

We were on back streets, among villas and walled compounds, some of them very grand, others almost romantic in their decrepitude, covered in vines, set in large gardens. And street dwellers and hovels too, as in the most expensive of Calcutta's neighbourhoods. Yet this one was substantial, with a thinner flow of traffic.

'This place looks familiar.'

'Alipore.'

'It resembles your neighbourhood,' I said. And I realized it *was* her neighbourhood.

She didn't reply. But any of these villas could have been hers.

'I'm glad you think of me,' I said, because I wanted her to say it again. I couldn't ask. It was often hard to obey her injunction against asking questions.

'Yes. But you're a strong, independent person, so you know how strange it is to need someone else.'

I wanted to say, *I'm not strong any more.*

'Charlie sees it. I think he's a little jealous.'

'He has his life,' I said, because I couldn't say, *He has Rajat.*

She looked out of the window as though glimpsing an answer. 'It'll do him good. I don't interfere.'

'I thought Charlie worked for you.'

'He helps with my foundation. But he attends to his own affairs.'

That was typical of her confident ambiguity. *His own affairs* could have meant anything.

'I'm so busy with my charities I hardly have time for anything else. I mean, besides the foundation there's my school, my clinic, the refuge. Well, you know. Keeping up with the funding and the accounting is a full-time job. And there's so much more. This is Calcutta!'

The pavements we were passing, in spite of the elegant villas behind the high walls, were thronged with women and children. At this spot, as she finished speaking, women in red and yellow saris worked on a building site, carrying gravel out of a pit, emptying one basket at a time in a heap by the side of the road – construction workers, dressed as if for a folk festival.

'I want to make an impact. I want to do something for these people. I don't want to be another tourist in India.'

She spoke in an urgent whisper, not in the valiant and weary way of a philanthropist, boasting of her charity. Her sincere undertone of modesty moved me and filled me with longing.

I had never known any woman like her. Such a woman, I was thinking selfishly, was so truthful, so loyal to her principles, she would never leave me. She would love and nurture me, would be a companion and a caring friend, would look after me with the attention she gave to the lost children. And that same passion could be translated to the bedroom, where generosity mattered most.

'It's always like this.'

She was speaking of the traffic, denser as we moved into narrower streets, among older buildings and shops, a neighbourhood of pedestrians and auto-rickshaws, a place with the look of a bazaar, not residential except in the broadest sense, for people seemed to be living everywhere, in lean-tos and shanties and on blankets by the side of the road. Many of these people were hawkers, selling beads and relics and garlands of marigolds, or were squatting among piles of fresh flowers, stringing them together. The car was slowing, a steel barrier across the road ahead.

'Blockages,' Balraj said.

'We'll walk from here. *Deka hobey.*'

I was glad to get out of the cramped back seat and I thought – not for the first time – that Indian drivers had the best seat; the esteemed passengers in the rear no legroom at all. As I swung the door open (Balraj was attending to Mrs Unger) I was surrounded by men offering to guide me or to sell me necklaces and holy lockets. Mrs Unger waved them off and led me, as a mother shepherds a small boy, keeping a few steps ahead, past the fruit sellers and the stalls into a narrow lane.

'Look.'

In the distance, an opening between two poor huts, a squalid creek with muddy, littered banks, where some women were scrubbing pots in the filthy water and others – women and children –

were picking through an enormous pile of rubbish that had been dumped by the riverside.

'The holy Ganga.'

She was still walking with confidence, striding past the men importuning her.

'And there.'

The sign of the old, low, pale yellow building was lettered MISSIONARIES OF CHARITY – MOTHER TERESA'S HOME FOR THE SICK AND DYING DESTITUTES. With shuttered windows and crumbling sills and cracked stucco, it could have been an old school or a warehouse.

'You can look in.'

'Voyeurism,' I said, but another sign caught my eye: THE GREATEST AIM OF HUMAN LIFE IS TO LIVE AT PEACE WITH GOD – MOTHER.

Mrs Unger saw it too. She said, 'Poor Agnes. I wonder if she achieved her aim of finding peace with God. She certainly found peace with millionaires and celebrities. How she loved visiting New York. She went to Palm Beach once and dazzled everyone. Goodness, what did she do with all that money? She certainly didn't spend it on that sad building.'

'It does look ramshackle.'

'Compare it with my Lodge,' Mrs Unger said.

'I see what you mean.'

'You know why she established herself here?' she went on. 'So she could be a permanent defiance of the temple.' She indicated a parapet and a gilded cupola. 'That's the temple.'

She set her jaw and continued walking stiffly in her determined way through the milling crowds and the occasional beeping car. Wagons, auto-rickshaws, cows, shoppers, beggars, holy men and saddhus – she parted the crowd and I followed, as though being carried into my childhood.

Then I took her hand and instead of consoling fingers I felt a sudden snatching grip, too tight, too hot, too damp, not leading me but pressing for support, her nails digging like a raptor clinging to meat. She wouldn't release me.

'Those people,' she said of the mob. She had gone pale. Her features were sharpened by anxiety and she wore a half-smile of fear. 'I always think they want to devour me.'

She had cut through the crowd without looking left or right. This apparent confidence, which was bravado, making no eye contact, had made her seem imperious.

But her hand told me the truth as she hung on. No one would have guessed that she'd noticed the crowd, though her hand resolved itself into a small, panicky animal. It was not until we were past all those jostling people that she slackened her hold and began again to talk calmly.

'You only hear about one side of the little woman,' she said of Mother Teresa. 'The saintly side.'

'I suppose there was another side.'

'With a saint? Always. A ghastly one,' Mrs Unger said in a subdued way, as if in sympathy.

'That building's famous as her hospice, though.'

'And it's a glorified morgue,' she said and seemed torn, 'because she adored suffering.' She held her breath as we passed another staring knot of people. 'I wonder who she was when she was alone. I think she had no faith except in herself. Nothing wrong with that, but like most crowd pleasers she didn't know when to stop.'

'That seems a little harsh.'

'I don't deny her charity. But she spent very little of the millions she was given. She believed that poverty made people better, but it can make them vicious. The Vatican has the money, all those windbags and paedophiles. Little Agnes was an egotist.' Mrs Unger was still gripping my hand, tapping her emotion into it. 'I don't fault her for leaving her order of nuns and starting her own band of sisters. She needed to be in charge. It's understandable that she was self-invented – it's always the way with so-called saints. Saints are always on their own journey. Agnes was.'

'How do you know?'

'I knew her. I helped her.' Mrs Unger was smiling, passing between a pair of imploring beggars. I glanced away from their cupped hands. 'She had doubts, you know. But I forgive her for being an atheist, poor thing. God had pretty much abandoned her. Instead of faith, she had a feral willpower and a love of failure and death and – excuse me –' she waved away a man on a bicycle – 'poverty and illness. Absolutely loved them, all these miseries that concentrate a person's mind on salvation. "Save me," people screamed at her and that hopeless scream turned her head. Well, of course it would. Who would not be attentive to people so desperate, especially if you can build a reputation on it.'

'How well did you know her?' I asked.

'I sometimes think I'm the only person on earth who truly understood her. She was tiny. Unphysical. She was well aware of the effect her little pickled face and twisted body had on other people. Famous people loved posing with her.'

I tried to imagine Mrs Unger and Mother Teresa side by side, but it seemed a preposterous pairing. I suspected that Mother Teresa would not have been terrified by the mob, as Mrs Unger obviously was.

'She was preoccupied with death. I have only cared about the living, about children who have their whole life ahead of them,' Mrs Unger said. 'She wanted to give people an easy death. Is that an accomplishment? What about giving them sixty years of useful life? But no, that didn't interest Agnes.'

I said, 'Where are we going?'

But she was too engrossed in this memory of Mother Teresa to answer.

'I can ignore all that, but what I cannot ignore is her hideous posturing and her need to be noticed. Is that saintly? She lived for people to see her. She asked for money, but she believed that wealth was the source of evil. She needed witnesses. There's the difference. I don't want attention. I need no witnesses. I gave her money.'

Then she smiled – the smile of ill humour – and waved her hand in the direction of Mother Teresa's home.

'And what's left? Only that obvious anachronism, the house of death.'

Ahead of her, a bearded man in a long white shirt and homespun *khadi* vest recognized her and looked eager.

'Yes, madam, here,' and he gestured in invitation.

'*Apni keman achen?*'

'*Bhalo achhi.* Health is good, madam. I have been waiting you, madam.'

The front of his shop was open – no wall. It was not a shop in the usual sense, but rather an open-sided pen with a tile roof. In a fenced enclosure with an earthen floor there were about a dozen black bleating goats. They were small, most of them, with glossy coats, making sad little cries, each one tethered with a rope around its neck. They nibbled at fodder, grass that had been stacked in a cradle.

The bearded man tugged one of the goats away from the others and heaved it off the ground, holding it in his arms. But Mrs Unger walked past him – in her white diaphanous sari, in the reeking goat pen, she seemed suspended above the trampled floor.

'This one,' she said, indicating a small, bewildered-looking goat that stood staring up at her, not bleating. The animal looked cuddly and confident, even a bit defiant.

'He's cute,' I said.

'The blackest. *Dam koto?*'

'One thousand rupees, madam.'

Handing him a block of notes that had a paper band around it, she kept her eyes on the chosen goat.

'A brave little thing,' she said.

What happened next happened fast. We crossed the lane, passed Mother Teresa's hospice again, and walked up a lane, entering the precincts of the temple she'd shown me earlier. A young man carried her goat tightly against his chest. Seeing her, some men at the temple cleared the way, shoving people, then nagging me to take my shoes off.

As I sat on a bench, untied my shoes and slipped them off ('And sockings, sar'), Mrs Unger stepped out of her sandals and went to the back of the temple. I found her surrounded by chanting, sweaty-faced men near a walled enclosure – just walls, no roof.

She wore a necklace of flowers and the goat too was garlanded like a beloved pet. The chanting of the men became louder in their excitement.

A man inside the enclosure wearing an apron-like skirt stood over a drum and began to smack it, a snare-drum sound of syncopation that got the crowd of men stamping. The drummer's arms were flecked with red. The sound and the louder chanting seemed to make the day hotter. My shirt was stuck to my back and my head was burning.

Speaking in what I took to be Bengali, Mrs Unger directed the man with the goat to enter the walled enclosure. The man walked through clusters of flowers and what looked like fresh paint on the stone floor, where a barefoot priest stood, streaked with ashes and daubs of holy vermilion on his forehead and cheeks.

The goat began to bleat as its head was jammed between two upright stone stakes the height of a wicket, its neck pushed hard against a stump. The drumming grew louder. The priest touched his fingers to his lips and then caressed the goat's head. He raised a long curved knife and, without pause, he struck down, like a butcher dividing a side of meat, and with the same thunk as the blade hit solid wood.

The goat's bleating ceased like an interrupted hiccup as its head tumbled to the stone floor, coming to rest at the base of the wicket, blood bubbling and spurting from the raw, ragged meat of the neck and spilling on to the blossoms, puddling near the priest's feet.

I had gasped in the act of saying 'Please, no,' but everyone around me was screeching with delight. Even in the open air I felt suffocated, as if I were in a small room. Though I had seen dead animals, flattened squirrels on the road and human corpses in coffins, I had never seen any creature slaughtered. A live thing bulged with blood, and now all the blood was puddled on the stone floor. My head hurt; I felt it in my guts; I wanted to vomit.

Mrs Unger bent low to kiss the carcass of the black goat and when she straightened up she was smeared with blood, red streaks on her shawl.

A shrill cry went up (*Joi Kali!*), joyous, cruelly triumphant, as she lifted her blood-smeared shawl from her head and draped it over the posts of the execution rack, along with a garland of blood-red lilies. The bystanders rushed forward, their bare feet slapping and skidding on the blood, and stuck their faces into the sticky folds of the shawl.

The carcass of the headless goat was hoisted on a hook. Using the same hacker, the priest skinned and swiftly butchered it, carving it into bloody chunks and joints on a platter, then directed it to be taken away.

The look on Mrs Unger's face was one of rapture, gleaming with sweat, the ringlets of her hair gummed to her cheeks, and she offered her face to the priest who, in one gesture of his dripping hand, marked her forehead with a fingertip of blood.

Murmuring, her face a mask of ruddied passion, she raised her eyes to the temple window, her mouth half open – as I had seen women in the throes of desire – her hands clasped, breathing deeply. She was speaking like a priestess possessed, but her words were drowned out by the chants and shrieks of the people who had watched the sacrifice.

Before we left, she led me into the temple. We shuffled past an inside window where the image of the goddess Kali, gleaming black and brightly marked, stared with orange lozenge eyes from a stack of blossoms and offerings. I was briefly frightened, jostled by the mob in this stifling place of incense and flowers and dishes of money and frantic pilgrims, who were twitching with gestures of devotion and gasping, seeming to eat the air, all of them smiling wildly at the furious image.

# 8

Her slightly bloodstained white sari billowed as she swept through the Kalighat bazaar, past the beggars and the flower sellers and the fruit stalls, the beseeching holy men, the clattering rickshaws, the beeping motorbikes. From the sounds alone you knew you were in another century – bicycle bells, the clop of pony hooves on cobblestones, the chatter of a sewing machine, the clang of a hammer on an anvil, the bang and bump of wooden wagon wheels.

Though her hand was hot, clutching mine like that of a panicked child, she seemed utterly serene. Now I knew that beneath Mrs Unger's impassive strength and certainty, she was wary of the big screeching mob. Well, who wouldn't be? But I was impressed by her bluff, showing nothing but indifference. She was unfazed and even in this filthy street of the market she appeared to take no notice of the men trying to get her attention. More than that, she looked fulfilled and a little fatigued, with a wan smile, spent, but with a glow like sexual relief on her face, lips apart, her eyes shining with pleasure though her face was rather pale.

Passing a heap of blossoms, the blood-coloured lilies I'd been seeing, I remarked on the redness. I tried to let go to touch the petals, but her fingers gripped me harder.

'Hold me,' she said, and as though to cover her fear she added, 'The *shonali* lily – Kali's favourite.'

Because she didn't hesitate and kept walking slightly ahead of me, pulling me onward, I saw how the bottom of her sari was soaked with a narrow red profile, a stripe of blood in a crimson hem where it had touched the floor of the sacrifice enclosure. And the light hairs on her arm prickled with tiny droplets of blood, more like dew than gore. If I hadn't seen where she'd been, I would have guessed that she'd brushed against fresh paint. It was vivid red in places, in other spots going brown.

'The puja was for luck,' she said, 'and to bless us in our next venture.'

That *us* cheered me. Seeing her car in the distance, Balraj leaning next to it, she raised her hand. Balraj put on his chauffeur's cap, straightened it and scrambled inside. But it took him several minutes to reach us through the crowd.

I now knew that Mrs Unger was uneasy on the street, yet she didn't betray it; she didn't look at anyone in the crowd. Her gaze was lifted to the gold bulge on the top of the Kali temple roof while she held my hand. And that was something else I knew: she needed me.

If you had money in India, I was thinking again, you never had to wait. Some people, like Mrs Unger, never waited, while others did nothing but wait to be summoned, to open a door; many obeyed without a command, acting when the person with money or power appeared, as though these underlings operated from a motion sensor.

I must not forget that, I thought; if I take this attention for granted I'll be like the money people, presumptuous and priggish. In this respect Mrs Unger was like the rest of them, expecting to be waited on, impatient when there was a delay. But at least she had the grace not to comment on it. She said nothing to me, but I could tell from the way she held herself that she was mentally drumming her fingers – beautiful fingers. It seems to be a feature of impatience that a person cannot speak, or at least hold an animated conversation, while she is waiting in this way – too preoccupied by the suspense and annoyance to hold or express a complete thought, and seemingly deafened by their annoyance too.

This, and her fear of the mob, made Mrs Unger human to me. I welcomed her lapses. I needed to be reassured that she wasn't perfect because usually – and especially when I was away from her – I felt she was faultless. Her apparent perfection intimidated me and reminded me of my weakness.

In the car, she said, 'We're crossing the river. You've been over there, of course.'

'To Howrah. To the Botanical Gardens.'

'Howrah's cleaner these days, but the gardens are a mess – terribly neglected. Luckily those trees don't need much attention, but it's turning into a jungle. Please let me finish –' I had started to speak – 'we'll be going past it. This is the Vidyasagar Bridge.'

We had gone up the ramp and around the high curve to the first span. Looking back, I could see Eden Gardens and the sports stadium; looking forward, the misleading green on the far bank of the river – misleading because it hid another crowded *bustee*, crammed with hovels and old shop-houses.

'It's amazing. You drive and drive in India and you expect to see the countryside at some point. But, no, it's just more city, the great sprawl of India, the bloated village.'

Mrs Unger shook her head at my saying this. 'I try not to see crowds any more. I look for individuals who need help.' She touched the bloodstain on her hem; it had dried to thin flakes which she brushed off. 'If you look closely at India's human features it's not so frightening.'

I considered this assertion and thought the opposite. If you looked closely at India's human features, the country was far more frightening. The starved eyes, the yellow teeth, people's bones showing through their skin, dusty feet in plastic sandals, the urgency in their postures, always contending. But Mrs Unger spoke with authority and she knew more than I did. I saw doomed people where she saw life and hope, because I was doing nothing and she was bringing help.

She was calm in the car, although the traffic was so heavy again we hardly moved once we were off the bridge.

'Where are we?'

'Blockages,' Balraj said. 'Shibpur.'

Mrs Unger said nothing, just shifted in her seat and peered ahead without any discernible emotion. After a while, inching forward, we saw the cause of the hold-up, a dead cow in the road, like something lightly upholstered, an old piece of bony furniture that had collapsed and lay broken, a single line of traffic detouring around it. A policeman blew his shrill whistle, managing the contraflow, jerking his arms in semaphore.

'Shame,' Balraj said, glancing at the carcass, hipbones and ribs and splayed-out legs, the dead animal looking as if it had dropped from the sky and flattened on impact.

Mrs Unger gave no directions. Balraj knew where he was going. Soon he turned off the road and towards a large stucco wall with a rusted pair of iron gates eight feet high that blocked the sight of whatever lay within.

The car hardly slowed down as a man in khaki stepped from his sentry box and went to the gate, shot the big bolt and pushed it open, first the left door, then the right, another example of someone in India whose job it was to watch and wait – hours, days – for the moment when the sahib arrived.

We entered a park-like compound on a gravel drive, passing shade trees and small flower beds where gardeners kneeled and yanked at weeds. In the distance, at the head of the drive, I saw several large tile-roofed buildings. I expected to see students. The gardens and the size of the buildings and the serenity gave the impression of a small college campus. Yet apart from the gardeners and some other groundskeepers there was no one in sight.

'It's another world,' I said, thinking of the traffic and the hovels outside the wall.

'These are my warehouses and godowns,' Mrs Unger said, but she wasn't looking at them. She was facing ahead where a white van was parked in front of a one-storey building, a little schoolhouse that looked as if it might hold a set of classrooms.

After we parked and were walking past the first warehouse, I saw that the big front door was open, a long-bodied truck backed up to a loading dock.

'So it really is a warehouse.'

'Export merchandise. No point in looking at it. It's all packed and ready to be shipped.' She was still walking towards the smaller building. 'That's for the American market. My shops, mainly. But I supply high-end retailers too.'

'It's a big operation,' I said, hoping she'd tell me more.

'This is only a corner of it. I have factories in other places. Most of what I make would be too expensive to manufacture in Calcutta. I don't have the space here.'

I smiled as Mrs Unger revealed her practical side, speaking of outsourcing and overheads and infrastructure and cost-per-unit yield. The woman I had seen as single-mindedly spiritual, advocating Ayurvedic cures and wholefoods, who had spent hours in the deep interior of her Lodge in (I supposed) Alipore, massaging me, making me hers, was also a shrewd businesswoman, brisk with facts.

More gardeners knelt at the flower beds near the smaller building, grubbing with skinny fingers around the clumps of pink and purple impatiens. They greeted Mrs Unger respectfully and settled lower, averting their eyes, as though abasing themselves, letting her pass.

Another man in khaki stood at the door to the one-storey building, someone else to anticipate our approach and snatch the door open. So it happened: Mrs Unger didn't break her stride, the door was swung open and in we went.

'You're late.'

It was Charlie. He kissed her – a bit too warmly, perhaps as a way of defying me. He was dressed Indian-style in a long white kurta smock, tight white trousers, black slippers.

'Traffic,' she said. 'And we stopped for a puja.'

Charlie said, 'You're bloodstained, as usual.'

'Where are they?' she asked, stepping past him.

'Right through here. It's the best we could do.'

Charlie did not acknowledge me. Had he been busy, I might not have minded. I knew what it was like to be preoccupied. But he was standing in his handsome self-satisfied posture – the Indian clothes made him seem more confident – as if modelling, and without looking at me. Turning aside, he ignored me with such abruptness I knew it had to be deliberate.

'This is a lovely old building,' I said, making a remark just to see whether he'd respond.

He didn't and both their backs were turned now, mother and son. I stood alone, gaping, and because he had snubbed me I felt conspicuous for having said something so banal.

Mrs Unger seemed suddenly fretful – I understood she was busy and couldn't blame her. This was the business that financed her good works. But Charlie's indifference to me seemed calculated. His resentment was palpable, emanating like a bad smell. It was both possessive and antagonistic, a stink of rejection and annoyance, a hatefulness that warned me against coming too close.

I tried again, another remark, out of sheer malice because his hostility was so blatant. I said, 'These floorboards are solid teak and so wide. Imagine the age of the trees, the size of them. Probably centuries old.'

A boring observation, just chatter, which was precisely what I intended – another test. And it had the effect I expected – nothing, or rather Charlie's effort at expressing nothing. It was more trouble for him to make it obvious that he was ignoring me than for me to make these silly observations.

Perhaps I wasn't playing. Perhaps I really did resent his taking his mother's full attention, as he resented my being there. He had his rights as a son, but I adored the woman and I had rights too. I was at least owed the recognition that his mother also cared for me, in a way he couldn't share.

Mother and son, touching, conferring, jostling, excluded me, while I watched from five steps behind. I thought that it was probably impossible to get between them or share their confidence. I thought too that whatever arrangements I made with Mrs Unger, I would always be regarded as an intrusion by her son. I could never be close to both of them, but that was all right with me. I had no interest in him and, as Mrs Unger herself had said, Charlie had Rajat.

The other oddity I noticed (and all this happened within a few minutes of my entering the funny old schoolhouse building) was that she was different here, as she had been different in the car and again at the temple, and different from my memory of her in her fragrant vault at the Lodge. In every new context she revealed a new aspect of her personality, and at times a new personality. I was reminded of the boldness of her letter to me, her fluttering submissiveness over drinks when I'd first met her, her beguiling assertiveness in the massage room. At the Kali temple and just afterwards, she had seemed regal, trailing her bloodstained sari through Kalighat. And now here, mother and manager, all business, headed through the big pair of doors to the holding pen.

Holding pen was how it seemed to me. This impression was emphasized by the mass of small children among the scattering of crouching women. Sometimes a mother can hold a child in her arms in such a way as to present the child as a shield. A few of these women did that, held the children in attitudes of protection, but protecting themselves, hovering, cowering behind these anxious-looking kids.

Only an hour or so before, I had seen something like this in the market at Kalighat, the sight of small tethered goats bunched together in fear and bleating like children. Both were about the same size too. The glossy sleekness and innocence of the goats were echoed by the scrubbed faces of these sweet-faced children, so tiny, so clean, so wide-eyed in terror. The mothers (they had to be mothers; no one else would have held them so tenderly) also looked fearful, raising their faces to the imposing foreign woman in her white sari, the tall young man in the kurta beside her with his hand resting lightly on her elbow, his expensive sunglasses propped pretentiously on his head. He was prematurely losing his hair at the crown and I felt this was his way of disguising the fact, a balding man's obvious ruse.

So I did not see children, I saw small, intimidated and bewildered goats, a great murmuring roomful of them, fearing sacrifice, anticipating their beheading. I was ashamed of myself for thinking this. It was the sort of gloomy intimation I often had in India. Among so many people they seemed not just doomed but expendable; existing only to die.

This awful thought was unfair of me and unworthy of Mrs Unger, who sacrificed herself every day to help such people. *I don't see crowds any more. I see individuals who need help,* she had said.

I needed to remind myself of her honesty and her effort, this beautiful woman who ran an orphanage, a school, a clinic and an Ayurvedic spa. I was a mere bystander, a tourist, a hack, a voyeur. Even Charlie, in his weird self-importance and snobbery, was a more sympathetic and worthy person than I was, roaming the streets and whining about my writer's block.

Charlie was greeting the women, introducing his mother, making his way through the crowd of children, most of whom were held by their mothers, many seated on the wooden floor, some of them standing, staring at the tall woman.

They fell silent as Mrs Unger walked among them, all their faces turned to her. At the far side of the room I noticed Rajat and, still feeling conspicuous, I went over to him to say hello.

'Quite a crowd,' I said, another banality, but socializing depended on banalities. The point of a platitude was to appear unthreatening, even a little dim.

'The monthly intake, but fewer than usual.'

'So this is a regular event?'

'Once a month. It's not that many – Ma won't take them all. She'll be disappointed.'

'I'm amazed she has room for them.'

'There's a monthly release too. It almost balances out.' He was looking past me and across the room at Mrs Unger. 'Ma's been to the temple.'

'How do you know?'

'Spatter,' he said, hissing the word. 'Bloodstained kind of suits her.'

I turned away from him to look.

'It's a good colour for Ma.' Then he spoke as though reading the label of a chip on a colour chart. 'Dried blood.'

I could not read Indian faces. I could not tell what emotion lay behind his expression. He stared at me, his lips fixed in a sort of smile that had no mirth in it, only (as I guessed) a sly contempt for my ignorance – another snub, perhaps.

In order to see his expression change, I said, 'I've been to the hotel.'

III

He went on staring. He said, 'Oh?'

'The Ananda,' I said.

'You told me that already.'

'I went back again.'

Now his smirk seemed pasted on. Was he ridiculing me for making this second visit? His eyes were blank and emotionless. I had no idea.

'I just want to forget all about it. It was a terrible experience.'

'There was one detail you forgot to tell me.'

'I told you everything.' He seemed to be defying me by not blinking.

'You didn't mention how the dead boy got to your room.'

'I don't know how he got there. Obviously someone brought him to the room while I was asleep.'

'Brought him how?'

'I have no clue.'

'You didn't see what he was wrapped in?'

In a harsh whisper he said, 'He was naked.'

Was Rajat being obstinate? I didn't want to help him with the word 'carpet'.

'You just saw him and nothing else?'

'What else would there be? Isn't a dead boy enough?'

Now I could read his expression: it was tight with the memory of seeing the dead boy, his eyes damp with fear, his lips twitching on his murmuring mouth. I would have felt sorry for him except that I was the one who had been assigned the task of proving whether what he said was true.

Across the room, Mrs Unger had bent to pick up a child from its mother's arms. She spoke to the woman, reassuring her, as she stroked the child's head – a little girl in a ragged purple dress that reached to her bare feet. As she hoisted her I could see how skinny the child was, gaunt and hollow-eyed, with the dull dry skin of malnutrition, the bright eyes of fever and a lassitude that made her limp and compliant in Mrs Unger's arms.

Carrying the child like a symbol of authority, looking even more like a mother, Mrs Unger greeted the other mothers, spoke to their children. She shifted the child to the crook of one arm, and the fact that she was holding her this way seemed to make her more approachable. She walked around the room, stepping among the seated and kneeling children.

'Namashkar,' she was saying and 'Apni keman achen' – hello and how are you? in Bengali.

They were fine, they said, Bhalo achhi, or more often, just OK, Thik achhey.

She patted the child she carried, or swung her and shifted her like a doll. I guessed the little girl to be six or so, but an Indian child that size could have been older. Poverty diminished them, shrank them, gave them extraordinary bodies, spindly legs or swollen bellies. Some children had faces like old men and some of the mothers looked like haggard girls.

Rajat was following her progress through the room. He said, 'She's thinking, "Why aren't there more of them?" But it's not that easy.' He watched her stoop to speak to a group of anxious children. 'She knows just how to calm them.'

'Why should they be afraid?'

Now he became unreadable again, with an expression that seemed like contempt for my ignorance, another snub for the big, uncomprehending foreigner.

He went on praising Mrs Unger, but I was thinking how he'd called her bloodstained ('It's a good colour for Ma'), and I could not take my eyes off the dark blood on the hem of her white sari, the blood that was dried and crusted on her feet.

Shaking her head, looking disapproving, she was deep in discussion with Charlie. He was taller, so he had to stoop slightly, and it was easy to tell that she was the authority figure.

'I'm sorry,' Charlie said to her as I drew close to them.

Still holding the child, she headed for the door, and I took this as a signal that I should follow.

'Bye, Mother.'

Another snub to me, because at this point I was right behind her, leaving the room. She had given me the big soft basket that served as her handbag.

In the car, she said, 'Charlie hates me.'

'He has his life,' I said, another banality. I did not know anything.

The small girl sat between us in the back seat.

'That seemed a good turnout.'

'Not good at all. The room should have been full. Think of all the children who are not there, who missed this chance. It breaks my heart.'

She seemed entirely unselfish speaking this way, wanting more work, seeing her role in terms of rescue. And I had my selfish thought again: a woman so concerned with human welfare will look after me. That was how she had seemed to me, like a benefactor. I had known her as someone wholly committed to giving. She hugged the small girl.

'Her name is Usha,' she said. 'Isn't she sweet? It means "dawn".'

'Was that her mother in the room?'

Mrs Unger smiled at me, as if I had said something very foolish.

'I am her mother.'

# 9

Was it possible to desire anyone more than I desired Mrs Unger?
I didn't think so, even in middle age, after all my lessons in love. I
had never felt this way, utterly abstracted and dependent, like
a small boy clinging to his mother. It was love of a rarefied kind: I
was her devotee. I had nothing to offer her except my loyalty.
She had everything to offer me. When I could not see her I felt
mournful, almost ill. Yet I preferred to be alone rather than with
other people – Howard or Parvati. It seemed disloyal to spend time
with anyone else. This devotion was the sort that deprived a person of family and friends; they were no use – worse, they were an
intrusion. And I needed my secret.

Howard persisted. He called to arrange meetings. Could I talk to
the Theosophical Society? Could I give a lecture at the university in
Burdwan? What about the Book Week in Ballygunge?

Normally I might have said yes, but somehow his requests
appalled me, shamed me, made me sad.

'I can't, I'm really sorry,' I said, and was almost tearful, thinking:
*I have nothing to say to anyone. I am empty.*

'I've got some great stories for you,' he said.

He liked telling me the more colourful ones ('You could use
this in an article'). One was about two American Foreign Service
officers, both of them men, who were involved in a murder-suicide.
'It happened in Equatorial Guinea, but maybe you could give it
an Indian background.' Another was about an American consul's
wife who sang Tagore songs and had a cult-like following. 'Maybe
something in the water here – a lot of foreign women get goddess
complexes.' And there was the Monkey Man: 'A large monkey
roams neighbourhoods, causing mayhem. He killed a commis-
sioner on the roof terrace of his residence. A bunch of vigilantes
went out to catch Monkey Man. There were hundreds of Monkey

Man sightings. People are still terrified of Monkey Man – possibly a hairy man, possibly a huge monkey. Wouldn't that make a great short story?'

It was the sort of thing people had been saying to me my whole writing life. If only he knew the fantastic narrative I was living with Mrs Unger, for which I had no vocabulary.

The rattling bell on my old room phone nagged me. I hoped it was Mrs Unger. It was Howard, and I was at once suspicious. Skilled at getting people to say yes, he had a special, softly insistent yet deferential voice for eliciting agreement. He was used to dealing with difficult people – stubborn Bengalis, pompous matrons, commissars of the Communist Party of Bengal, obnoxious State Department types – and though he was now a public affairs officer, he had served time as an assistant consul, dealing with any number of mendacious visa applicants.

'Paul Theroux wants to see you. He's in Calcutta.'

'I've never met him,' I said. 'How does he know I'm here?'

'I told him. He's a huge fan.' That had to be bull. 'I mentioned that you once asked about Mrs Unger.' Before I could dismiss this, he said, 'He also asked about her.'

My whole body went slack. I felt my throat constrict, my voice go small.

'Is that why he's here?'

'I don't think so.' Howard put on more of his special 'selling' voice. 'He was supposed to open the Calcutta Book Fair, but it was scrubbed at the last minute over a lawsuit by some local people who said it would create pollution. Isn't that funny? You might be able to use that in a story.'

But I was still thinking of *He also asked about her*, and I was too numb to reply.

'We were having a drink at his hotel yesterday and out of the blue he said, "Does the name Merrill Unger mean anything to you?"'

In a voice I barely recognized I said, 'What did you say?'

'I said that I knew someone else who'd asked me the same question.'

I could not speak. Since I'd met her, I'd felt I had her to myself –
and she had me. We were each other's secret. Even her sly, inquisitive son could not have known what went on between us. We
met covertly, by assignation, and she worked her tantric magic on
me in semi-darkness, by the light of flickering oil lamps in her vault
at the Lodge.

Foolishly, early on, I'd dropped her name to Howard, not
realizing that he'd remember. I thought I'd been so offhand. But as
a Foreign Service officer he was alert to the slightest suggestion of
any new fact or query. His job was to know as much as possible
about the Americans in Calcutta, to keep track of them, to make
connections. He didn't know much about Mrs Unger, so on this
slender association he wanted to find out more. Arranging a meeting, putting me in touch with someone like Theroux, he might find
something out – about us, about her. I had taken Howard to be a
friend, but no matter how casual he seemed, a diplomat was never
off duty. His first duty was to the flag, and keeping the flag waving
was his job.

'I don't know him,' I said. 'I've never met him.'

'This is your chance.'

Howard was shrewd, but he had no idea of the antagonisms that
exist among writers.

Howard's geniality masked his calculating mind. On the pretext
of a chance meeting, the reactive chemistry of bringing people
together, he would find out more about me and Theroux and Mrs
Unger. It was the triangulation of the diplomatic world, holding
a party ('Have another drink!') to see what information could be
shaken loose.

I didn't want to cooperate or let myself be suckered into this.
Mrs Unger was my secret, my mission, my single reason for staying
in Calcutta. I was in possession of the dead hand that might pluck
open the door to the truth. Yet Howard had been helpful to me
and kind; I needed favours from him in this dense and difficult city.
So I had to agree, but I warned myself in advance to be cautious, to
give nothing away. More than saving myself, I wanted to protect
Mrs Unger from this notoriously prying man.

What I knew about Theroux was what everyone knew about him. He was known for being intrusive, especially among the unsuspecting – strangers he met on trains, travellers who had no idea who he was, people thinking out loud in unguarded moments. I suspected that much of what he wrote was fiction, since he'd started his writing life as a novelist. And I knew the temptation to improve quotations or to dramatize chance encounters and far-off landscapes, to make people and places more exotic. But he was too explicit to be convincing. Life was seldom so neat, and never neat in a city like this. I indulged in a little fictionalizing myself, but I always felt this colouration was in a good cause. Like most writers, he was ruthless in using whomever he met.

I resented his book sales and his bonhomie and his breezy manner. From his work you could see he was the sort of writer who smiled and encouraged you to chatter and afterwards wrote a pitiless account of the conversation, playing up his knowingness. He was not cruel, but he was unsparing. He noticed everything – the scuffed shoes, the pot belly, the clichés – travelling the world, generalizing and jumping to conclusions. 'In the Pacific the chief is usually the man whose T-shirt is not quite as dirty as everyone else's' – that sort of thing.

I prized my anonymity – Theroux did as well, though he had a reputation for using it to blindside the unsuspecting. As a traveller I did not want any witnesses to my experiences. It was my privilege as a writer to write about myself without someone looking over my shoulder. In short, and for the love of God, I did not want this man to know me.

What every traveller craves, what every writer needs, is the illusion that he or she is a solitary discoverer, whether of actual or imagined territory. This is obviously a conceit, but it is necessary to preserving the mood that allows a writer to make a place his own. Theroux was proprietorial about the places he described. If he were in Calcutta, he'd want to own it. But I had put in too much time and effort here to hand it over to him or share it. I wanted to own Calcutta. I wanted Mrs Unger to be mine. I didn't want to give information. I didn't want to be witnessed.

If I refused to meet him he'd be suspicious, and Howard would be annoyed with me. If I agreed to meet him, I risked giving myself away and putting my relationship with Mrs Unger in jeopardy. But it seemed I had no choice.

Suppressing my fury, I said, 'Maybe we could meet for a drink. I'm pretty busy.'

I didn't want a drink, I wasn't busy, I badly missed Mrs Unger and here I was condemned to meet someone who was apparently competing with me – to talk about her while all I wanted was to see her.

'Great. He's staying at the Fairlawn.'

Typical of someone looking for 'colour' instead of the truth (as I was). The Fairlawn occupied a decaying mansion. It was a Calcutta institution in every sense, run by the domineering Mrs Smith and her family: stodgy food, mutton chops and boiled cabbage and bossy waiters. In any other city it would have passed for colourful and fun; in Calcutta it seemed joyless, even menacing, the sort of place Theroux might use as a setting for his Indian fictions, which put me on guard. The Fairlawn was within walking distance of the Hastings, near Madge Lane. I'd passed it going to the Indian Museum. I avoided staying in such places and instead got a comp room at a luxury hotel that was willing to trade a room night for a mention in one of my travel pieces. But I had not written anything, so I'd run out of welcomes.

Wanting to get this over with, I said I'd have to meet them the next day. Howard agreed so quickly that I suspected that Theroux's wish to see me was not casual at all. He was determined to corner me. He wanted something from me. And so I was again forewarned.

'Say five, drink time,' Howard said. 'He's a good guy. You'll like him.'

This sounded like an order. It also made me suspicious. And I hated hearing Howard praise him.

The next afternoon, entering the courtyard garden of the Fairlawn, seeing them under the striped umbrellas, I decided to surprise them. There are two methods of meeting nosy, hyper-alert strangers like this. One is walking up to them from the front door, smiling as you advance. The other is approaching from behind, the wrong door. The disadvantage of encountering them head-on is that they have time to study you, to size you up, to think of questions, to assess your movements – a person's gait and posture can be so easy to read, and such a giveaway. He'd be able to scrutinize what I was wearing, my shirt, my shoes. Footwear often figured in his descriptions. Coming from behind, I'd surprise him and prevent him from making any calculations.

That was what I did; slipped in through the side door, detoured around the trees, sidled past the other tables where people were drinking and passed behind the two men. I was deliberately early on this hot afternoon, to catch them off guard.

'Hi, Howard,' I said, bursting into view, stepping in front of them and taking a seat. I could see that I'd startled them. They were drinking Kingfishers and facing the Fairlawn's side door, expecting me to emerge and make a long revealing walk to their table.

'This is Paul Theroux,' Howard said, seeming rattled by my sudden appearance. He signalled to a waiter and tapped his bottle of Kingfisher, meaning one was needed for me.

'Jerry, great to meet you at last.' The *at last* had to be insincere, as though he'd been wanting to meet me for years. I knew this could not be so. 'What brings Jerry Delfont to Calcutta?'

The use of someone's full name to a person's face in a question like this has always annoyed me for being stagy, an interviewer's mannerism – more insincerity. And the more depressed I became about my failure as a writer, the more I hated my name, so this was not simply annoying but hurtful.

'This and that. Just passing through. How about you?'

'Same here. Passing through. I'm one of those people Kipling described who spend a few weeks in India, walk around this great Sphinx of the Plains and write books about it, denouncing it or praising it as their ignorance prompts. In other words, no big plans. You?'

'No plans at all,' I said. 'Waiting for the monsoon is about all.'

'I know what you mean. I'll be glad when it starts. This heat is awful.'

'It's hard to work in it,' Howard said.

Theroux said, 'I'm not doing any work. Jerry?'

'I wish. Too hot.'

Forgive this banal dialogue, which by the way continued a little longer. The reason I write down the empty phrases is that I want to show how oblique Theroux was with me, oblique while seeming genial and forthcoming. He was condescending and evasive; he gave me no information; nor did I give him any.

All this time – I suppose it was a technique he'd learned as a travelling writer – he was observing me closely. His words meant nothing, but while he talked to hold my attention he was able to study me, the very thing I'd hoped to avoid. He glanced at my shoes, my linen trousers, my loose linen shirt, and he was trying to guess my age, to judge my evasions, as if looking for a weakness. His relaxed posture was meant to reassure me, but his twitching eyes were those of a predator.

'This city doesn't change,' Howard was saying.

And I had to admit that, stalling, uttering clichés myself, I was doing the same to Theroux, sizing him up.

Meeting a writer in the flesh is always a letdown, since the image you have from the writing is formed from loaded or misleading words. On the page the writer is an intelligence, an efficient and fluent being, clear-sighted and alert: the reader invents a face for this man. In the flesh the writer is usually misshapen, overcautious or hesitant; fallible in the way that flesh is fallible; bruised, squinting, older and shorter than you expect – even, quite often, un-balanced. I met Hunter Thompson once at a party in New York and he seemed timid and oversensitive and insane, like a crazy child. Writers never resemble the jacket photo. They are always smaller and heavier. Theroux's hair was thinner, but no writer's hair looks in the least like his hair in his photograph.

This fox in prose looked hot and obvious, fleshier than his picture, not vulpine at all but preoccupied, flexing his fingers in a displacement activity to use his hands, as though he wanted to be writing down what I was saying or making notes. In spite of the humidity he wore a rough-spun cotton *khadi* vest and baggy trousers, a collarless shirt, leather walking shoes, no socks, an expensive watch. His round-lensed horn-rim glasses were the type Indians called 'Netaji spectacles', after the glasses popularized by the nationalist Netaji Bose. Though he smiled pleasantly enough, his eyes were busy behind his specs, too busy, always on me, up and down the whole time. I was reassured that he appeared older than his picture; he'd lost his looks, if indeed he'd ever had them; but he was sinewy with determination, that ruthlessness I mentioned before. He was friendly in a way that bothered me, because I knew he didn't mean it and must want something.

'I haven't seen the Jerry Delfont byline lately,' he said. That irritating verbal mannerism. I winced, hearing my full name again. 'Usually you're everywhere.'

'I've been pretty busy,' I said and I knew from the forced encouragement tightening in his expression that he didn't believe me. I hadn't been busy at all, not in any way he would have understood.

'Are you on an assignment?'

'In a way,' I said and we both knew that this meant no.

The form and tone of a person's question often indicates that he wants to be asked the same question. 'Have you been to Bhutan?' means 'Ask me about Bhutan. I've just been there.' But his manner wasn't like that. He didn't want to answer any questions. He was the interrogator, at the periphery, behind the light.

And with each question came a compliment.

'I always look for your pieces in magazines. They're so topical.'

'I try to keep on the move,' I said.

'You travel light. I envy you.'

Another canny reference. 'Travel Light' was one of my magazine columns.

'You do a lot of TV,' he said.

Was this a gibe? It seemed so.

Howard said, 'I hadn't realized that.'

'I was on cable. It's not the same as network TV.'

'You're good at it,' Theroux said. 'You should do more of it. You could have your own travel show.'

I took this to mean I wasn't much of a writer, that my real talent lay in gabbing to a camera. Maybe he didn't mean that. But the problem in talking to him was that I wasn't sure exactly what he meant. I *was* sure that all this time he was verbally dancing around, using a magician's misdirection while peering at me.

'You do TV, don't you?'

'No,' he said. 'Never. I wouldn't be any good at it.' Was this a compliment or a put-down?

'How long have you been in Calcutta?' he asked.

'About a month. Maybe more. I've lost track of time.'

'That's travel at its best,' he said, sounding pompous and self-important. 'The open-ended thing – no view to going home.'

'Since I don't have a home, it's pretty easy,' I said, to set him straight.

'Footloose.'

'Not really. I have a tenant in my place in New York. I use the rent money to travel.'

And I thought: *Goddamn, why did I give him this information?*

'How about you?' I said. 'Where do you live?'

'It's hard to say. I've never been happy living exclusively in one place. And we Americans are not natural expatriates, even writers like us.'

Utterly evasive, and *writers like us* was just a way of patronizing me. He wrote books, I wrote magazine pieces; but by referring to us both as writers, he was grandly including me in his company. Did he really think I believed him?

He was older than I imagined but affected a kind of eager curiosity that I associated with someone younger – someone on the make. And that was another irritant. But mostly it was his inquisitive eyes that I minded.

'We have some Americans here that almost qualify as expats,' Howard said. 'Indian visas and work permits are problematical, but there are some Americans in India who might regard themselves as residents.'

Though I knew what he was driving at, I didn't help him.

'Missionaries,' Theroux said. 'Indians hate Christian God-botherers. Now and then they persecute them. It's funny, we've got all sorts of Hindu proselytizers in the US. Remember that sex-mad guru with all the Rolls-Royces and funny hats?'

'Bhagwan Shree Rajneesh,' I said.

'Bhagwan means "god",' Theroux said. 'He promoted himself to god!'

Howard said, 'It's used in a different sense, kind of an honorific.'

'Whatever,' Theroux said. 'It was tantric sex he was selling, to cast a sexual spell over his flock. I associate him with poly-morphous perversity. And visa fraud.'

'Anyway, he's dead,' I said.

'The Americans who come to Calcutta tend to be philan-thropists,' Howard said. 'An awful lot of them started out working as volunteers with Mother Teresa. It was almost a rite of passage, part of the India tour. Seeing the sights, then a few weeks feeding the incurables.'

'Mother Teresa believed that poverty was a good thing,' I said, trying to remember what Mrs Unger had said.

'Funnily enough, she collected millions in donations,' Theroux said.

Howard said, 'I see these people all the time.'

'Thoreau said, find a do-gooder and you'll see that at bottom there's something wrong with his life. "If he has committed some heinous sin, what does he do? He sets about reforming the world." Why else do pop stars and celebrities get involved in these causes? Their lives are so miserable. The things they do are so worthless, so meretricious and overpaid. They need to atone, to make themselves look better. And being bossy do-gooders feeds their vanity.'

He had become animated and seemed uncharacteristically sincere as he became vexed.

I said, 'Maybe they want to give their lives meaning. I did a piece on Liz Taylor. She really cares about AIDS research and she's raised a lot of money – millions.'

'I guess that's what happens to actresses who can't get a part in a movie any more,' Theroux said. He was poking one finger into a plate of peanuts on the table, stirring them, a way to show me that he had no interest in what I was saying. 'Know what these are called in Bengali? *Cheena badam*. Chinese almonds. But they're peanuts. What does that tell you about pretensions here?'

I said, 'Liz Taylor's using her fame for a good cause.'

'With all respect, Jerry, that's what they all say, all these lame high-profile mythomaniacs.'

'What's wrong with doing good?'

'They're not doing good. They're promoting themselves. They think money is the answer, but they have so much money they should know that money is not the answer. They're doing harm. Here, have some Chinese almonds.'

'So what's the answer?'

'Like the guru said, "What's the question?"'

'Mrs Unger isn't high-profile,' Howard said.

At last, after all this time, her name. It had been hovering over the conversation for the past fifteen minutes.

Theroux turned to me. 'What do you think?'

I went vague. 'About what?'

'Mrs Unger.'

I sipped my beer and tried to look indifferent. I said, 'I don't really know her.'

Howard reacted to this with just the slightest hitch of his spine, a straightening, a fractional head-bob, and I knew that Theroux had registered the involuntary twist of Howard's reaction as well as my own flat denial. I should not have denied her. Both men knew I was lying, but worst of all Theroux pretended to believe me. His bland expression of credulity was like contempt for me, the heartless and unblinking gaze of a hunter lining up a prey animal through a gun sight – an animal that has just revealed a weakness, a slowness, a limp, perhaps.

'I can tell you a few things about her,' Theroux said. 'She stays below the radar. She's been married two or three times. She first came to Calcutta about ten years ago, like many others, to work at the Kalighat hospice with Mother T. Got disillusioned by Mother. Drifted to the establishment next door.'

'The Kali temple?' Howard asked.

'Right. She's said to be a practitioner.' While Theroux talked, he hardly seemed to look at me, yet he was monitoring me closely. 'It's said that she's a *dakini*, a kind of priestess, and that she taught tantric massage to a French actress who'd come out to work with Mother T. The actress later had an affair with a big Hollywood tycoon and bewitched this rich guy with Mrs Unger's tantric method. How about that for a story?'

'Why don't you write it?'

'Why don't you?' Theroux said. 'Oh, sorry, that's right – you don't know her.' He peered at me for a reaction before adding, 'Look her up. She's never been interviewed, yet she runs one of the largest private charities in Calcutta. She'd be a huge "get" – isn't that what they say on TV about people in demand?'

'I don't do much TV these days.'

'I thought you said you were pitching a new travel show. She'd be perfect for a Calcutta segment.'

'Or a chapter in one of your books.'

'I have plenty of material,' he said. 'You want material? Hey, I got it.'

He reached into his briefcase and became absorbed in leafing through a folder of newspaper cuttings, sorting them.

'I love these Calcutta stories. They're like urban myths. There's a woman here, Mrs Chakraverti, who calls herself a witch and supposedly had an affair with Elvis. She advertises her powers. Or the crazed woman two weeks ago at Howrah who was jealous of her sister-in-law, so she threw her baby in a pond when no one was looking. Two cases like this in one week! Also' – he was holding another flimsy cutting – 'lately, servants have been teaming up with *dacoits* to rob their employers, sometimes murdering them. There was a case recently in Ballygunge, just down the road. The newspapers came out with a story on how to know whether your servants are planning to kill you. I love this stuff.'

'I just read the matrimonial classifieds,' Howard said.

'Me too,' Theroux said. 'Or what about the abduction classifieds?'

He was not looking at me and yet, even turned aside, his body was like an instrument measuring my reactions.

'"Search for kidnapped girl,"' Theroux read. '"Sumita Chandran, ten, four feet five inches, kidnapped on twelve Feb. at Howrah." Or "Anikat, eight months old, missing since January." "Sultana, five, disappeared in 2007. Nitesh Kumar, seven. Prafula, five."' He closed the folder of cuttings. 'Forty-four thousand children missing every year. Eleven million Indian children are designated as "abandoned".'

Howard said, 'They end up in the sex trade or as adoptees. Or in the sweatshops.'

'Mrs Unger helps them. One of the few who cares. That's the story. That's why I'm interested.'

I decided not to respond, but he seemed to register even this resistance.

'I wish I could find her,' he said.

'That shouldn't be too hard for you.'

He smiled. 'Or you.'

'But you're interested and I'm not.'

'Stop piggling with your samosa, Howard!' he said.

Howard licked the flakes of pastry from his fingers and said, 'Piggling?'

'Piggling, piggling!'

Theroux thought he was fooling me with this sudden distraction, but I knew that teasing Howard was his way of throwing me off, because he had become self-conscious in his serious questions about Mrs Unger. His teasing also showed how confident he was with Howard, who was obviously his friend, and it was a way of excluding me.

'You're not interested in missing children?' he asked.

'I'm not interested in Mrs Unger.'

And again, in denying her I was revealing more than I cared to, and he knew it. He was jealous of my access. He knew something and I wasn't cooperating. I began to eat a samosa, wondering if he would ask me anything more about Mrs Unger. But he simply smiled and nibbled peanuts.

'How much longer will you be in Calcutta?' I asked.

'I have no idea,' he said. A flat-out lie. 'How about you?'

'Who knows?' Another lie.

We were writers lying to each other, as writers do. The greater the writer, the bigger the lies. Why are they incapable of telling the truth? I say 'they' because I had no illusions. Secretive, protective of their ideas, keeping close, trying to throw you off. ('Stop piggling!') And yet at that moment, realizing that I was lying, I began to think that I might have a real idea. That I might be a writer.

A writer of magazine pieces, of stories, I had no pretensions to writing books. Theroux didn't want me to know him, didn't want anyone to know him, which was why he did nothing but pretend to write about himself, never quite coming clean, offering all these versions of himself until he disappeared into a thicket of half-truths he hoped was art.

Later, what I remembered most clearly were his eyes, searching, inquisitive, evasive, probing, a bit sad and unsatisfied, trying to see beneath the surface and inevitably misremembering or faulty, because you can't know everything. He was like someone trying to see in the dark.

I was convinced that he knew I was close to Mrs Unger and he had tried everything to get me to disclose it. He wanted to know what I knew. But it was my story. I had given him nothing, yet he made me intensely uncomfortable, and as I sat there saying nothing I felt he was taking something from me. I was like one of those tribesmen who believe that photographers will take their soul by snapping a picture. He gave me that feeling.

But worse than that, I felt undermined. I said, 'Now I really do have to go.'

'Great meeting you, especially here,' Theroux said with a theatrical sweep of his hand at the Fairlawn garden. I knew he didn't mean it, or perhaps he really had divined something of what I knew of Mrs Unger.

Howard said, 'Keep in touch.'

I was exposed. Howard had set me up. Now he knew another side of me and Theroux, who hadn't known me at all, knew me better than I wanted him to. I was not just uncomfortable, I was diminished, made smaller by his attention. He had helped himself to a slice of my soul.

This smirking, intrusive, ungenerous and insincere man was jumping to conclusions about me, making up his mind and forming fatal errors out of his impatience and knowingness. I hated his horrible attempt at appreciation as he sat smugly inside his pretence of surprise. He was someone who could not accept things for what they were and be at peace. He needed to tease, to provoke, to get me to react, as though – so to speak – he had a mallet in his hand and was constantly rapping my knee, like a doctor testing for a reflex. But that image is too kind. He was more like someone poking a wary animal. It was not only cruel, but the torment evoked an uncharacteristic and untrue reaction. What right did he have, and why did he want to know about Mrs Unger?

All this time, penetrating the garden from the street, the wall of sound, constant in Calcutta – the traffic and the shouts, the bicycle bells, people calling to each other, every word like a warning in the city that was never silent. No matter where I was, the street noise, the reminder that Calcutta was dense with restless people, where the stinks were so sharp they seemed audible, the diesel fumes of taxis and buses, the reek of garbage, of shit, of risen dust that was also like a high-pitched whine, the vibration of dirt, the sweetish tang of decay, the presence of oil smoke from the lamps and candles of veneration. The only place that was truly silent and fragrant was Mrs Unger's vault.

Just before I left them, Theroux had said to me, 'But if you do see her, if you do get close to her somehow, you're a very lucky guy. It would be a gift.'

And so I crept away among the tables.

Their high spirits as they saw me off did not mask their serious-ness. And I knew they remained in the garden of the Fairlawn to talk about me. They were saying: a lightweight, a trimmer, an evader – what's he hiding, why is he lingering here? Howard was humane and not a mocker, but he was curious and he had a diplomat's love of post-mortems. He was the good cop. He had used Theroux as an invasive tool to draw me out.

I told myself that I didn't care what they thought. What bothered me was that in his questions, his sideways looks and his insincere postures, especially his pretence of agreeing with me, Theroux had held up a mirror. In the end he was no more than that, a mirror, showing me my own face and feelings, making me intensely self-conscious. He was doing what writers do, reminding me of who I was.

He had made a reputation out of fooling other people, yet he didn't fool me. He made me confront myself, my failure, as he flashed back my reflection in the writer's mirror that he hid behind. I was like him in some ways. I was the lazy, idle, pleasure-loving side of this man. He pretended to be casual, but he was intense and never at rest, forever uninvolved. I was the procrastinator. He knew that I wasn't driven and competitive like him, and I knew that he envied me for my involvement with Mrs Unger. I also knew that he was going to write about me, about meeting me, and that he'd get everything wrong.

So much for Theroux and his false intimacies. What Howard didn't know about the mirror was that it was cracked. It was the deep flaw in all writers' mirrors. In most of them – in Theroux's for sure – you saw the writer's boiled eyes, staring wildly through the crack.

As I lost myself in traffic and people at Hogg Market, I kept thinking: *I lied to him. I denied everything. He made me do it and he knew I was lying.* But I didn't care. I had Mrs Unger to return to.

A few days later, Howard called and said, 'He's gone.'

I knew who he meant and was glad that I didn't have to see again the man who had shown me who I really was.

# IO

Somehow – was it something I ate at the Fairlawn? – I fell ill. I had eaten a samosa, not much, but just a nibble of something foul could lay you low in Calcutta. 'Tummy trouble' did not begin to describe my complaint. I had cramps, a headache, muscle pains, an unslakable thirst and a case of the runs that convinced me that I was slowly dying a drizzling death, a liquefaction from within that would reduce me in a short time to no more than a stain on the sheet. I tried to rehydrate with salted water, but still I drizzled. And I was in pain so severe, and was so weak, I could hardly speak. Three days of this, then I was able to stand without feeling dizzy, though I felt like a shrunken and arthritic old man.

'I think I had amoebic dysentery,' I said to Howard afterwards.

'Probably just diarrhoea,' he said.

'How do you know?'

'It's only amoebic when you see a fifty-dollar bill on the floor of your bedroom and can't pick it up. By the way, Parvati wants you to call.'

I was still waiting for Mrs Unger, for the pleasure of entering her vault. In the meantime, half in flirtation, half in friendliness – so it seemed; what did I know? – Parvati kept me up to date with her doings. I needed the distraction, but it was awkward merely being near Parvati these days. I was obscurely repulsed to be next to someone so virginal, with her pale fragrance of innocence, like the smell of soap, someone fresh out of a bath – and my head still ringing with the ripe, almost wolfish odours of ecstasy from Mrs Unger. After the overwhelming sensuality of this woman, being with Parvati was like being with a child: nothing to say, no common language. It was as though I was violating an old taboo.

To me, unmarried Indian women were like schoolgirls, in their good humour and with their restrictions. There was a line in Indian friendship that was never crossed, at least with an Indian woman. Casual meetings were out of the question, nothing physical was permitted, no touching, not even an air kiss. Any talk of physicality was forbidden. It wasn't possible for me to be alone with an Indian woman and a mere chaste and discreet stroll on the Maidan needed supervision. I had never held Parvati's hand. She performed the sexiest dances, her body swaying, her hips thrusting, her hands in the air, her eyes flashing like a coquette; yet off the dance floor she reasserted her virginity and was untouchable. And that was not the worst torment for me.

'I want to learn sexy things,' she said to me on one of those days when I wanted to be with Mrs Unger.

'Like what?'

'Whistling. Through my teeth, very shrill. Like hailing a taxicab.'

'Teach me how to break someone's arm using *kalaripayatu* and I'll show you how to whistle.'

She laughed and made a martial arts gesture, and as I parried, said, 'I want to know how to drink whisky. I want to know algebra. Sexy man things.'

This frivolous conversation was permissible because we were at a party on the rooftop verandah of the consul general, the place filled with people. And far from this frivolity, somewhere in Calcutta, Mrs Unger was attending to her lost children, mothering them, saving lives. It was the opposite of the world of morbidity at Mother Teresa's anteroom of death, tucking old people into bed for the big sleep.

So I was almost ashamed to be at a party, but Parvati was like a younger sister, as most desirable Indian women seemed – innocent, forbidden, but burdened with responsibilities. As Indian men never ceased to be boys, Indian women seemed to me creatures without an adolescence, passing from small giggling girls to clucking middle-aged matrons. I felt protective and forgiving towards Parvati, but I had never seen any future for us, even as friends. Her parents would find her a marriageable man of her caste and I would have to respect the Indian taboo against a man's being friendly with someone's wife.

But with Mrs Unger's philanthropy and unselfish effort on my mind, I was usually disturbed by Parvati's talk of poetry and dance. Her obsession with art and music could be jarring. She invited me to her dance recitals, fluttered her lovely eyelashes and told me all the places she wanted to go. She did yoga every day and was sympathetic to my struggle to write. She was always working on a poem, sometimes several at once, with a deftness I envied. She wrote sensual poetry. She passed the poems to me, folded, like money she owed me, always handwritten in her graceful script.

One, about becoming a dancer, ended with the lines

> So when I'm home, lying vanquished
> In my own bed, searching for what is slow
> And lonely, I pare my knees apart, point my toes.

Another contained the image

> . . . the muted lisp
> Of morning's tongue pushes against the sky.

'What do you think?'

'What do I think? Coruscating.'

She laughed. She said she wanted to loan me a book by a Bengal novelist. 'Pop by my flat. You must read Sarat Chandra Chatterji.'

Though Howard had told me she lived with her parents, I took this to mean that the flat was hers. It might have been. On a side street near a mosque in Shobhabazar in north Calcutta, it was four flights up on a landing that faced the minarets and a building draped with drying laundry. The dark staircase smelled of disinfectant and cooking. I was breathless from the climb when I knocked. An old woman opened the door, her harassed face puffy with the heat, a servant judging from the way she was dressed, wrapped in a plain cotton sari and barefoot.

'Won't be a minute!' Parvati called from an adjacent room that was blocked by a folding screen.

'*Chai? Pani?*' the old woman asked as she plucked at her gauzy sari.

'I'm fine,' I said and clarified it by gesturing with my hands. An offering of water in Calcutta had sinister implications for me. The very word 'water' was like poison.

An inner door clicked open. I expected Parvati, but from the reaction of the servant, compact, cringing, I took the woman approaching to be her mother. She straightened to appraise me. She was not old, but I saw no resemblance to Parvati. She was darker, heavier, flatfooted in gold sandals, wearing rings on her toes, and she twisted her wrist bangles as she frowned at me. She was clearly disappointed, as though I were hardly human, a peculiar animal, a pest.

'You are alone?'

What did that mean? I was still standing. I said, 'Yes.'

'Your employment is American consulate?'

'Not exactly.' What had Parvati told her and why wasn't she here to help me? 'I do a little writing. I was giving lectures at various places around Calcutta, sponsored by the consulate. Maybe that's what you were thinking of.'

She waggled her head. 'Please sit. You won't have tea?'

Helpless, not knowing how to deal with the silence in the shadowy room, I said, 'Thanks. I think I will.'

'Ragini, *chai*,' she said to the servant, who stood to the side, still cringing. And seating herself across from me, she said, 'And how are you knowing Parvati?'

'Through her poetry, of course.'

'Tcha.' This was less a word than a way of sucking her teeth.

'And her classical dancing.'

'Tcha.'

Behind me, I saw a flash in a mirror as the outer door opened – a sight of laundry and minarets – and a man came in, obviously fresh from work and heat; a crease of disturbance on his face made him seem like an escapee. He glanced at me with undisguised alarm and disapproval, as if he'd encountered an intruder. His leather briefcase was bulgy and bruised, and although the day was hot he wore a dark wool jacket and a shirt and tie. He unbuttoned his jacket but did not remove it. His heavy clothes seemed like armour and gave him an air of pugnacity, as though he were dressed for combat. Not taking his coat off seemed hostile.

The woman spoke to him in Bengali. I caught the word 'Parvati' and guessed at what she might be saying.

This man (her father, I assumed) could have been my age, yet in his stern, heavy-faced way, his brows and his hooked beak making him look owlish, he seemed much older – out of shape, fattish, with delicate hands; fleshy, with the air of a clerk, in baggy pants and thick-soled shoes. I thought how in travel, especially in India, I met people from an earlier time, another era.

'You're the chap from the consulate?'

I smiled at his wife, hoping she'd set him straight. But she stared at me and said nothing.

'No. As I said,' and smiled at the woman again, 'I'm just passing through.'

I wanted to say: *And, don't worry, I don't want to marry your daughter.*

We sat, the three of us, in three chairs, in hot, silent formality, as the lilting voice began in the mosque's crackling loudspeaker, calling the faithful to prayer.

The man looked unloved but like someone who'd always been obeyed. Certain Indian men seemed to me like this. No matter how accomplished and successful, they remained like big hairy boys, ungrateful and tantrum-prone and spoiled.

The servant Ragini set the teacups down on side tables as the man muttered to her. She cringed and turned that reflex into a bow.

It was as though I'd come for an interview and, before any questions were asked, the interviewer had written me off as unsuitable. They saw me as a bad man; not just a thief but a thief from another world. I had travelled all over, but I could not remember a time when I'd been seen this way, implausible and tainted.

'Kinda hot,' I said. The man glanced away from me; the woman rocked her body a little. The call to prayer was still crackling. 'Monsoon's coming.'

They were like sentinels. Their silence made me stupid. Worse than my coming to ask a favour, or to see Parvati, I was here to steal from them, to rob them of the only thing that had value in this place; not their daughter but their daughter's honour – to steal her virginity and leave her bleeding.

'Sorry to intrude,' I said.

They sipped their tea, which was more offensive to me than replying.

I *was* intruding on them. I had no business there. Had I been a young Bengali man, a potential suitor, they would have been chatty. But I was all wrong, an alien.

'Which part of America?' the woman asked.

'New York.'

'Crime,' the woman said with satisfaction, her earrings trembling. 'So dirty. So dangerous.'

The man waggled his head in agreement, as we sat in the heat, breathing diesel fumes and listening to the roar from the street and the howl from the mosque.

I did not belong in the privacies of Calcutta, only in the big public stew with the mob that swallowed everyone up. No one belonged here. How had Mrs Unger managed? But she was afraid of mobs.

'My husband has been to America. Punch?'

'For a conference. Workshops.'

His name was Punch? I said, 'Parvati tells me you teach at the university.'

'Indeed,' the man said, and no more.

'What do you teach?'

'Faculty of English studies.'

'My favourite subject. I've done some teaching myself. What period?'

'Seventeenth century. Recusant poets and dissenters. Thomas More to Ben Jonson.'

'You write too?'

'For the journals.' *Jarnels*.

I had nothing to offer. Recusant poets? I was a barbarian, here to steal his daughter. And now, at last, I heard her.

'Sorry to keep you waiting,' she said. 'I see you met Daddy and Mummy. I was dealing with a computer meltdown.'

'I was just about to leave,' I said. 'If you've got the book.'

'Oh, please, don't go. Have some more tea.'

'If he has business elsewhere, let him go,' her father said.

And so Parvati handed me the book, and I thanked them and left, descending the stairs to lose myself in the anonymity of an alien in the streets, where I belonged.

The effect of that brief stop at Parvati's – never to be repeated – was that I wanted to leave India. It was all very well to be a sightseer here, but their reaction told me that I was unwelcome. I knew that I could exist with other writers and tourists in the superficial world of Calcutta, struggling on the surface with the other short-timers and sensationalists. I didn't know the language, as Howard did, but I was so infatuated as to be lost with Mrs Unger.

And I had the dead hand. That was the only thing that kept me here. It represented the innermost India, a pathetic trophy and the key to a mystery I had not yet solved. If I could have taken it with me, I would have gone. But I had to stay here and protect it, to attach it to its owner, whoever that might be.

Parvati's parents disapproved of me, as they would any man who cast his shadow over her and darkened her chances of a good match. They would certainly have hated me if they'd known how I spent my days longing for Mrs Unger. Parvati would have been devastated too.

I would have gladly said to them, 'That woman is the noblest person I've met in India – an ideal in your own terms! She asks for nothing. She uses her own money and all her time to improve the lives of Indian children.'

The rest had to remain my secret. It was just not possible for any-one to imagine the physicality of my craving, how I was touched by her and yearned for more of it. How I longed to be alone with her. What it was like to be held by her, her hot, dark breath at my ear: *Do you want me to stop?*

For Parvati, despite her sensual poems, my associating with Mrs Unger would have been a crime.

All this was simultaneous and I couldn't tell Parvati of Mrs Unger or vice versa. And Mrs Unger made me strong enough to be able to endure the wait until she was free to see me. I liked having her as a secret and I knew it was desire because nothing else mattered and everything seemed possible. It even seemed logical that I should be sitting in a very ordinary hotel on a back street in Calcutta, waiting to be summoned by a woman I had known for three weeks, who had introduced herself in a teasing letter she never now alluded to – had perhaps forgotten.

Another party at the consul general's, for some visiting academics, Howard making the introductions, Parvati in a green silk sari trimmed with gold, others dressed the same, in silks like extravagant plumage. I was uneasy in the presence of beautiful Indian women who arrayed themselves like courtesans, with nose jewels and dangly earrings, extending their slender arms, gold bangles jingling, and offering nothing but teasing fragrance. I resented the ancient rules of courtship that framed their lives and made them inaccessible. Parvati was like that, a challenge, as radiant as they were, but wiser. 'They're pukka Brahmins,' she told me, when I asked about her parents.

That was a coded way of suggesting that I was unclean to them. She confirmed that though her father's name was Surendranath, he was known as Punch. Then she sized me up and said, 'You're not here, as usual.'

Odd that even in her detached way – she hardly knew me – she could be so perceptive.

'Where am I?'

'You're far away.' She put a folded poem in my hand.

I opened it and read the first lines:

In you, a single blue country
Laid bare of inconsistencies.
A bone of truth caught in a cage of fire.

'A love poem,' I said. 'It's very good. It's a dream. You're amazing. You're a brilliant poet. You practise martial arts. You do seductive dances. And you live with your parents. How is that possible?'

'It's the Indian way. Even if I marry I'll probably live with my parents. I don't have any brothers. My sister's still in college. Who'll look after them?'

'What do you mean "if" you marry?'

'I hold views on marriage,' she said.

'Thank you for this poem. I want to see all your poems.'

But even saying that, I felt disloyal to Mrs Unger. I didn't want to be there. I was more uncomfortable with Parvati's good poems than her weak ones.

But it was true, as she had said, that I was far away. A woman in her detached, somewhat elevated position was extra-sensitive to a lapse in my attention, the more so because we were unphysical. She was more alert to gesture and tone, to the pulses in the air around me, than a hugger or a hand holder would have been. This was the upside of Indian romance: without sex, fascinated in virginal alertness, every other instinct was sharpened, almost to the point of hysteria. She knew from my eyes, the way I breathed, my posture, the tiniest inflection, from my very odour perhaps, that my heart was somewhere else. In an overformal society where insincerity was the norm, where most relationships, including marriage, were based on polite or hostile untruths, Parvati was expert in seeing through my meaningless compliments and evasions.

Compared to this, being held by Mrs Unger while I lay naked on the wooden table was the real world. With her, every word mattered and was unambiguous. We spoke the same language. We were free. She was generous and humane and was mistress of the great Lodge, shelter to abused and abducted children. Next to this, poems and dances were trifles of showing off, mere niceties with the subtext *Look at me!*

And Mrs Unger had love left over for me. *No, I don't want you to stop*. That was my yearning, lavish, frank, risky, naked, physical, un-Indian. *Don't stop*.

As I hoped, Mrs Unger summoned me about a week after the long day at the Kali temple and the compound at Shibpur, a few days after my unsettling meeting with Theroux at the Fairlawn. Balraj drove me to the Lodge. I caught his glance in the rear-view mirror as we entered the back street of villas.

'Alipore?'

'Alipore.'

She met me at the door, holding a small girl by the hand.

'Recognize her?'

I couldn't remember the Indian name. I said, 'Daylight.'

'Usha. Dawn. See how happy she is?' She led me into the Lodge. 'The other children are here. They're settling down nicely. They feel right at home.'

With that, she let go of Usha's hand and took mine, but with a tightening insinuation in her grip. I wanted to nuzzle her hand, the way a dog licks its mistress's fingers. Love is a yearning to clutch and hold, to be clutched and held.

The Lodge was alive: children's voices rang in the room and upstairs the drumming of running feet, the shriek of laughter; the aromas of cooking and flowers; the monotone of chanted mantras, repetitious and soothing, a kind of holy gargling. It was cool here too and the high perimeter wall muffled the sound of traffic. This was the other world that I longed for and had found, not exotic at all, not the gaudy and overformal India but a version of home – secure and safe in the embrace of this lovely woman.

We descended to her vault without speaking. I took my clothes off while Mrs Unger lit the candles and adjusted the volume of the Indian chants. I lay face-down in the heat and she traced the contours of my body with her fingers for some minutes. After that, she began digging her knuckles into my shoulders, now and then pouring hot oil on my back. She was able to penetrate deep within me, reaching to the meat of my muscles, taking her time. She worked on my head, my face and my jaw, squeezing her thumb in the declivities of my shoulders, and it seemed to me that her unhesitating fingers and hands were following familiar paths along the length of my body, because her confident touching reassured me.

'I need you to turn over.'

So I did, and she slipped a damp cloth over my eyes. She bent over me – I felt the cool sweep of her hair linger on my skin. In a refinement that was new to me, she began to nibble and lick at my nipples and to chafe the areolae with her fingertips.

'Do you want me to stop?'

My voice was a croak of encouragement as the heaviness of her hair continued to spill like a silken shawl across my stomach. Her hands were all over me, four hands it seemed, or more than four, and as she touched she made me weightless, lifting me off the table in a prolonged ritual of levitation. She went lower, her hands and lips – multiple mouths – taking possession of me, not giving what I wanted, but offering urgent promises. She anticipated what I wanted, which was a pleasure beyond desire, something like a refinement of gluttony, sucking the life from me, all the while soothing me with a satisfied purring in her throat.

I was folded into darkness, then came suddenly awake as though in a new room. I yanked the towel off my eyes.

'Was I asleep?'

'For quite a while.'

'Sorry.'

'I love watching you sleep.'

My body was heavy. I lay, unable to move, while Mrs Unger caressed my head, her sari like a wisp against my skin.

'Will you do me a favour?'

'Yes. Anything.'

She laughed. 'You don't know what it is.'

'Anything,' I said.

'I want to go to Assam. Will you go with me?'

'Yes. Any time.' I was going to elaborate but stopped myself, and she heard the catch of qualification in my voice.

'Go on . . .'

'Charlie will hate me even more.'

'He hates Indian trains.' She pinched me affectionately. 'You sound as if you care and I know you don't. But why should you?'

Because I was not sure when I'd be back in Calcutta, I took a taxi the next day to Dalhousie Square and walked to police headquarters to see Dr Mooly Mukherjee. I deliberately had not brought Howard along. I wanted to receive the news of the child's identity in confidence. In the lobby, I was given a badge and ushered to his office as before by a *chowkidar*, strutting with ceremony in front of me.

'Do come in,' Dr Mukherjee said warmly, inviting me to sit. He shut his office door, stroking his moustache as he did so.

His friendly manner should have indicated that Dr Mukherjee had good news, but I had been in Calcutta long enough to find his smile ominous. His warmth meant that he had no news, that he knew nothing; he was going to break it to me gently that the dead hand was a riddle.

He was smiling as he said, 'Normally, body part can provide us masses of information and usable data. This' – he held the plastic pouch with his thumb and forefinger – 'is one of those rare instances when we can find out very little. It is a mystery.'

'Age? Sex?'

'Certainly male child. Maybe ten years of age. Could be a bit more or less.'

'Is there any way you can match the fingerprints?'

He smiled under his moustache, lifting it with his smile, because the news was so unusual.

'Not possible in this happenstance.'

'Because you don't have matching fingerprints on file?'

'Because' – and he smiled again – 'body part is not having fingerprints.'

'I don't understand.'

'Fingertips perfectly smooth. Not a single whorl or loop.'

'They've been tampered with!'

'Not at all, in my opinion,' he said. 'That is why I enquired as to occupation. In some trades fingerprints are abraded. Masonry work. Men who make mud and clay images for puja. Rough carpentry. Tilery. Ironmongery. Pavers – lads making roads.'

'What are you saying?'

'Such people lose fingerprints by process of abrasion. Instead of print, smoothness is there. As I said previously.' He sighed, seeming irritated by my bewilderment. 'This person was perhaps engaged in just such occupation. These are the fingers of a hand worker, someone using his fingers many hours a day. Brickwork. Who can say?'

'So you didn't find anything?'

'You are entirely mistaken, sir. What we did not find is very revealing. This body part is interesting for what is not there.'

'What shall I do?'

'Keep safely. It is a piece of a larger puzzle. You need more pieces.' He tapped his finger on his desktop and wagged his head knowingly. 'Cholche cholbe, we say in Bengali. Keep on – it continues.'

'The rest of the body was cremated, I understand.'

'Possibly other pieces of puzzle will occur in other forms.'

I took the plastic pouch from him; he had been gesturing with it. Out of respect, I didn't want to put it into my pocket. It seemed offensive even to be holding it.

'I examine many pieces of evidence in the course of my investigations,' Dr Mooly Mukherjee said. 'Spectacles can seem sad – one imagines the person's eyes. Shoes or sandals – the foot always leaves a distinct imprint or shape. I have had occasion to examine human ears, the result of violent altercations. Bite wounds – the dentition is apparent, a reminder of our animal nature. But this, sir, this small boy's severed hand with its indication of hard manual labour, is the saddest thing. It says nothing and it says everything. It is like a holy relic. It is a most melancholy object.'

He spoke with dramatic pauses, stroking his moustache,

speaking to the window, a kind of oration, and when he had finished, he stepped to the door and opened it.

'Left at pillar. End of hall to the staircase. Please leave ID badge with receptionist.' He indicated with a downward swipe of his hand that he had something more to say. 'Ultimately, I should be immensely relieved to hear that body part underwent decent cremation, with proper puja, in fullness of time.'

No fingerprints on the dead hand. As if the skinny, half-mummified little thing were not melancholy enough, this news made it seem sadder in its anonymity, like a corpse without a face.

'It's what I used to do,' Mrs Unger said a few days later, the afternoon sun showing in streaks of dust-glow beneath the great open canopy of Howrah station. Balraj supervised a porter who carried her large bag on his head, my smaller one in his right hand and our basket of water bottles and tiffin tins in his left. She had the tickets; she'd even hired bedrolls for us both.

'Platform jix,' Balraj said with a glance at the departure board.

She said, 'Let's go before the crowds get there.' She snatched at my hand and I felt all her anxiety at being in public, exposed to the mob. Though her grip was hot and tight, her nails sharp, when she spoke again she sounded casual. 'I like arriving fifteen minutes before departure. And there's no one here to frisk me.'

'I want to frisk you. I want to pat you down.'

Inclining her head so that Balraj couldn't hear, she said, 'That might not be enough.'

I was elated. We rarely talked like this – the facetious and forgiving innuendo that lovers use. But today was something special. It was our first night together and on an express train to Gauhati in Assam.

'This way, madam. What bogie, madam?'

'Looks like ten,' she said, lifting her ticket to verify it.

Balraj passed this information to the porter and snapped at him to hurry. He seemed impatient and now I saw why. We were being watched by a hard-faced woman in a filthy sari, her face smeared with make-up, her big feet in broken sandals. Her hair was matted and thick with dirt. She whined a little and she nodded to get our attention, seeming to peck at us with her sharp nose.

Even beyond the barrier at platform six the ugly woman followed, legs wide apart, carrying a shoulder bag. Mrs Unger saw her but said nothing and when the woman tried to get closer, Balraj blocked her way.

We found our coach and our compartment, a four-berth sleeper. She said, 'Don't worry, I paid for the other two berths, so we'll have it all to ourselves.' The berths were narrow and unpromising. I could not imagine lying next to her on one of these badly padded shelves.

An aggrieved and nagging voice just outside in the corridor made me look up. It was the ugly woman – *bhikhiri*, Balraj said, a beggar, and he stood in front of her, screening us, as the porter swung our bags on to the upper berths.

'Sorry, madam,' Balraj said, apologizing for the gabbling woman.

'Give her some rupees,' Mrs Unger said. And to the woman, '*Dam koto?*'

'She wanting two hundred, madam.'

Mrs Unger smiled at the amount. The woman was still talking in her scratchy voice. She seemed to be threatening and her reddened eyes looked hostile.

'What is that language?'

'Assamese, madam. She wanting to speak to you.'

'What about?'

'She say she not normal, madam.'

Mrs Unger reacted sharply, made a face, shook her head, then said, 'How unfortunate. But how does it happen that she's in first class? I think we should call the conductor.'

Balraj said in a respectful but cautioning way, 'Please listen to her speak, madam.'

Seeming to marvel at Balraj's audacity, Mrs Unger softened. '*Namashkar. Apni keman achen?*'

'She not well,' Balraj said.

The woman clutched her ragged sari with heavy sunburned

hands and turned her beaky face on Mrs Unger. She began to shout, showing red teeth and dark gums.

'She say she wanting money. You have money.'

'That's true. Go on.'

'She having no money. She say, "I not normal." She say, "God make me different, not like you. People treating me in bad way because I not normal."'

The rough-looking beggar woman was becoming angrier as she spoke. I had seen many panhandlers. They repeated the same phrases, pleading for food and 'No mother, no father!' But this one was giving a speech, denouncing Indians, proclaiming her abnormality, and all of it seemed threatening, her voice still harsh with menace.

Because I did not understand anything she said, I looked closer, scrutinizing her, and saw that she was not a woman. She was a man, middle-aged, wrinkled and graceless, clownish in a torn sari, with big filthy feet and swollen hands, a wooden comb jammed into his matted hair, and still demanding money, beginning to shriek, showing his green, gummy tongue.

'If you don't give, madam, she will open sari and make nuisance and shame.' Balraj, in his panic, was reaching into his own pocket for rupees. 'She will show private parts.'

But Mrs Unger had summed him up herself and was counting hundred-rupee notes. Seeing her, the man – I no longer saw a woman in this sari – became calmer and licked the spittle from his lips and reached out, his big hostile hand like a weapon.

'That's more than you asked for. *Onek dhonnobad,*' Mrs Unger said.

After the strange creature whined his mild thanks – '*Dhonnobad. Thik achhi*' – and touched the money to his forehead; after Balraj got off and saluted us from the platform; after the whistle blew and the train set off into the late-afternoon sun, Mrs Unger shut the compartment door and took the seat facing me and spoke in a subdued voice.

'I'm glad that happened. That was extraordinary.' She was silent for a while, breathing softly. 'I needed that.'

146

I began to say something about the Hindu concept of *maya*, illusion; about the Jain word *anekantvad*, 'the many-sidedness of reality'. In beetling and practical India, where everyone occupied a narrow slot in society, this obliqueness and vagueness and evasion, ill-informed observation, arcane philosophy reduced to the sort of chit-chat that foreigners like me made in India, usually third-hand, 'Someone was telling me . . .' But I didn't complete the thought.

She had been smiling, but the smile slackened and her eyes glistened and went out of focus. Very slowly her smile broke, her face softening as though a thought was crawling beneath the loose skin of her features. It was the sort of expression you see just before a shout, a face about to swell with laughter. Several attitudes rose and fell until I no longer recognized her helplessness. The face of someone you've never seen cry before is shocking because it seems another face entirely, and you can't imagine why it is so cracked and ugly and weak.

Mrs Unger lifted her hands and began to sob into them. I made a move to sit beside her to console her, but she must have seen me through her fingers and she waved me back.

She seemed to draw great anguished breaths from deep within herself, sorrowing with her whole body. I said nothing. I watched her weep, hoping that she'd understand that my close attention represented the sympathy I felt. But it was more than sympathy. It was fear too, seeing this strong woman reduced to helpless tears – and why?

The train clanked over those loose rails at level crossings that are so frequent at the fringes of big Indian cities. Mrs Unger still sat across from me, upright, her knees together, her lovely hands resting on them, facing me but not seeing me, her eyes large and so unfocused as to be luminous, tears streaking her cheeks. Then she took out her bag and, using her mirror, dabbed at her face and tidied her dampened hair.

'That was perfect. I'd wondered how to begin. But that was the right beginning.'

'A grubby transvestite looking for a handout.'

Her reddened eyes found me. 'A person living two lives.'

She said it softly, correcting me, not in any melodramatic way but with an intensity that seized my attention.

'You have something you want to tell me. Something serious.'

'I don't really want to. It's better when secrets are kept.'

'Then don't tell me.'

'I feel I have to. You know too much already.'

'Do I?' I felt I knew very little about her, but that I had no right to ask for more.

'You know what I'm like in the dark – with you, alone.'

'In your vault.'

'Darkness reveals who we really are.'

'I hope so.'

'But now you know I have a secret.'

'The only part that bothers me is that it's somehow related to that strange person, the man in women's clothes. So what are you saying?'

I was more than bothered; I was seriously alarmed. I had never seen Mrs Unger naked and for all I knew – and I felt utterly ignorant and credulous – Mrs Unger could have been Mr Unger.

She didn't blink. She was staring at me as if to say, *I defy you to see what it is that's strange about me. It's right in front of your face.* She wasn't mocking, yet a smile was implied, as a pinhole of light in her eyes, a glitter of that same defiance.

This was all a little too playful for me. Anyone can face you and say *I'm not what I seem, guess my secret,* torment you by forcing you to guess. It was a cruel way of making a fool of you, wringing an admission – but of what?

'I think it would be good if we didn't have any secrets,' I said.

'Not good. My secrets sustain me,' she said.

I said, 'I've never known anyone who was so forthright.'

'I'm talking about one secret,' she said. 'I wonder how you'll take it.'

'Nothing could possibly change my feelings for you.'

'You might find it shocking.'

'I want to be shocked,' I said, daring myself. 'I want to share your shocking secret.'

*It be so strange to you. You must not cry out*, Mina Jagtap had said, passing me the dead hand.

Mrs Unger smiled at me the way an older person smiles at someone much younger, that *You'll learn* smirk of superiority. I became very nervous and thought: *Is she going to tell me she's a man?*

In my anxiety I looked out of the window for relief and saw that the sun was at the level of the palm trees in the middle distance. A half hour out of Calcutta and we were in the countryside, a chewed-up landscape of trees with shredded foliage and small straw-roofed bamboo huts and the usual biblical scenes of robed women carrying water jars and boys herding goats and men in turbans leaning to steady wooden ploughs that were pulled by sleek black buffalo. The daylight dimmed as we watched, the lamps not yet lit in the train, and in this gathering dusk Mrs Unger became calmer and more certain.

'I'm black,' she said simply.

'You're not.'

'I'm black,' she insisted. In a low voice she added, almost in sorrow, 'I hate confessions. They're so stagy.'

I sat back, flattened against the seat cushion, so I did not appear to be staring.

'I know I don't look it, but I am. If you were black, you'd know it immediately. I can pass for white among whites, but I can't pass for white among blacks. We have ways of knowing.'

The obvious question was on my face.

'We black people.'

She had become very serious and somewhat vexed, as though exasperated at having to explain something so complicated to someone so simple. Certainly she'd got my attention and because I didn't know what to say or where to look, I was just gabbling.

'It would be much easier if you didn't say anything.' She was rocking forward as the coach rocked, the train turning by a wide river. And then her face trembled as we banged over an iron bridge. 'It's not a long story.'

'You don't have to tell me.'

'Just listen,' she said in a mother's firm tones. 'I was born in

149

Georgia. I won't tell you where; you've never heard of it. I was one of seven children. I wish you could have seen us together. There weren't two of us who looked alike. I was second oldest. The eldest, my brother Ike, was quite dark and had black features. Then there was me. Number three had tightly curled reddish hair. Number four was pale, with dark hair. And so on.

'My grandmother was black, my mother – her daughter – was dark. My father was white. But never mind all these distinctions. We were a black family living in a black township and all of us kids went to a black school. Everyone knew our pedigree – it's the country way. Georgia was still segregated then and I hated it. I'll spare you the details.

'I wanted to go to college up north, to get away from all this. So after high school I applied to a college in Boston. My local church arranged for me to stay with a family in the Roxbury area. They ran a sort of boarding house. A few days after I arrived, the woman of the house said to me, "You think you're better than we are, white-looking and uppity, but you're nothing but a little black girl just like us. Just like us – and don't you forget it."

'I thought to myself: Did I come all the way from Georgia to end up in a segregated part of Boston, in the same sort of place I just left? I stayed for one semester and then went to New York City. It wasn't easy, but it's a big city and I just disappeared there, as people do. And the barriers weren't so rigid.

'I didn't want to live among black people, who seemed to resent me. I wanted to pass for a white person. I didn't want black baggage and I didn't want my family bringing me down. I lived alone. I finished my degree and on the way I met a lovely man and married him. He'd been married before – was a widower – and he had a small son. That was fine with me, because I knew I didn't want any children of my own.

'Harold died. The boy, Chalmers, became more my companion than my son. Then I married Ralph Unger, the Anglo-American – the late, unlamented Ralph. He resented Charlie. You can see how fond Charlie is of me. I think I've done a good job. I was left a lot of money and I realized how lucky I'd been. I resolved never to marry again and to use the money in the best possible way. Well, you've seen what I've done at the Lodge.'

In the course of speaking she'd turned away from me towards the window, where night had fallen and only pinpricks of light flashed, lanterns in those bamboo huts or stammers of flame from cooking fires. She'd spoken without much emphasis, almost without emotion, a statement rather than a confession.

'So now you know my secret.'

I thought of myself as unshockable, yet when she'd finished her story I was speechless. As with a real shock, I had no questions, no answers either, only a dumb gaping funk in the half-light of the railway compartment, and my unvoiced self-recrimination: *I thought I'd heard everything, and now this.* I didn't doubt her, I doubted myself.

Also (even worse), that accompanying doubt in which, with one shattering revelation, the whole logical and obvious world becomes deceptive – suddenly, nothing was what it seemed. A lot of people would subscribe to that cliché. I certainly did, only half believing it. But presented with the evidence, I could only sigh. I felt like a fool, as though in a shell game she'd shown me a pearl under a cup and moved the cup among two others while I watched, and lifted it, and the pearl was gone – and she lifted another cup and there was the pearl, but a new one, black and more beautiful. And I hadn't a clue.

'I know you wouldn't lie to me,' I said. 'But I don't see it.'

'If only you could see my mother or my brothers,' she said almost wistfully.

'I just see you.'

'I'm like them.'

I could not imagine her in any other way. I could not recast her as black nor find any feature that was different from my own.

'Anyway, now you know why I was so moved by that woman at Howrah station. That man in a sari. That's how I feel most of the time. Like an impostor.'

'I'm glad you told me.'

'I can see that you're shocked.'

'No,' I said and wondered how convincing I sounded. 'I'm happy. You trust me with the truth. I want to show you that I'm worthy of that trust.'

A knock at the door – the conductor to punch our tickets, the meal seller behind him with boxes of food. Mrs Unger dealt with them, speaking Bengali. After they'd gone, she took out the food she'd brought in tiffin tins, a cylinder of stacked containers, rice and dhal and vegetables and yogurt. Eating off trays on our laps was the mundane ritual I needed to bring me back to reality, though we ate mostly in silence.

'I'm glad I'm here,' I said afterwards.

'Good. There's lots of things I need you to do. Lots of ways to help. Now it's bedtime, but there's only room for one person on these berths. Let's turn in. We'll be in Gauhati at seven. We'll talk then.'

She called the sleeping-car attendant – barefoot, wild hair, pop-eyed, hungry for *baksheesh* – and he unrolled the bedding and made our beds. He got his tip and, after he'd gone, I kissed her lightly on the cheek. I thought I would agonize all night. But rocked by the train I slept and dreamed of her.

# II

'Bodoland,' she said, looking up as the train, going rap-rap-rap, raced past an embankment of palm trees, banana groves, more bamboo huts and women washing clothes in a creek, four of them, side by side.

I remembered what she'd told me and I felt somehow like a conspirator. But because of it I had never felt closer to her. Taking me into her confidence, she had made me feel that I mattered to her. She never used the word 'love', but I felt nothing but love for her. It was always *bhoga* for her, the intense sexual pleasure of the tantric massage.

I said, 'I'd do anything for you.'

She kept her gaze at the window. 'Bodoland looks so peaceful. Look at those lily ponds and the children playing. You'd never know that Bodos have a liberation front. That these smiling people commit murder, blow up bombs. That they have the true pedigree – they are aristocrats. That they're angry.'

'I didn't know. How would I? They look content.'

'People write about landscapes like this and because they're so far from home they feel they have to make it pretty. Look, it's not pretty at all. It's not ugly. It's a great featureless emptiness, an awfulness of trapped people and peasant misery. You gape at it. It gapes back at you.'

She was drinking a cup of tea, smiling out of the window as I lay in my berth.

'Who would want to possess it or blow it up? Who could possibly care that much? Yet they do, in their multitudes.' She was still smiling. 'It's not the weirdness of humanity. It's the weirdness of the Indian personality. And the way people write about them. The travel books! The novels!'

Hearing this, I thought back to the garden of the Fairlawn and winced at recalling how I had been subjected to the scrutiny of that flitting, pitiless man.

'There isn't a single truthful book about India. There are long-winded family romances. And whimsical novels. And the experimental junk. India reveals itself, but no one looks closely. It's a culture of evasions. This country is very dirty. It's impossible to tell the truth here. The truth is forbidden, especially in writing. Anyway, a truthful book about India would be unbearable – about spite, venom, cruelty, sexual repression, incest and meaningless crimes.'

That also made me recall the Fairlawn, the newspaper cuttings about infanticide and servants murdering their employers and the Monkey Man. I mentioned this to Mrs Unger.

'That's nothing,' she said. 'There are monsters and freaks all over India. Real monsters, grotesque freaks. No one writes about them. No one sees them. They write about buffoons – the Monkey Man! They praise the call centres and the steel mills. "We have computers!" They write about happy families, not about child-strangling, the mobs, rural suicide, the bombs on trains and in marketplaces where people are blown to bits. "What a colourful bazaar!" Nothing about the savage crowds and bombs. Nothing about diseases.' She smiled her bitter smile. 'They're content. And they're furious too.' She canted her head. 'See those purple hills?'

'Yes.'

'Bhutan,' she said. 'We'll be in Gauhati soon. That's the Brahmaputra River, though you can only see the embankment. We have a hotel in Gauhati.' She turned away from the window and smiled at me over her cup of tea. 'You might do something for me there.'

On a long curve, the compartment filled with light that warmed the stale air and Mrs Unger lit a stick of incense to freshen it. I stepped out to use the mucky toilet and on the way, passing the propped-open door, I was surprised by the cool breeze eddying in the vestibule and the sight of fog lying in patches, like large grey wisps of wool, unravelling and ghosting across the freshly ploughed fields. The river – mostly sandbanks here – was visible through the thicknesses of bamboo, in wide clumps. I could see women setting off across the smooth dunes, past the beached boats and black hulks, with basins of laundry on their heads, seeking the watercourse that was hidden from view in this dry season. Then the tea gardens, then the low hills.

I was hoping after all this time for something substantial. It was not a pretty landscape. It was a chewed and ruinous one, a flood-plain in a time of drought, before the monsoon. Gauhati rushed upon us, a progression of well-made shacks rising to humble shops and three-storey slapped-together buildings. I was back in the compartment, tugging the bags from the upper berth. Mrs Unger sat calmly. She touched my shoulder to restrain me.

'We're being met. The porters will take care of this.'

And, as she spoke, a man in a wool hat with a sign saying UNGER appeared outside the window of our coach as we drew into Gauhati station.

'That funny little man is ours.'

She greeted him in Bengali, with *Namashkar* and the usual how-are-you that I was beginning to learn, *Apni keman achen?* And she must have asked him his name, because he replied, 'Ravi Baruha, madam, speaking English.'

'Our bags are right inside, compartment ten.'

Ravi Baruha nodded to his own lackey, who rushed in for the bags and soon was balancing one on his head and one in each hand, Baruha leading the way.

'We want to visit the Kamakhya temple later this morning and tomorrow we're on the train to Silchar.'

This was news to me – not just the temple, but Silchar. I was reminded that I was in her hands.

'Train departs eight a.m. for Lumding,' Baruha said. 'Change for Silchar.'

'I have the tickets.'

'Long journey, madam.'

'We are on a mission.' She nodded at me.

Outside the station, we boarded a van. I sat next to the driver and the porter crouched in the narrow space at the back, tangled in the luggage. Baruha said, 'New hotel. Just open. Many facilities.'

But I listened without interest, for all this time, since early morning, since Bodoland, I'd been deep in thought, glancing at Mrs Unger and, when she was turned away, studying the nape of her neck, the texture of her hair, the gleam of her skin, her slender hands, her feet in her sandals, her profile, her pretty mouth, remembering what she had told me. *I'm black* was a mystery to me.

I was used to gazing at her, but this was in adoration. I was lost in a new kind of scrutiny, but all I saw was what I had seen before: the face, the body of the woman I loved, if anything paler and prettier than ever, a loveliness and purity I wanted to hold, because in holding her I was holding all her good works. I yearned to put my mouth on her – not so strange a desire. It was the elemental hunger all passionate lovers feel, something almost cannibalistic, the intensity of tantric *bhoga*.

'Indians have a genius for making something new look fifty years old,' she said under her breath as we entered the hotel. 'They never quite finish and it's never quite right. All of India is a work in progress. Do I mean progress? Never mind.'

At the front desk, the clerk said, 'We've been expecting you. We've put you in our Palace Suite. Good journey?'

'Excellent. Thank you for asking.'

After the paperwork and the porter and the rackety elevator with its gates of steel mesh, we were shown to a suite that overlooked a sports ground – some boys playing cricket, the crack of the bat, scattered shouts. Mrs Unger pulled the curtains.

We were alone at last in the half-dark. I had the sense in this new setting that we were strangers. I was plunged into a self-conscious silence. I didn't know what to say. I desired her, but how to begin? Lying across from her in the opposite berth in the rocking train all night had simply confused me. I was tongue-tied and felt awkward, not to say tormented.

But she knew that. She could always assess a situation and was never at a loss for words.

'First a bath,' she said. 'And then the temple. After that, you might give me a massage. You know how. That's how I learned, by getting one from a *dakini*. Do you feel up to it?'

'*Dakini?*' Where had I heard that word?

'Priestess, healer,' she said. 'Never mind the words. Tantra is full of them. But it's the deeds that matter.'

Priestess was an apt word for her. It was how I had seen her at Kalighat, in a rapture after the goat sacrifice. I held her. Instead of kissing her I pressed my head against hers and felt the blood pounding at my skull.

We took showers separately and afterwards went down to the hotel lobby. The driver Ravi Baruha signalled to us with a wobble of his head that he was in attendance.

I had imagined Gauhati to be a small riverside town, but it was a sprawling city in bad repair, with tucked-away bazaars and slow-moving traffic, bicycle rickshaws and old buses wreathed in diesel fumes. The wide river was so shrunken in these months before the monsoon that it seemed like a shallow lake streaked with low islands of sand. The streets smelled of earth and oil and had a tang that reminded me of bark mulch.

'Fancy bazaar,' Ravi Baruha said in the Bengali way, *bajjar*. 'Big and famous. Pan bazaar. Many attendees.'

The temple crowned a rocky hill just outside the busy part of the city. The area was one of Gauhati's landmarks – scenic in the Indian sense, meaning that it was a magnet for mobs and vandalism. 'Scenic' in India always implied blight.

It seemed to me a Mrs Unger observation, but when I said this to Mrs Unger she gave me one of her I-couldn't-agree-less smiles.

'You're looking at surfaces,' she said. 'Always a mistake in India. You're distracting your mind with all the wrong things. You could say this road is a mess' – our car had begun to climb the steep road of loose boulders and litter and yellow wilted trees; it *was* a mess – 'but this is the way to the holy temple, a holy road. We're so lucky. I love those ragged prayer flags and those faded pennants.'

'I wish I had your gift for seeing into things.'

'Close your eyes, maybe. You'll see more.'

But I didn't, because the sharp bends and the steepness were making me feel car-sick.

'Go as far as you can,' she said, as Baruha parted the crowd by tapping his horn.

He dropped us at a barrier near the crest of the hill. Beyond it and above, past the food stalls and the relic sellers and the ice-cream vendors and the hawkers of posters, fluttering flags and marigolds and strings of plastic beads, all this kitsch, was a stone fortress and a gateway, the entrance to the rambling temple complex.

The way that Mrs Unger stiffened from her aversion to mobs was so extreme it bordered on horror. It made me wonder why she'd come to India, where every street was crowded; the whole of India was a mob. And when she murmured about her dislike of Indians in a mass, surging towards her, she seemed to become small and fragile, to visibly shrink; and she wanted me to care. Yet I kept thinking that she was like a visitor to Alaska complaining of the cold.

The Indian mob to her was a dark creature. More than a pushing tide of toothy men, it seemed to represent a menacing intelligence, a monster loose on the street, all its many limbs thrashing towards her. She was the victim of this predator that rippled through traffic, stopping cars, reaching for her with grasping hands. *I always think they want to devour me.*

Even the yelling we heard from three streets away, a distinct syncopation of shouting, angry laughter and screechy chants – it might have been a wedding party – this commotion was a mob to her. And that roar of voices and slapping feet quieted her and made her withdraw. She always took my hand in her hot, damp fingers and held on.

'I never have any idea of what they're saying. *Zindabad*, yes, "long live", but long live what? They always seem to be destroyers.'

I agreed, yet she seemed to thrive in India, and I wondered what it was she saw that I didn't.

'Kamakhya temple,' Mrs Unger said, still gripping my hand. 'The grieving Lord Shiva carried the corpse of his beloved Kali on his shoulders as he danced across the earth. The gods were appalled.

Vishnu intervened and chopped the dead Kali into fifty-one frag-
ments. Wherever a body part landed, a temple was built. One of
her little toes came to earth at Kalighat. I wonder if you can guess
which part of her body landed here?'

We were passing through the gateway, past pillboxes and low
towers of red-smeared stone. Holy men, looking regal yet dispos-
sessed or disinherited, sat upright before brass bowls as pilgrims
hurried forward excitedly. The temple had the look of a hill fort,
the remnants of one: a perimeter wall and parapets, the stonework
like battlements around its enclosures. It was well protected, its
chapels like sentry boxes, with images carved in deep relief into
the black blocks and, as a form of veneration, wiped with paste that
had crusted in the heat.

'That's a hint,' Mrs Unger said.

The goddess was depicted on the side of one shrine as the
carving of a woman squatting with her legs open, the thick lips of
swollen genitals exposed and gaping. All around us, devotees –
women mainly – were chanting and praying.

I said softly, 'Was it Kali's vulva that dropped here?'

'Yes, her *yoni*,' Mrs Unger said. She paused in front of the bold
carving, the wide-apart legs. 'Isn't it marvellous? A whole temple
dedicated to it. That's why this is the most sacred of the tantric
pilgrimage sites.'

'What's happening here?'

'The goddess is showing her *yoni*, inviting a puja.'

'What kind of prayer would that be?'

'An adoring mouth,' she said and pursed her lips in a kiss.
'Adoring fingers on the sacred spot.'

Beyond this stone shrine was a pavilion, open sides, tile roof.
Men and women crowded into it as though at a sideshow. We
joined them and a gleeful yelp went up as a bare-chested priest
brought his hacker down on a black goat's head, just as I had seen
at Kalighat. The head toppled on to the bloody floor – a puddle of
blood six feet across, the grateful praying watchers standing at the
edge of it, their feet splashed with the blood, rejoicing at the sight
of the beheading.

'Do you know how lucky we are to be here?' Mrs Unger said.

I followed her into a smoky stifling temple and she squatted and put money into a basket. Priests sitting cross-legged blessed her as she lit sticks of incense. She was intent, kneeling, concentrating on a shadowy cloth-covered image, murmuring prayers.

I had no idea what to do. It was far from anything I knew about India. In this remote place, midmorning in the heat of another Kali temple, I was like a child who had been taken to a place of pilgrimage by his mother. I would have gone out of the temple but I didn't dare to lose sight of Mrs Unger, didn't want to stray. I was clinging to her, feeling helpless and a bit dazed by the clouds of incense, with the passivity of an anxious child.

I had been startled by her rapture at Kalighat; I was equally impressed by the intensity of her devotion here, because I was used to seeing her in charge. And she was prayerful here, bowing down, offering pieties in an unexpected posture, compact, submitting to whatever image was hidden there, covered by a cloth.

It was weird and enigmatic. Indian gods and goddesses could look ferocious, but nothing I'd seen could compare with the fierce spell cast by this shrouded foot-high figure, a brooding mummy-wrapped bundle. The very folds in the blank cloth exhausted me with fear. I could not imagine what lay beneath this terrifying shroud.

Her veneration seemed to invigorate her. Though we returned to the hotel in silence, she was excited, expectant, eager to be alone with me. I knew this without her saying anything. It was noon, yet our suite was so dark I fumbled locking the door, and when I turned I saw her lying face-down on the bed.

By her touch, in a vault just as dark, she had taught me the way to proceed. And so I began. Touching her, I realized she was naked, not wearing her white silk sari, as it had seemed: this was her warm flesh, her characteristic odour, not floral perfume but something heavier and more animal. She smelled of vines, of ripeness, of cut-open fruit, of a stickiness I could taste.

Tentatively at first and then with more command, I moved my fingers from zone to zone, the seven chakras: the dome of her head, her brow, her ears, her throat, her heart, her belly, the base of her spine. The idea was to work slowly, to insinuate with my fingers, to find the organs and massage them; to reach the inner meat of the muscle, where the nerves lived; to apply gentle pressure to stir the blood. I worked on her body as she had worked on mine. When my eyes grew accustomed to the darkness, I saw the bottle of warm oil on the side table and I used it on her.

She was still face-down. I had found her heart and throat and belly by reaching beneath her, by stroking and using the flat of my hand while pushing from above, enclosing her between my palms.

'Yes,' she said several times, and it was more a groan of satisfaction than a whole word; but even so, she said no more than that.

I knew I was doing it well because of the way she sighed, whimpering slightly to encourage me. That was when I straddled her – as she had straddled me – and worked down her backbone to her buttocks, caressing them, clapping my hands against them. I was surprised by the ripple of her hard bum muscles, the way she could clench and release.

All this took more than an hour and might have been closer to two. I was excited, so far from Calcutta, in this semi-ruin of a city sprawling by the low duney banks of the river, in this nearly empty hotel. Thrilled, seated on her long slender body, as pale as those dunes, my knees containing her, my knuckles against the globes of her glutes. I tried to remember everything she had done to me, repeating these moves on her. A grateful receiver of her adoring attention, I had become a methodical and scrupulous masseur – she had shown me the way.

'An hour or two isn't enough,' she'd said to me once. It took an hour just to warm up and two hours at least to achieve *bhoga* – delight. And so I went on riding her, smoothing her, oiling her and pushing her with my palms, plying her chakras with my fingertips – the first time I'd ever touched her in this way. I loved her sighs of acceptance and the way she turned slippery, her whole body, like a great oily reptile I was riding, digging my elbows into her buttocks and (another of her techniques) using my chin and my mouth on the base of her spine, feeling the warmth radiate throughout her body.

161

Even in the half-light of the hotel room, all the blinds drawn, she glowed. I remembered her saying in the train, *I'm black*. I gloried in it for being our secret. I was a monkey clinging to a goddess, desperate to please her.

'Now,' she said after a long while of my caresses and I dismounted, crouching beside her, as she shifted and rolled over, naked, arms to her sides, her legs parted.

She used both hands, her clutching fingers, to spread her sex like a flower. Or so it seemed to me as I watched, like an opening lotus with reddened and thickened petals.

'Find the sacred spot,' she said in a whisper. 'Search for it slowly.'

Obeying her, I stroked her beautiful blossom very gently until I had opened it further and my fingers were slick. And I knew when I'd found it, because I had seen her before captured by ecstasy.

'*Yoni* puja.'

I must have faltered – she knew I was baffled.

'Pray with your mouth,' she said softly.

And so there I lay, for the longest time, like a mating insect, until at last, rapturous and writhing on the bed, she sighed. She let out a long groan as dramatic as a death rattle, almost as deep as grief, and at the same time clapped her thighs to my ears.

We slept and when I woke I didn't know where I was. I began to marvel that we were still in India, in distant Gauhati, but she shushed me and turned me over. She worked on me in much the same way that I'd done to her, devoting two or more tantric hours to my pleasure. It was a great novelty and a relief to be with her alone, uninterrupted, in this far-off place: no car, no driver, no waiting to be summoned or sent away.

Midway through the massage, she applied delicate pressure and held me, as though suspended on a lengthening wire of sexual tension – a pulsing of energy, a rippling of sexual health, not an orgasm but something akin to skimming lightly, feeling intense pleasure, a swelling just short of bursting. At that point, with my temperature way up, she stroked the base of my spine, as she had done before, as I had done to her. But this time I sensed the release of an expanding plume of warmth from my lower back and it spread through me, as if she were pouring hot oil over me. Seeing how I seemed to soar, she whispered, '*Kundalini*.'

By the time she was done, night had fallen, and we lay entwined, exhausted, the light of passing cars now and then raking the walls of the room.

In the darkness before dawn, we woke and bathed and packed our bags. At this hour, some people were already mopping floors and poking the corridor walls with long-handled dusters.

'We have an early train,' she said. 'It'll be all day to Lumding and then overnight to Silchar.'

'Wouldn't it be quicker by car?'

'We'd never reach Silchar. We'd be stopped at a roadblock and robbed, or killed.' She was smiling. 'We're off the map here. This is the land of rebels and *goondas* and tribals. It's dangerous, even deadly. That's why it's so full of life.' Before I could say anything, she added, 'You have the gift. You have the hands.'

'You gave me the gift.'

'You knew how to receive it.'

She had a mother's touch. And no wonder she was able to help all those children, I was thinking – restore them to life and give them hope and purpose.

We left Gauhati at eight, on the day train to Lumding, the coaches half empty. We drowsed through the day in our own compartment. Lumding, just a junction in the bruised green hills, appeared in the early evening. We were late. No time to linger on the platform; the night express to Silchar was standing at the station. The conductor, glad to see us, with a wink for *baksheesh*, showed us to our compartment. It was an old sleeping car and though I could not see any food or people, it smelled of stale food and human bodies. But our beds were made and the door locks worked.

The train laboured all night, hooting through the hills of southern Assam. I couldn't see much outside, but I could sense a landscape of trees and streams. The air at our open window was murky in the deep valleys, cooler on the slopes, thickened with a dusty leafiness of sour jungle. Most of the passengers were in the front coaches, the hard seats, the floor littered with peanut shells and fruit peels, trapped-looking faces behind barred windows, Assamese in shawls, tribal people in embroidered vests, wearing necklaces of red beads.

In the darkness of the night, listening to the anvil-clang of the train on the tracks, I sensed that she was awake.

'I've never known anyone like you,' I said.

'I'll take that as a compliment.'

'When I first met you, I thought, here's a woman who's never had to struggle. Yet you've done nothing but struggle.'

'There's no end to it, ever.'

The clanking of the train worked this sentence into my head. After a while I said, 'I want to help you.'

'You have no idea what that means to me.'

'I'm devoted to you,' I said, relieved to be able to say it.

It was not love. The power and uncertainty I associated with love I did not feel with Mrs Unger. I didn't want anything in return: I wanted to serve her, needed for her to accept my attention. I was grateful to her for making any suggestion to me, thankful for her request – the feeling I associated with a son for his mother. Sentiments I'd never felt for my own mother, I felt for her. I wanted to obey her.

'Anything,' I said.

'The time will come,' she said. Then her breathing became regular, as I listened; and I slept too.

At dawn we were among low, mostly bald hills, the old train rolling on the scooped and flattened outskirts of Silchar. Shallow valleys and tea estates, each one well planted with slopes of deep-green bushes, as orderly as a botanical garden, all the bushes trimmed like topiary. Where the land was flat there were corrugations of newly ploughed fields. The tea pickers were visible on some of the slopes, looking as if they were tidying the bushes.

Empty and green, the valleys gaped at the crawling train, and the whole scene had a sunlit grandeur until, at growing intervals, I saw the hovels of farmers, the skinny children, the careworn women washing the breakfast pots in a muddy creek.

Mrs Unger was also watching, but unlike me she was not judging or trying to sum the place up. I was making notes for my scratchy diary, while her attention was witness, concentration intensified by memory – nothing new for her but the shock (so it seemed to me) of seeing something familiar. It was the expression I had seen on her face the first time I met her, how I'd felt about myself when I'd thought *ruthlessly worldly*. But I had been wrong. Hers was the face of compassion and understanding in the presence of suffering.

'But it's beautiful too,' I said, in the way I sometimes thought out loud, the fragment of a reflection.

She knew what I meant. 'Yes, but better enjoy it while it lasts. Silchar is another story.'

Silchar station at ten in the morning was the usual Indian free-for-all, passengers relieved to be out of their hot three-tier coaches where they had sat all night among peanut shells and banana peels. They scuttled across the tracks pursued by porters and rickshaw touts and hawkers with buckets of cookies. Busy rats, most of them plump and bold, nosed amid the litter on the line, making the scraps of paper and plastic bags quiver as they swarmed.

As at Gauhati, we were met, this time by a shy young man in a tweed jacket. He stepped out of the crowd and introduced himself, sounding as if he were about to sell us something.

'Mrs Unger, I am Sudeep. I will be your guide. May we fetch your luggage?'

Snarling, he summoned a porter, stern with this underling, then smiled at us and led the way down the platform and out to the front of the station, where a car was waiting.

'You got my message?' Mrs Unger asked in the car.

'Indeed so, madam. All is in readiness.'

I stared at them, hoping for an explanation, but they continued to speak in generalities.

'And the situation hasn't changed?'

'Situation, madam. Still very much same situation.'

I lost interest in their generalities as the old car we were riding in began to shake – and to shake my head with it. The car tipped and banged on the broken road, the potholes four feet across and some of them deep enough to swallow half a tyre.

'Is this a back street?'

'Main thoroughfare, sir. Mahatma Gandhi Road.'

It was a ruin. We bumped among scooters and bullock carts and cycle-rickshaws, their bike bells tinkling. The shops along this main road were one storey, paint peeling, signs faded, not many shoppers. I had thought Gauhati to be a step into the past, but Silchar was a stride into the distant past.

'We are cut off,' Sudeep was saying, replying to something Mrs Unger had said, and he was also answering an unasked question of mine. 'But air is fresh. Cool climate. Very healthy.'

In the dusty air, the shop-houses tilted sideways on the sloping main street, which was worse than unpaved. It had been paved and shattered, potholes all over it, and its only smoothness was beaten earth. The cycle-rickshaws toppled along it, their skinny drivers standing on their pedals. The place was so poor there were no obvious beggars – no one to beg from, though many people stopped and stared, seeing Mrs Unger and me alighting from the car.

'So, it's arranged for this evening?' she asked Sudeep.

'All arranged. You will find me here.'

The hotel's bare lobby and plastic plants were being dusted by a woman in a green smock. Mrs Unger dealt with the check-in formalities and once again I felt I was being mothered, shepherded, paid for. We went upstairs, took showers, then had a meal in the hotel's dining room – the only diners, perhaps the only guests in the place. Afterwards, Mrs Unger said she wanted a nap.

We lay together on the bed. The accumulated fatigue of the trip to Lumding and the night train to Silchar had knocked me out and knocked her out too, but just before she subsided into sleep she murmured, 'Baby,' and touching my face, 'Baby.'

When we woke, night was falling, dusk at the windows, and I heard bike bells and crow squawks and the cries of hawkers.

'Find Sudeep downstairs,' she said. 'I'll be down in a little while.'

Sudeep was of course standing in the lobby, in the posture of a sentry, awaiting his orders.

'You are coming from?'

'Calcutta. Have you been there?'

'I have not been to mainland at all,' he said.

'Mainland?'

'Indeed, never. Only to Shillong and Gauhati.'

That was new to me, but since we were so far east, like an island surrounded by Bangladesh and Burma, it seemed appropriate to refer to greater India as the mainland.

'All is in readiness,' he said to Mrs Unger when she came downstairs.

In the car, I tried to count the days since we'd left Calcutta, but the nights in the train and the days of massage and sleep defeated me. Perhaps four days – or was it five? All this time we'd penetrated deeper into Assam, the landscape growing stranger, leafier in the valleys, where the tea bushes provided a sort of continuity. But the orderliness of the tea estates was misleading. The villages had grown poorer and smaller, and Silchar, like a dead end, was weighted and slowed by its decay.

But Sudeep was upbeat. 'It is crossroads,' he was saying. 'So many lorries passing hither and thither. We are vibrant. But there are *dacoits* on the road to Imphal. *Goondas* as well. Shillong also treacherous. Extremists are there.'

'Where are we going now?'

Mrs Unger said nothing. Sudeep said, 'As requested, Nagapatti.'

I felt it was some sort of test of loyalty, though I would have agreed to go anywhere with her. As we had gone farther into Assam, we had reached a new stage in our relationship. She must have seen that I was devoted, utterly loyal too and dependent on her.

Mrs Unger was doing me a great favour. She was bringing me into her world. I saw it as an initiation for which I had to be suitably passive. She had taken me by the hand and brought me by degrees to this remote town, which reflected a deeper intimacy between us. In the hotel in Gauhati she had encouraged me to stroke her as she lay, legs open, like the image of Kali I'd seen at the temple. She had hardly spoken, yet her posture was a physical

167

expression of trust. She had luxuriated in my caresses, but I was the acolyte and she the priestess who had liberated me and shown me the way.

Now we were banging along the back streets of Silchar, the potholes deeper and more jarring in the dark. Oil lamps hung from stalls but illuminated nothing but themselves. The road ahead was black. We went about half a mile, not far, though we went slowly, almost at walking speed, and when we came to a road junction, Sudeep told the driver to stop.

'We will proceed by foot.'

The road stank of mud and cow shit and motor oil, and the light was so poor it was hard to see where to walk. Again I marvelled at Mrs Unger's boldness. She was unfazed – white sari, white shawl, sandals – seeming to glide along the back street.

'I know where we are. Nagapatti is down that lane.'

She set off confidently, Sudeep just behind her, and I was at the rear. As my eyes grew accustomed to the dark I could make out the contours of the lane, the lurking boys, stray dogs; some men squatting before a brazier of reddened coals, drinking tea, glanced up, muttering as we passed.

Luminous in her sari, Mrs Unger glowed like an angel, her shawl over her head, moving quickly, her feet hardly seeming to touch the ground. And yet when she saw more people in the road, backlit by their fires, she took my hand.

'Madam,' Sudeep said, his voice rising in a cautioning tone.

But we were ten steps ahead of him. She paused, turned to the right and walked down another lane, where a head-high bamboo barrier had been erected. The thing was flimsy but effective. It blocked the opening of a narrow road: you had no idea what went on behind it. As she slipped past this barrier, she let go of my hand. I followed her. Then she stopped and stood looking down the lane, saying nothing yet serenely triumphant.

The lane was well lit – more than well lit: it was highly illuminated by bright lights and open fires. It was busy, a sort of market scene full of standing and crouching people. Looking closely, I saw that all of them were women – not women but girls and children, grouped around the wood fires that were burning on both sides of the lane, in front of the shops and the houses, as far as I could see. The girls and even the older children, hundreds of them, were garishly made up with red lipstick and blue eye kohl, wearing thin blouses in the chilly air, warming themselves by the fire.

Smoke and flames and the close-together bungalows and huts; girls around the fires, girls on the verandahs, girls leaning on the railings and crouched on the steps. Some had vicious faces, but most looked pathetic and lost. A few of the smaller girls were holding babies and other small girls, hardly more than twelve or thirteen, kneeling near the lanterns, pursed their lips at me and smiled wickedly.

In the smoky air, a whole long lane of child prostitutes and transvestites. An old fat hag was seated just inside one open doorway, attended by a retinue of little whores, painting the fat woman's toenails and massaging her feet.

'I've never seen anything like it,' I said lamely. 'It's like a vision of hell.'

'You're shocked again,' Mrs Unger said. She looked unmoved; she seemed almost jubilant. 'It's not hell. Hell – if you believe in it – is forever. But these girls can be rescued. That's why I'm here. Do you think I'm slumming? A few years ago I came here. I've been back many times. See those old women eyeing me? They know I'm going to hurt their business. But I'm willing to bargain with them.'

I was thrilled to think that Mrs Unger had come here to help these girls – more lost souls. As I considered this, a hand had taken hold of my elbow – a good grip; I couldn't shake it loose. I looked down into the tiny pleading face and desperate eyes of a girl who could not have been more than fifteen. She tugged at me and licked at her lips with a little darting tongue.

Mrs Unger was turned away. She said, 'I don't see any customers.'

Sudeep helped me detach the girl's hand from my elbow, but she went on trying to snatch at me.

'It is their misfortune, sir.'

'Who are they?'

'Tribals, sir. From the mountains, sir. Nagaland. Some are Mizos and whatnot. They are awaiting the lorry drivers. But your friend – madam – will help them find their freedom.'

A few were gesturing to me, calling out, beckoning, striking the poses of coquettes.

'We'll come back tomorrow to negotiate,' Mrs Unger said. She seemed vitalized, her eyes shining with flames. 'But I wanted you to see it like this – at night, with the fires. You have to admit this place is full of energy.'

Our arrival had silenced them and made them watchful. Who could this foreign-looking woman be in her white sari? And what of that foreign man who stood stunned and staring? After a while their chattering resumed, perhaps conjecturing who we were. We walked the length of the lane, girls on both sides, so many of them, all of them in make-up – powdered faces, rouged cheeks, smeared mouths, blue and green eye shadow, their hair fixed with combs; but even so, they looked like schoolgirls dressed for a pageant or a school play that was about to begin. Most of them were barefoot, but some tottered on high heels they'd not yet mastered. They called out, they grabbed my arm and pinched my hand, and a few begged money from Mrs Unger, who walked slowly among them – tall, in her elegant sari, utterly calm, offering soothing words. She had never looked more like a priestess.

Sudeep caught up with us at the far end of the lane. He said, 'I have addressed a few of women. They are agreeable to negotiations.'

But Mrs Unger was looking at me. 'See?' she said. 'It's possible to bring a little hope. Even here.'

The next day I accompanied her to Nagapatti again. Even in daylight the place looked vicious, the girls wearier, the fires smokier. The firelight of the night before had lent it an air of debauched glamour. But today the sky was overcast and clammy, and the lane stank of woodsmoke. The incense stung my nose. I could see the girls' skinny legs and dirty feet, and some of the small children were crying miserably.

It was my job to sit outside and turn away potential customers, while Mrs Unger and Sudeep negotiated to obtain the release of certain girls. Only one man wandered by, unshaven and dirty, a truck driver probably.

'Come later,' I said, and he was so surprised he shrugged and obeyed.

I stared at a bewildered girl, who stared back at me. I didn't know what to say. She went on staring and then made a kissing noise at me. She cupped a breast with one hand and touched herself with the other.

Flustered, I said, 'See that nice woman?'

The girl clung to my leg. Her fingernails were bitten and painted pink.

'That nice woman is going to help you.'

Still she held on to my leg and leered at me.

That evening we flew back to Calcutta. I had not realized it was possible to go so far.

# 12

And, at last, I began to write. I surprised myself at the ease of it. I thought I'd been lost, done with the written word. But no, I was at work again. I had something to write about and I had the energy.

Most people thought of me – probably think of me still – as an adventurous traveller, welcoming hardship, willing to take risks, going to extremes to find the subject of a magazine piece. The hard and lonely life of a wanderer. 'Your amazing tales.' I was, for most of my readers – for many people who knew me – invisible. My career had been made out of a series of calculated vanishings, inspiring people to imagine what I was up to. Stick around too long and get cosy and conversational and people realize you're human.

If you go far enough, if you stay away long enough, people imagine the worst and begin suffering the hardship on your behalf, and they credit you – they certainly credited me – with stamina and ingenuity. So the distant traveller acquires a kind of power – and more than power, virtue – for the very fact of being away, mooching around in inhospitable countries. Heat, dust, swamps, bad roads, mobs, skinny children, scolding men, nasty boys, mushy food, rats, roaches. I did nothing to dispel the notion. I became the conspicuous absentee. The fact was that I usually stayed in good hotels and sometimes great hotels, the sort of luxury that can exist only in countries where people are servile and underpaid.

Remove Mrs Unger and her magic fingers from the trip to Assam; remove the happy hotels and the helpful servants – the guides, the *dhobis* with a bag of my laundry, Mr Baruha sitting next to the driver, Sudeep awaiting orders; remove the comforts, don't mention the pleasures, and what's left is the grubby train, the bamboo huts, 'Bodoland', the slum urchins and the child whores in Nagapatti – the horrors of travel without any compensations.

But my travelling life had been all about compensations. I would never have lived in this wandering way if the pleasures had not outweighed the difficulties – I mean, far outweighed them. I hadn't chosen my life out of a desire to confront danger but rather because I was lazy and evasive, ducking out or moving on whenever I felt like it, whenever something was expected of me, when I had to be grown-up and accountable.

I lived like a prince, which is to say I had no responsibilities, and at the same time I was (as a traveller) credited with being a hero. I mentioned at the beginning of this story how I had managed to live my life this way, pretending to be big and busy – 'I have to be in Bangkok on Monday' – while merely looking for outlets for my pleasure-seeking.

I had come to Calcutta out of pure idleness, not to write but to give lectures. Howard had invited me; the American consul general was my sponsor. Bengalis were highly literate and most of the ones I met spoke English well – so well that they wouldn't stop talking. My lectures were simple. The Indians in the audience sat waiting for me to finish (sometimes impulsively interrupting) and then took turns talking, not questions but long, ponderous pronouncements about art and life. In their vain and wordy pretensions (harmless, really; I found them lovable) they wanted to be regarded as thinkers, challenging whatever I said, this verbose show of wisdom being the embodiment of the Indian ideal, the philosopher, the sage. Their love of discussion was comic, especially in Calcutta, which was falling apart as all the Bengalis went on yakking, yakking, yakking.

I was no different. I was an evader and a fraud in much the same way and for many of the same reasons. Why make hard decisions and assume responsibilities if you can procrastinate by yakking? Talking was the answer and in my case had displaced my writing. Writing was difficult. Talking about writing was a low and profitless form of discourse, and probably the laziest.

I travelled because I was idle, I talked because I had nothing to write, I moved on or ducked out when someone asked me a searching question. And I was averse to being near anyone who was creative. Parvati, for example. She was full of energy, she wrote poems, she danced, she practised martial arts, she was lovely and unmarried: she exhausted me. I was envious and dispirited when I was with her. Maybe I saw something of my younger self in her and was ashamed to see I was no longer creative.

It is very hard for an older writer, tired and out of ideas, to be in the presence of a young writer, especially a gifted one, who is full of hope. I praised Parvati's image of the muted lisp of morning's tongue pushing against the sky, but really I hated it for its brilliance. The better Parvati's poems, the more graceful her dancing, the sadder I became – sad for myself, in the selfish way of someone who suspects his creative life is at an end. It was unfair to Parvati for me to behave this way. I consoled myself by protecting her, keeping my feelings to myself.

She can't have known that I avoided her out of envy and self-disgust. Still she called me, invited me (with a chaperone) to tea and emailed me her new poems. She insisted I go to a dance recital. I went because the theatre was so near to my hotel, but the provocative beauty of her dancing – the lovely virgin stroking the air with sensual fingers – made me so melancholy that I had to leave.

The next day she demanded to know why I'd slipped out of the auditorium early. She had come to the Hastings with two girl-friends who stood guard in the lobby while we sat whispering in my corner of the upstairs verandah.

'Didn't you realize I was dancing for you?'

Feeling obligated, I said, 'But I have nothing to give you.'

'I only want your friendship,' she said, 'that's all. Can you imagine what life is like for someone like me in India?'

'You're a great beauty, you're gifted. You have everything.'

'I'm an unmarried thirty-two-year-old – that's on the verge of being an old bag. You laugh!' – who wouldn't? – 'I told you I have views on marriage. Want to hear them?'

'Of course' – though I didn't.

'Good, because no Indian man wants to hear them. My parents don't want to hear them. India doesn't want to hear them.'

'Tell me.'

'This is the most unromantic country on earth,' she said. 'Never mind sex outside marriage – there's no romance either. No hand holding, no kisses. How I would love to kiss someone I loved. But I can't. We are a trapped and frustrated people.'

'I see that, but maybe it's what makes your poems so steamy. Your dancing too.'

'Maybe, because I'm dying and deprived, but it's not worth it. I want to live and when I meet someone like you I think real life is somewhere else.'

'But you're a wonderful writer.'

'I'd rather live more and write less.'

As she spoke, her beauty dissolved. I no longer saw her as a figure of loveliness. She became a voice, a passionate and sad one, and she was now real to me.

I said, 'But what does any of this have to do with marriage?'

'India has a market economy,' she said. 'There are no suitors here, only customers. The little chap that shows up at my house with his parents as a prospective husband is a customer. His parents are shopping for a bride. I'm the goods – damaged goods. They want to see my teeth, they want to read my horoscope. They might want to make an arrangement. Money's involved – big money sometimes. You've seen the adverts.'

'Matrimonial classifieds. I love reading them.'

'I hate them. I hate the system. They're like coded versions of the personal ads you get in the American papers. "Friendly guy would like to meet young pretty girl" – except in India it's for keeps. And what would my advert say?'

'I wonder.'

'"Over-the-hill Bengali woman, not looking for anyone."'

'You write poetry. You dance. And what about your martial arts?'

'They're not a plus in a culture that wants cookery and child-bearing. My mother-in-law would burn my poems. I wouldn't be able to dance – married women don't do such things. And a talent in martial arts is not a recommendation for a prospective bride.'

'So what do you want?'

175

'To dance for you.'

'I like that.'

'And to meet a man who has a life of his own. Not possessive. A partner. Maybe gay.'

That day she left me a poem about being eight years old and running into the sea, with the lines

> The sea pulls me in around the ankles,
> Grabs the sand from underneath, shows me
> A glimpse of my life, what it will be like later.

What I am trying to describe here is the situation I was in before I met Mrs Unger and in the early days of my getting to know Mrs Unger. I can't say 'friendship' or 'love affair' because she loomed so large, and I felt myself to be her inferior in every way, as a traveller, as an Indophile – intellectually and morally most of all.

I began to change, to see myself and the world differently by knowing Mrs Unger, by seeing her work. The trip to Assam was the defining journey. I, who thought of travel as evasion, had found that travel, as Mrs Unger did it, was purposeful. But more than that, in the course of the journey I had come to know her and to depend on her to such an extent that I lost the selfishness that had prevented me from seeing the world clearly. She had released me and the person she was seemed so unusual, I knew I had someone to write about, someone real.

Calcutta had been a blur. She had helped me to see its true face and to understand it. Her house in Alipore was full of life – the life of children being taught, fed, protected. I was like one of those children: she had rescued me in the same way. I understood their joy and their relief; they were safe, they were happy, they had something to live for.

Assam had been a revelation. The train trip had been liberating. I kept replaying her story about being black and how she had told me that after we'd been accosted by the fierce she-man. Gauhati, the Brahmaputra River, the Kali temple, the journey to Silchar by way of Lumding, the tea estates and the slums and at last, like a vision of hell, the child whores of Nagapatti – all of it was new to me, the hyper-reality of India I had never guessed at before. But writing about it would have been impossible without the steadying and inspirational presence of Mrs Unger, who helped me make sense of it all. She had brought me to these scenes; she had shown me this spectacle; she had penetrated this world and by making use of it had taught me how to use it. An important experience of this trip had been her tantric massage, her healing hands on me, the locating of my creative energy, the release of my *kundalini*.

That would have made me laugh before. 'She helped me find my *kundalini*' – the American searcher, usually a woman, who, turning India into an opportunity for navel gazing, becomes a licensed busybody. Injunctions like 'Out of the mind and into the heart.' But I wasn't laughing any more.

She was a woman of action. I know I have portrayed her so far as a rather humourless and passionate woman, a compulsive do-gooder, overwhelming me with her personality. But I was a small, peripheral part of her life – I saw just how small on this trip. This revelation was a spur to me. I had come to the end of my writing life, so it seemed, because the only subject I had was myself. The mistake my sort of writer made was to falsify my travels, pretending to be an adventurer, when I was merely indulging myself as a tourist. My imagination had shrivelled and my writing had dried up, and when I did make an effort to write something I was aware that I was repeating myself. No wonder I envied Parvati, whose writing was so vibrant. I had a dead hand.

But now I had a subject, someone I would have found impossible to invent, and no one knew her as I did. She had few vulnerabilities, but they went deep. She was human and her frailties helped me know her better. Her closest secret was her fear of the mob, her anxiety whenever she saw large numbers of people, the packed-together crowd that seemed to her like a many-headed creature. Her fear was so fundamental it was like a fear of India and a form of guilt, like that of a fugitive seeing an angry mob and expecting it to pounce. *I always think they want to devour me.* She reacted to mobs, seeming to struggle, and afterwards she was weakened as if just the sight of so many people was an exertion.

She managed this fear in a way I had seen many foreigners do. She had chosen her own India. She'd invented an India that suited her, and when the crowd got to be too much she escaped to her simpler, spiritual vault. She confined her movements to specific places; she looked for safe corners; she avoided the bazaars and markets and mobs.

As for food, she was fussy to the point where she would sometimes refuse to eat; rather than eat something doubtful, she would not eat at all. That point where a religious person becomes rigidly observant, when piety becomes stubbornness and even paranoia. 'Take that foul dish away,' she might say to a waiter. She sounded imperious and sure of herself, but I knew better: she was afraid and when she was afraid she slipped into her Englishness. *That foul dish.*

She must have guessed that I saw beneath her certainties, that I understood her fears; and that made her cling to me. I'd seen her cry. In anyone else, crying was an extension of their laughter. With Mrs Unger, crying was a form of collapse. I'd seen it only once, but it was so anguished and final I felt she'd never get over it, never return from it, never be the same again. Perhaps she needed me too.

Mrs Unger was a character in all senses of the word, multidimensional, someone I admired especially for her ability to create. Out of the *bustees* of Calcutta and the *chawls* of Assam, the exploited girls on the back street and the lost children in the slums, she was giving life. It was a species of rescue, an act of will. She was the person a writer longs to meet, because she was someone almost unimaginable – a good person, not a saint but a woman of action and vision, and for me (I wasn't quite sure how to describe this part) an object of desire, someone adorable. She had given me hope.

The animal sacrifices she had made in Kalighat and encouraged in Gauhati were not aberrations. They were life-giving – that's what sacrifice is, a profound offering, an enhancement. I saw the glittering blade, heard the heartbeat tapped out on the drum, saw the warm black goat jammed between two posts and, in a flash, its head struck from its body, the blood pouring on to the blossoms and the muck of the stone floor of the slaughterhouse. That blood released me. The sight of it stayed with me. Life sprang from blood; life went on.

And I remembered how Mrs Unger's white sari was never without the slight stain of blood, a dark stripe at the hem or a blood spatter on the lower part of her sari that looked like freckles, the same size and brownish colour, a sort of umber. It was visible only close up, but I knew it was blood – blood that made her white sari whiter, purer.

I sat on the upper verandah of the Hastings and wrote the beginnings of what I imagined might be a novella, something I'd call 'A Dead Hand'. I needed to fictionalize, to give myself latitude to invent. The title was one that it seemed had been chosen for me, because, unable to write, I'd felt I had a dead hand. And the moment an actual dead hand had come into my possession, I recaptured my ability to write. I was now awakened, in the live hands of Mrs Unger. I kept her name for my main character because I didn't intend to take any liberties with her.

In the first pages I wrote about receiving the old-fashioned letter, about meeting Mrs Unger at the Oberoi Grand, the invitation to the Lodge in Alipore and the experience in her vault, her healing hands. The very word 'vault' was evocative to me and represented the passion and secrecy of our meetings. She had admitted me to her vault in every sense.

I was privileged to write about that rarest of beings, a thoroughly good person who had found a way of using her fortune to improve people's lives. She didn't preach, she hadn't founded an order of nuns, she wasn't a celebrity – she avoided all publicity. She was practically unknown. I freely surrendered to her; I wanted to belong to her. As a result, I had a character; I even had a narrative. She had healed me too. The sight of the child whores, the tribals on the back street in Nagapatti, was something I would never forget. Analysing my feelings, I began to see that, though I was horrified by the small girls, selling themselves, I was also fascinated and aroused to think that, for a pittance, I could have had any of them. And that unworthy feeling helped me distinguish between the expression of mindless lust and the elevating desire I now knew. I would not have experienced any of this except for the intervention of Mrs Unger.

Almost as satisfying as her good works was her beauty. At first, I had seen her as rather severe, almost forbidding, holding court, a little too majestic with Charlie and Rajat on either side of her. But time softened that image and deepened my understanding. She had clear skin with a rosy blush on it and her hair, drawn back Indian-style, gave her an impressive forehead above her piercing eyes. The Calcutta heat kept moisture on her glowing face and the tropical sunlight emphasized the sculpted planes and angles of her skull. Her nose was sharp, like an instrument of enquiry; her lips were full and soft. She was slightly buck-toothed and her side teeth were prominent, so her lips were usually parted, making her expression more sexual, somewhat hungrier. Her breasts were lifted against her billowing shawl and her loose sari, her nipples like subtle pegs against the silk. I loved her slender feet, with a stippled floral pattern that might have been painted or tattooed.

Even wearing sandals she was almost as tall as me. She walked purposefully and yet upright, with grace, like a dancer, but a tall one, singular and strong. Parvati would have seemed like a school-girl next to her. Mrs Unger had a way of holding her left wrist with her right hand, turning the bangles and the gold cuff with her fingers as she spoke, as though the jewellery were an outward symbol of her power or a badge of her authority. She wore an anklet, a gold chain; she had gold rings on some of her fingers and a nose jewel, a ring with a pea-sized diamond at her right nostril. Yet these jewels were warm, the gold like flesh.

She was perfumed, trailing a sweetness that was so enticing I wanted to taste her, to lick her shoulders, to eat her – and she must have known that, because she had allowed it, had urged me to go deeper, to penetrate her not with my wand of light (her expression) but by insinuating myself inside her. Yet to think that this woman was so lovely within, had such a good heart, a great soul – this was all the inspiration I needed to write. In the days after our return from Assam, in the steamier pre-monsoon heat, I was reborn as a writer.

In this unlikely place for a rebirth, the shaded upper verandah of the Hotel Hastings, above the thickened dust of its lane off Sudder Street, I was given new life. I was happy. I was grateful too. I had thought my creative life was over; I was ashamed to be pretending that I was a writer. That thought must have kept me travelling: I didn't want to stay anywhere long enough for someone to see how little I wrote, how futile I felt. 'I've got to be in Bangkok' or 'I'm going to Vietnam in a few days' or 'I have an assignment' – the restless movement, a pretence of being busy, kept everyone from seeing that I had nothing to write, that travel was my habit of evasion and, like all habits, a dreary repetition, a folding and refolding of feeling, a diminishment. All habits are tinged with sadness, for being habits.

Everything had changed. I loved writing about Mrs Unger. I enjoyed recapturing the pleasure of being with her. I described her lips, the hair that straggled on the nape of her neck and was always the same, uncombable, the fingers that had touched me, the skeletal angles of her jaw and the glow around her eyes. Recreating her, I was aroused, and the form my arousal took was a visceral happiness.

As an outsider, the travelling writer sees only surfaces. I was a recommender of hotels, a sampler of meals, a tester of comforts. I had described disturbance before and the derangement of the world, the appearances of places I'd skimmed across. But I had never known a whole worthy person; I had always doubted that such a person existed. Everyone I knew was just getting by. They were like me, tenuously attached to chaotic societies, but we were parasites, living life outside, in bars, in hotel lobbies, hiding in big cities or at the edges of villages, at the beach, on the verandah with our feet up, calling for another drink, more peanuts. Lives with no further purpose than survival and sex. So that was my subject. I had no idea where I was going and neither did my friends. Writing about these uncertain people was a way of writing about myself.

Now I had Mrs Unger – her energy, her certainty and sensuality, her sense of direction, her self-esteem. Unlike the other Americans I knew, she never dramatized her being in India. I had never met anyone with that amount of restraint. She didn't boast about her charity; she was generous without being conspicuous. She was content. Writing about her lifted my spirits. I was back in the world again. I had a wonderful reason for staying on in Calcutta – no need to slip away. I was at last proud of what I was doing, writing a true account of a meditation on virtue.

Through the dead hand, as if this withered yellow thing had pointed the way, I had discovered something new and unantici-pated. I wrote fifty or sixty pages. No one had ever written about anyone like her. She was not a sentimental do-gooder wishing herself on the poor or helping old people to die, praising their suffering and their poverty, but rather a glamorous woman quietly improving the lives of lost children.

Howard called: 'You still here?' Parvati called: 'What are you up to?' I didn't say. 'A Dead Hand' was my secret. And I had much more to write – I hadn't written about Theroux's intrusion, the train trip, 'I'm black', Assam, Nagapatti. All that lay ahead, so much experience to draw upon. I was absorbed in this long story and I saw that, though happiness was the rarest of subjects, happiness had liberated me. I thought of nothing else but doing full justice to Mrs Unger and my luck in having opened the wrong door and met her.

I was so concentrated on this work that I forgot everything else. I made no plans. I saw Mrs Unger a few times, always quietly, always in the incense-filled vault of the Lodge. She massaged me with the tantric pressure of prolonged and unexpected touching, adoration of the fingertips – and all of it these days was a further lesson in how I was to touch her. The best of tantra, taking turns.

And, after such caresses, I always went back to my work refreshed.

This was about two weeks of sustained creativity, the happiest period of my writing life I had ever known. And it ended as suddenly as it began.

'Packet for you, sir,' Ramesh Datta, the desk clerk, said one day as I went down to lunch after a morning's work, just as many weeks before he had said, 'Letter for you, sir.'

He said it casually and because of that I didn't take it seriously. Something from Parvati was what I thought, with a kind of irritation – a very good poem. I'd have to read it and respond.

But it wasn't that at all. It was something else entirely and it reminded me of everything I'd forgotten.

*Part Three*

# 13

My name was nowhere on the little parcel, which was square, too large to fit into my pocket and thick, yet light, taped on two sides. It was about the size of a sandwich and just as soft. Indian paper is fragile – the wrapper was already bruised and torn at one corner. No stamp, only HOTEL HASTINGS in blue ballpoint in block letters, and slightly grubby, as though someone had carried it by hand. I imagined a boy clutching it in sweaty fingers. *Tell them it's for the ferringhi.*

I was reminded of Mrs Unger's letter, the fat envelope that had started me down this road. Had it not been for that letter, I'd be far away from Calcutta now. A letter without a stamp seemed to me portentous. I could not imagine what was in this parcel, but I knew it mattered.

'Who brought this?'

'Runner, sir. Small boy.'

I did not want to seem too inquisitive. I suspected it was something to be kept secret. I didn't want anyone to know about my private life, my passionate attachment to Mrs Unger, my resumption of writing. At that point, with the unopened parcel on the lunch table beside my plate, I still believed that my writing life had been revived, that Mrs Unger was a goddess who had restored my creative vitality.

Although I longed to open the thing, I resisted, fearing witnesses. What if it were bad news? Its unusual size and shape somewhat alarmed me. I was afraid it might contain another melancholy body part, something small and withered. I finished my lunch, pretending to be casual, then I shoved my chair back, stepped outside on to the verandah and, glancing behind me, seeing no one, picked it open.

As the brittle paper wrapper disintegrated in my hand, I held its contents, a square of carpet. It was like a swatch, a store sample, but roughly cut, velvety with a floral design and part of a margin on one side, tightly woven and dusty on the underside. No other obvious markings, though the pattern on the upper side was distinct: green strands, yellow petals, on a deep red background. It had been coarsely scissored, like a bite out of a big rug.

No message. I sat staring at it. My first thought was to search for bloodstains or any identifying marks. I found nothing; even the pattern was unrevealing, not to say banal. But as an unexpected chunk of material, it was so odd as to seem meaningful – that is, a deliberate riddle. I could not at first imagine who'd sent it, but I related it to what I'd been told by Mina at the cemetery: *Carpet was parcelled. Body was inside.*

I sat back and sighed. This was like blunt trauma, a colossal interruption of my writing. My work lay on the table. I knew that I could not return to it until I had solved the problem.

That was the strangest thing of all. During the trip to Assam and in writing about Mrs Unger, I hadn't thought about Rajat and the hotel, the discovery of the corpse, his running away and how, from the very beginning, I'd been asked by Mrs Unger to solve this mystery and vindicate Rajat. So overwhelmed had I been by her that I'd neglected to follow up on the information I'd found: the rudeness of the Ananda's manager, the details that Mina Jagtap had given me.

*How did this parcel find me?* The thought fluttered through my mind. But it was naive of me to wonder. Calcutta was a city almost without tourists. I had been here more than two months, walking the streets and openly asking questions. Though there must have been many foreigners in the city, it sometimes seemed that I was one of about a dozen resident *ferringhis*. I was easy to spot. That explained how the parcel found me, but not why.

I immediately suspected Mina. Who else? She knew I was enquiring, she'd been fired from the Ananda, so she had a reason to help me. No note: the swatch was self-explanatory – cut from a carpet, probably the one that had held the body.

Wanting to please Mrs Unger, to remind her that I was still

pursuing the problem she had posed to me, I called her cell phone, an emergency number she'd given me. 'Emphasis on "emergency".' I got one of those messages: *The mobile customer is either currently out of service or out of range.*

I wanted to show her that I was on the scent. I got into a taxi, with the square of carpet in my briefcase, and went to the Lodge in Alipore. I had never dared to go uninvited before, but today I had an excuse – this ambiguous clue. I could prove that I was busy on her behalf and grateful to her.

Writers talk to themselves and travelling writers talk to themselves constantly. People on their way to a meeting prepare their lines. I began to rehearse a little speech in my head.

'See what I've done?' I would say. 'You asked me to investigate the bizarre event at the Ananda and I've obeyed you. I have a few leads. The dead boy was brought to the hotel in a carpet and I have a piece of that carpet, sent anonymously to me at my hotel, probably by someone who wants me to know the truth. I think it might be a former employee. I've got it right here.'

The gate to the courtyard was padlocked and the courtyard itself was empty. I called out to the *chowkidar*, who stood in the shade holding his badge of authority, a long thick club.

'*Namashkar.*'

He pretended not to hear, but I kept calling and embarrassed him into coming over.

'Please let me in.'

'Cannot.' He looked solemn and stubborn but confident, happy to be unhelpful.

'I have to see Ma.' Everyone knew her by that name.

'Not available.' He smacked the club against his palm, as if to remind me that he was in charge. The club was dark from being handled.

I felt awkward talking to him through the iron bars of the gate, especially here, where I'd always been welcome. I could hear the children screeching inside, some of them singing.

'I'll write Ma a note. You can give the note to her.'

I imagined writing *I must see you at once.* She would forgive me for intruding. I was making progress in solving the mystery. I had a dead hand, I had a piece of carpet, I had a witness.

As I began to scribble my appeal on a page of my pocket note-book, the *chowkidar* said, 'Not here.'

'Not in the Lodge?'

'Not in Calcutta.'

'Where is she?'

He gestured past the wall with his big club. 'Gone to UP.'

*You-bee* was what he said. I knew he meant Uttar Pradesh.

'Where in UP?'

'Pactory. Meerjapur.'

'Out of town', 'on a buying trip', 'away for a bit', 'picking up some children' she always said to explain her absences. She never told me where. This was more specific, a factory in Mirzapur. I was not sure where Mirzapur was, but I knew it was not near Calcutta.

In the taxi on the way back to the Hastings, I asked the driver where it was.

'Varanasi side,' he said.

'Far?'

'Five hundred twenty kilometres.'

'How long to drive?'

'Not drive. Train better. Fourteen hours.'

I considered going there so that I could say, 'Look what I've got!' But I thought better of it. It would be ridiculous and premature to show up with the dead hand and the piece of carpet. I needed more evidence. I wanted to amaze her, to show her that I cared. I hoped that she'd be pleased, that she'd reward me. I longed to see her smile at me, to touch me with her secret blessing.

At some yellow hour of the Calcutta night, sleepless in the light pollution of street lamps, alone with this problem, I thought: *It must have been Mina who sent it.* But had she got this fragment of carpet from the hotel itself? She wanted to help without being directly implicated. I needed to spend a night at the Ananda.

I hated the sight of the hotel. I associated it with death and deceit. I disliked the manager, Biswas, for his rudeness, for being so unhelpful. And he had abused Mina. He'd fired her for showing me the register. And in this hot weather there was no more uncomfortable part of Calcutta than high-density New Market – the milling crowds, the stink and noise of traffic, the litter in the streets. Here were the cheapest hotels, with pompous names: the Savoy, the Ritz, the Astoria, New India, Delight, Krishna Chambers and, among them, the Ananda.

Seeing me approach with an overnight bag, the girl sitting just inside the door raised her head and called to someone.

Mr Biswas loomed behind her, materializing out of the hot shadows, wrapped in the puffy gauze of his dhoti, wearing a *khadi* vest. I had forgotten how hairy his ears were, how yellow his fingernails, how red his teeth, how sour his expression.

He must have warned the girl to look out for me. It didn't matter. He knew me only as a nuisance. He wasn't seriously threatened; he was annoyed because I hadn't rented a room.

'Remember me?'

'How could I forget you, sir?' he said, swelling a little with belligerence.

'I need a room.'

'As you wish.' He said something to the girl in Bengali and, hearing him, she reached for my bag.

I clung to it. It was ridiculously light – suspiciously so. 'Never mind.'

'We are here to serve you,' Mr Biswas said. Every word he spoke sounded either sarcastic or insincere.

'A single room. What are your rates?'

'Standard is four hundred. Facing street. Deluxe is more. Surcharge for garden view. Supplement applies to suite.'

Mina had told me that Rajat had stayed in number fifteen. I asked for that room.

'Garden view. Six hundred rupees. Payable in advance.'

That was about sixteen dollars. I handed over the rupees. Mr Biswas licked his thumb and counted them, then gave them to the girl. He was eyeing me sideways, working a wad of betel nut in his mouth. He spat a gob of reddened saliva at the side of the doorway, a fresh streak among dried-out drips.

'Passport,' he said and beckoned with his skinny fingers.

We were still standing on the top step of the Ananda. I slipped my passport out of my pocket, held it away from him and said, 'I want it back.'

'After transfer of details, full name and visa number.'

Only then did he allow me into the hotel. He took his place behind the window of the check-in desk and opened my passport. He pressed it against the desk with the flat of his hand, then spat into a bucket, licked red betel juice from his lips with an even redder tongue, then turned the pages slowly.

'I will send to room.'

'I'd rather wait.'

He shrugged and went on turning pages, and when he found the page with my India visa he used a key on a bracelet to unlock a drawer beneath the desktop. He slipped out a large bound volume that I recognized as the register and slowly copied my name, my date of birth, my visa number and place of issue. Then he replaced the volume and locked the drawer again.

'Your papers.' He handed me my passport.

I had hoped to get a look at the register again, for Rajat's details. No such luck.

'This way, sir,' the young girl said.

I followed her up the stairs, liking the way her sari tightened like a sling around her swaying bottom as she climbed. She carried a thin grey towel, a small rectangle of soap wrapped in wax paper and on one finger the loop of a key, which was wired to a large wooden tag inked with the number fifteen.

'What's your name?'

'Chitra, sir.'

'What happened to Mina?'

'Gone, sir. Sacked, sir. I am Mina replacement.'

'Why was Mina sacked?'

'She giving manager angerness.'

'What happened?'

'He beating her, sir.'

'Why did he beat her?'

'I not knowing.'

'Where's your home?'

'Assam side, sir.'

'I was in Assam recently.'

'Are you enjoying, sir?'

'Very much.'

'Thank you, sir. Tea gardens beautiful. Also trees. Also Brahmaputra River.'

I remembered Mrs Unger saying, *The real aristocrats of the world are the native peoples, the so-called tribals in India, the Mizos, the Nagas in Assam*. But all I could recall of Assam was the Kamakhya temple, its floor running with blood; the child whores of Nagapatti; and the hotel room, Mrs Unger lying beneath my trembling hands. *Show me what you've learned from me*.

We had come to the second floor. Chitra led me along the corridor, away from the bright front window and the growl of traffic – bells and horns and human cries, a density of noise. She opened the door to number fifteen and paused at the threshold to let me pass.

'Toggle switch for fan here,' she said, flipping it, and the overhead fan croaked and began to turn like a heavy bird beginning to rise, groaning on its outstretched wings.

She placed the towel and soap on the bed and stood before me awkwardly, bowing slightly. She had a sad face and her attempt to smile made it sadder: narrow shoulders, a thin, breastless body, bony hands, skinny feet.

I held out some money, two hundred rupees that I had counted on the way up the stairs.

'Thank you, sir.' And at once the money disappeared into her sari as she hid it without looking at it.

'Chitra, I need you to help me.'

She stared, fearful, widening her eyes, pressing her lips together.

'I want to look into some other rooms.'

She ungummed her lips. 'All locked, sir.'

'But you can unlock them.'

'I cannot, sir.'

She looked anguished and without another word she backed away and shut the door.

I lay on the bed listening intently – would Chitra tell the manager what I had said? I was so anxious that I was rigid, afraid to move lest I miss hearing something; and in this state of nerves I exhausted myself. I slept suddenly, dreamlessly, then woke gasping in the dark, jarred by a slamming door. Still in my clothes, I did not at first have any idea where I was. The bed stank; the dust in my nostrils alarmed me. I had the notion that someone intended to kill me. That was when I opened my cell phone and shone it around the room.

Without turning on the bedside lamp, using only the light from my cell phone, I got up and listened at the door. I could see that it was not yet nine – I'd been sleeping for about two hours. I opened the door carefully and saw that the corridor was in shadow, the only light the reflected glare from the window that gave on to the rear. I crept from one door to the next, noting the numbers, hoping that I'd find one ajar. They were locked and silent. This was not a busy hotel.

The stairwell was in shadow too. Peering down, I could see where the small lobby emitted some light on to the lower landing, but above me was only darkness. I climbed into this darkness, holding up my cell phone, taking care not to make the stairs creak.

I could just make out three numbered doors, one of them partly open. Keeping motionless, listening closely, I tried to determine whether anyone was inside. No voices, no snoring. Putting one foot slowly in front of the other, nudging the door with my knuckles, I eased it open wider.

As I lifted my cell phone it seemed to explode in my hand, jangling – a call. In a panic I stabbed at the answer button to silence it.

A squawk from the room and a rattle of an iron bed frame: a man had risen in the shadowy interior, glowing in his pyjamas, flopping forward, and began berating me in Bengali.

'Can you hear me?' came from my phone, a woman's voice.

'Sorry,' I said to the advancing man and, into the phone, 'Yes, yes.'

It was Mrs Unger. I hurried to the stairs (the Indian in the room still hissing at me) and cupped my hand over my phone. 'I have some news.'

'What is it? Where are you?'

'In the hotel.' I was whispering, padding down the stairs, now at my own landing, hurrying to my room.

'I can't hear you.'

'I've made a breakthrough. I've got a very good lead. I can't talk now.'

'Are you all right?'

'I'm fine. I need to see you.'

'I'll be fascinated to know what you found. It's so important to clear Rajat. I'm sure that he was so upset he was imagining it.'

'It's not just that. I want to be with you. I've been missing you. But I'm also doing some good work – writing. I've got you to thank for that.'

'I want to energize you.'

'You've done that.'

'If you don't mind!' A shout from behind a door, the voice of an angry woman.

I was in the corridor outside my room, but excited, hearing Mrs Unger, I'd begun to raise my voice.

I slipped into my room, saying, 'They can hear me. I'll call you back.'

'Don't bother. Concentrate on what you're doing. I can tell you're preoccupied.'

Mrs Unger's call could not have come at a worse time, disturbing the man in pyjamas whose door was ajar, the shrieking woman in the room across the hall from me. But I was also secretly pleased: Mrs Unger could see that I was acting on her behalf, going to some trouble for her. She'd interrupted me in the act. I was happy, proving that I wanted to help her. I knew that she was somewhere being virtuous – helping a child, healing someone who was miserable or ill, making a sacrifice. It was important for me to show her that I was on her side. That night, I dreamed of her, but it was an ugly dream, of Mrs Unger transformed into a demon, and I woke up ashamed and hot.

# 14

The poor in India wake up early. At dawn everyone looks destitute. It sometimes seems as though they never sleep. I heard rattling in the corridors of the Ananda. In the dusty light I looked out and saw Chitra with a bucket. I found something incongruous about a young woman in a bright flowing sari, draped in yellow, carrying a mop and a sloshing pail. I remembered the women in colourful saris at the building site, lugging gravel in baskets. Chitra looked graceful and out of place. She looked cursed, as if a spell had been cast upon her and she'd found herself with a bucket and a mop.

'Good morning, sir.'

'*Namashkar*, Chitra.' She seemed pleased that I'd remembered her name. I watched her as she walked to the end of the corridor, rapped on a door, lifted a keyring from a chain at her waist and fitted a key to the lock.

Moving quickly, I got to the door before she closed it. She began to object, but I put my finger to my lips, shushing her. That made her smile. I then handed her two hundred rupees. She smiled again and she folded the money into her bodice.

'I'm looking for something,' I said softly.

What was I looking for? I hardly knew. A clue, a connection, a floral carpet, something to link the dead child to the hotel. My idea was that I was more likely to find this unknown thing in one of the empty rooms.

I watched Chitra mop the floorboards and the bathroom tiles, filthy mop on dirty floor, shoving scum back and forth. She then used a straw hand broom to whisk the dirty carpet. This was a gesture at cleaning, going through the motions; the carpet was industrial, grey, not woven, nothing special.

What I took to be a stain in the next room she cleaned was a dead mouse, flattened, dried out in death. Chitra swung it by its tail into a plastic bag. In the third room the bed had been stripped to its lumpy and discoloured mattress. Chitra seemed not to notice anything, but only to go about her work, slapping the painted wood floor with her filthy mop, whisking the carpet with her old-fashioned broom.

What was I looking for? The answer was: anything. I was sweating with distraction, because everything was a clue and nothing added up.

'What you are doing, mister?' The yell behind me was like a thump on my head. I turned and saw the manager's furious eyes, his reddened teeth, Mr Biswas at his craziest. He shifted a lump of spittle-sodden pan from one cheek to the other, then shook his bony fists and began to scold again. 'You having no business in private rooms!'

'I lost something.'

'I am having a brace of complaints about you – giving a nuisance in the night. You are making me headaches. I can charge-sheet you!'

'I was looking for something.'

All this time I was backing away from Mr Biswas, half enjoying his fury, half fearing it. I wanted to hit him.

'Look somewhere else. Do not look here. You are creating intrusion.'

'OK,' I said and sidled towards my room.

'You must leave,' he said. He was screechy and agitated in his loose dhoti, his hair uncombed. I guessed that he had just woken up.

'I can't leave.'

'Immediately. Take your things and go. Get out.'

But I was at my door now. He had startled me at first, but now I was able to compose myself a little.

'I must eject you.'

'It's only six thirty.'

'You must go, sir,' he said, clamping his mouth shut, though there was a froth of reddened spittle at his lips.

'I paid for breakfast. I'll leave after breakfast.'

'I will refund you twenty rupees. You will take breakfast else-where.'

'I will have breakfast here.'

'Then you will take breakfast now, without delay.'

This snorting, vituperative man, with his fangy face, in his puffy skirts, alarmed me, but also made me think that I was on the trail of this mystery. He was just the sort of bully who'd abet a murder or a disappearance – a sour face, a mean and heartless manner. He had manhandled Mina. He snapped his fingers at Chitra and muttered something in Bengali.

'You will take something to eat. Then you will vacate.'

He turned and, holding his dhoti, a bunch of gauze in his fist, a skinny aunt in a frenzy, he descended the stairs, his sandals slapping.

'May I bring tea, sir?' Chitra said.

'Good idea. And a roti.'

I lay on my rumpled bed, my heart pounding. The fuss with the manager had unsettled me, because it had been so sudden and because he seemed such a brute. I was out of breath, damp from the heat, trying to imagine Rajat here – the dead boy on the floor, the unrolled carpet. I felt mocked by my helplessness, ashamed of having come here in the absurd presumption that I might be able to puzzle out the mystery. I had found nothing.

But why linger? I was hot and weary from the early-morning confrontation. I took a quick shower – a cold piddle from a rusty pipe – dried myself on the small towel that was as thin as a dish-cloth, put on some clean trousers and a fresh shirt, folded my pyjama bottoms and stuffed them into my shoulder bag. Bunching my other cargo pants, I felt a bulge. So I emptied the pockets of the grubby rupees, the insubstantial coins, the receipt the manager had given me the evening before, my wallet, my passport, the fraying piece of carpet.

In my amateurish way, looking literally, I'd thought that I might see a carpet at the Ananda with a chunk taken out of it – this chunk a piece of the puzzle. But the carpet in this room, like the carpet in every room I'd seen at the hotel, was grey and dirty. I was a fool, pretending to be a detective.

A knock – 'Tea, sir' – and Chitra entered carrying a tray, a pot of tea, a cup, a dish of sugar, a pitcher of milk, a spoon and a plate of cookies.

'What's that?'

'Milk Bikki, sir. Dry biscuit.' She lifted and shook the plate of cookies. 'No roti available.'

I scraped the piece of carpet out of her way as she lowered the tray to the small table. She faltered, tipping the load, the cup and tea things slipping to the tray's edge and almost toppling. She had looked aside at the square of carpet and whinnied in fear and recognition.

'You know what this is?'

'Mina, sir.' She was whispering, retrieving a fallen spoon from the floor.

'Where did she get it?'

'I cut for Mina.'

'Where did you cut it? Where did you find it?'

She took a breath. She widened her eyes. She said, 'I find every-where.'

I smiled at her reply. 'Show me.'

She stepped to the door, which she'd left open, and glanced into the hall. Seeing no one, she went to one of the rooms I'd seen her clean and opened the clothes closet. And there on the floor of the closet, cut to fill the space, was a red carpet, identical in colour to the square I had, with a yellow loop of the floral design.

I stooped to look at it, but she was paddling the air, beckoning me to a new room. This one too had a carpet in the closet, a large rectangle, obviously part of the same larger carpet.

'All wardrobe, sir.'

Two more rooms had similar pieces of the carpet on the floor of the closets. I examined them all quietly and quickly, realizing that I'd made a connection. One of the pieces was seriously stained, brownish; something had seeped into the weave. I removed it and rolled it up and put it into my bag.

'I will thank you not to come back,' Mr Biswas said to me in the lobby, glaring at me, his hairy ears twitching.

But I smiled. I was happy. I had what I wanted and had not even realized that it was what I'd been looking for.

'You are not welcome, mister, at this premises.'

I waited at a coffee shop near the Hogg Market until nine, then called Howard at the consulate and asked him to meet me for lunch. 'Still here!' he said. 'I thought we'd got rid of you.'

Over noodles and spring rolls at the New Cathay on Chow-ringhee, I told him I was growing to like Calcutta.

'I'm glad. At first glance it's a horror, but it grows on you. It's a little limiting for a single guy, though. I can't get a date without a chaperone. I've invited my ex-wife back, just to have someone to go to a movie with. How are you making out?'

'I'm doing a favour for a friend.'

He stopped eating and said, 'In India, "friend" always means woman.'

'It's not Parvati.'

'Too bad. She always asks after you.'

'She's too good for me.'

Howard said, 'You always call when you need something. What do you need?'

'I'm sorry.'

'I'm just teasing you.'

'But I do need something.'

'I want to help. With you, I always feel as if I'll end up in a story. That's nice. It'll give me credibility.'

'Remember that guy at police headquarters, Dr Mukherjee? The forensics man. I want to see him again, but I need you to tell him that I'm honest. I've already aroused his suspicions with one piece of evidence.'

'I'll vouch for you. I see him all the time. Americans are constantly dying in India, usually old ones, of heart failure. But sometimes young ones in suspicious circumstances. We get Dr Mukherjee to run the tests and sign the death certificates.'

'You'll assure him that I can be trusted?'

201

'I'll remind him that you're one of us.'

'That's really good of you.'

'You're an American. You've got a problem. I'm a consular officer. This is my job. Besides, it's too hot to go back to the office.'

In the taxi, Howard said casually, 'Does this have anything to do with Mrs Unger?'

'Why do you ask?'

'You mentioned her once a while back,' he said. I didn't say anything, so he went on. 'Which is odd. I mean, the only other person who asked about her was Paul Theroux. But when we met you at the Fairlawn you said you didn't know her.'

'Did you believe me?'

'Yes, but Paul didn't.'

'Did that guy really leave? I don't trust him.'

'He said he wanted to take the train from Battambang to Phnom Penh.'

'He would. The bus is quicker!'

Perhaps hoping to calm me, Howard said, 'Mrs Unger has no profile in Calcutta. She's never in the news. And yet she's here all the time.'

'She doesn't like publicity.'

'How do you know?'

He was very shrewd, but then, he'd lived in Calcutta for three years. In the nicest way, he'd caught me. I said, 'She told me.'

He nodded and, though his expression was mild, I could see his eyes in a rapid calculation.

'She's an amazing woman, an incredible philanthropist,' I said, but I felt helpless saying this. There was no way I could adequately describe what Mrs Unger meant to me and it seemed disloyal merely to mention her name like this. 'I respect her privacy. Theroux just wanted to use her.'

The receptionist at police headquarters recognized both of us, but she responded more warmly to Howard. He was friendly and memorable and he spoke first in a courtly way in Bengali.

'Dr Mooly Mukherjee. Consular business.' He handed her his diplomatic card, stamped with a gold American eagle.

As the receptionist called to announce us, she gave us two security tags. Then she beckoned a *chowkidar* to usher us upstairs.

I began to regret that I'd depended on Howard, because he was now involved in my quest. His presence made me self-conscious, and I had denied knowing her. I knew he was wondering how well I knew Mrs Unger. But if a crime had been committed, why should I hide it from him? I would probably need him.

The *chowkidar* knocked on the office door and, hearing a grunt, he showed us in.

'Dr Mukherjee. *Namashkar*,' Howard said. '*Apni keman achen?*'

'Top hole, thank you, Mr Howard.'

They talked for a while about a recent case, an American who'd died in Darjeeling. 'Heart-related,' Dr Mukherjee said. 'Altitude was factor. He left immense debts. It turned out that he was a blighter and a mountebank.'

Then Howard said, 'And I think you know my friend?'

'Ah, yes,' he said with less enthusiasm, and I knew what he was thinking: he associated me with the dead hand, the sad little thing with no fingerprints.

'I'd like you to test this.' I opened the plastic bag and showed him the stained piece of carpet I'd found in the closet at the Hotel Ananda.

'Test for what? For fibres? For DNA?' He stroked his moustache, speaking slowly. 'Traces of drugs? Bodily fluids? Gunpowder? Chemicals? Food particles? Hair strands?'

Howard had begun to laugh softly at the litany of questions.

'We are thorough!' Dr Mooly Mukherjee said, still tweaking one tip of his moustache.

'Please test it for everything. There's a suspicious stain on it. Who knows, maybe a bloodstain.'

'I will be judge of that,' Dr Mukherjee said, taking up a clipboard that held a printed form. 'May I ask origin of carpet sample?'

I squirmed a bit, then said, 'It came into my possession.'

'You have become a repository of many items,' he said. 'I can only wonder if they are related. Let's say, "Of unknown origin".'

'That's good. How long will it take you to do the tests?'

'For simple tests, a few days. We might have to send it to the lab. Here's my card. I'll write my mobile number.' He did so on the back of the card. 'Phone me Thursday afternoon. We might have some results then.'

'He's a good man,' Howard said when we left the building. He was curious, I could tell, resisting the obvious question, being pointedly discreet. And he had not referred to my earlier request, when I had foolishly revealed that I had a dead hand that wanted to be identified.

In the silence, I said, 'I can't tell you why I need to know this.'

'It's much better that I don't know,' Howard said. 'I don't want to have to write a report. Knowing things is a big burden in the consular business. Even though I'm a PAO, it puts me under an obligation. I'm glad to help. And I like the evidence.'

'That's not evidence. I'm just helping a friend.'

But he could see I was being defensive. 'The piece of carpet,' he said. 'It's pure Henry James. The big clue hidden somewhere in the weave. Puzzle it out and you have the answer. You know the story? "The Figure in the Carpet".'

'Yes, I do.'

'One of the many things I love about Calcutta is its Victorian texture. Not just the grandiose architecture, but the people too. Women need chaperones. They don't marry for love. Dr Mooly Mukherjee is a Victorian figure. His moustache is dated. Even the words he uses. "Repository." "Blighter." "Mountebank."'

Talking this way gave a bigger meaning to our visit to police headquarters and by linking it to literature he dignified it. He was right about 'The Figure in the Carpet'. And so although I was looking for bloodstains, or anything criminal, we were able to talk about it in euphemisms, and that helped us to be a little more dignified too.

And it calmed me. We agreed to meet again soon. I could not tell him what I was doing. There was only one person I could tell.

# 15

I had missed Mrs Unger. I had come to depend on seeing her once or twice a week for the sessions of tantric massage and I had yearned for her while she'd been away – her week in Mirzapur. I was like an old-fashioned woman waiting for a man to call, passive, dependent, helpless. She said that tantra was all-encompassing ancient wisdom that included sex, as it did every aspect of life. Yet for me the massage was not a sexual act but a way of prolonging desire: at its best it had no end, at least not an explosive finality, but rather a tapering glow of intense well-being.

'Better than sex,' I'd said to her.

She liked my saying that, yet still I was possessed.

My week in Calcutta without her had allowed me to plan the stay at the Ananda that resulted in my securing the stained piece of carpet from the closet. I guessed that the entire carpet had been cut and distributed throughout the hotel. And now I had the police working on identifying anything that had adhered to it. I had studied the scene of the crime. I'd used my time well, I thought. I'd have news for Mrs Unger. And now I was able to see her again.

Knowing that I was going to see her later in the day filled me with pleasure. The foreknowledge of desire, the certainty of a meeting, something every lover knows, is a vitalizing power, a source of happiness and optimism. She had that effect on me. She had that effect on everyone she knew, inspiring an eagerness, a willingness to make a sacrifice.

I longed to please her. The greatest gift of love was – without thinking – losing one's ego in a passion for someone else, becoming unselfish, wishing to serve and satisfy that other person, wanting her to smile.

That was easy to do for Mrs Unger because she gave so much of herself to others. Her goodness, the big-heartedness that made people thrive, motivated me to want to please her in the same way; she sacrificed so much herself that my making a sacrifice for her was a pleasure. The more inconvenienced I was by serving her, the happier I became, because she deserved it.

I found what many lovers find, that it is hard to give anything to someone who is truly generous. Her strength, and perhaps the key to Mrs Unger's personality, was that she didn't need anything from me, or anyone. Her criticism of Mother Teresa was that she needed to bask, to meet celebrities, to collect money, to be acknowledged. Mrs Unger scorned all of that. She seemed to exist in an atmosphere of pure kindness and serenity, offering blessings. What could I give her? A clue to the body in the room would be welcome, but not much else. Even that was unselfish on her part, for all she cared about was clearing Rajat's name. 'He must not be hurt,' she said. 'He has a lovely soul. He has fairy energy.'

I could see how the children thrived in the Lodge. That was how I felt at my hotel, writing those pages about her, having recaptured the ability to write that I had believed – dreaded – had deserted me. She was both the inspiration for those pages and the subject of them. Knowing her, being vitalized by her, touched by her, I was returned to being a writer and, finding that creativity, I had found a self I thought I'd burned out. But no, I'd rediscovered it, and in so doing I'd rediscovered a younger self. She had rejuvenated me. All she said was, '*Kundalini.*'

I didn't want to wait to be summoned. I wanted to get a taxi outside the Hastings and ride to Alipore, full of expectation, un-bidden, to show my loyalty and love. But I resisted, because the last time I'd done it, she'd been away in Mirzapur, wherever that was.

The night at the Ananda had interrupted my writing schedule, yet I was able to resume working on the pages of 'A Dead Hand', advancing my description of Mrs Unger and the stories of her philanthropy. She could easily have remained in New York or Palm Beach – she had the money. She could have spent all her time in pure idleness, among the wealthy, going to charity events, looking glamorous. She could have done what Mother Teresa did – hobnobbed with the stars, pretending to be a saint, dining out on her horror stories. But instead, Mrs Unger, who shunned publicity, was in Calcutta anonymously, enduring the heat and the noise, the unending mob, the crowded pavements, the traffic, the squalor. She chose to devote all her energy to neglected children.

This was my subject. While debating whether to visit her unannounced, I kept writing 'A Dead Hand'.

'Gentleman to see you, sir.' I looked up and saw Ramesh Datta, awaiting further instructions.

I didn't want anyone to see me writing. I considered it my secret and my strength, especially these pages.

'I'll be right down.'

I assumed it was Howard with news of Dr Mukherjee's forensic report. But it was Rajat. He'd been sitting in a wicker chair. The chair screeched as he leaped to his feet, recklessly, like a schoolboy when a teacher enters a room.

'I happened to be passing. I thought I'd say hello.'

This could not have been true. He'd never dropped in on me before. What was on his mind?

'Nice to see you. Would you like a drink?'

'A cup of tea only.'

Ramesh Datta had been standing by, listening. He signalled to Ramachandra, who hurried forward.

'Two teas, sir?'

I said to Rajat, 'You want a samosa?'

'I am not taking.'

'Tea cake?'

'I am not taking.'

'Biscuit?' I was asking just to torment him and say the odd words and hear his refusals. 'Milk Bikki? Fancy biscuits? Gulabjam? Sweetmeats?'

'I will take unsalted nuts.'

'Mineral water for me.' I sat down and Rajat returned to his wicker chair, sitting at the edge of the cushion, his elbows on his knees.

'How are you getting on here?' he asked. 'You seem to find the city congenial.'

207

'I like seeing Mrs Unger. I think you can understand that.'

'A gracious and distinctly formidable woman,' he said.

Victorian, Howard had said of the Bengalis. I was by now able to take their florid and slightly pretentious phrasing in my stride.

'Oh, yes,' I said. But I was thinking, *She's much more than that*.

'I know she charged you with vindicating me,' he said. 'Have you made any headway?'

He seemed terribly nervous, so nervous he could not manage to be subtle; he was without any guile. He'd come straight to the point.

'I don't see my job as vindicating you.'

'What then?'

'I think something like searching for the truth.'

I knew this was pompous, but pomposity was a normal mode of discourse in Calcutta. *Don't be audacious*, Parvati sometimes said to me. Rajat began to speak but, seeing Ramachandra bringing the tea tray, he held off, smiled at the waiter and did not speak until we were alone again.

'It was the worst experience of my life. Can you imagine waking up in a strange hotel room with a human corpse?'

Instead of answering, I said, 'I'm wondering if you made the right decision in running away.'

'The alternative was much worse – being implicated in a murder.'

'Why do you say murder?'

'That's how it would have been viewed by the law here.' His knees were pressed together. He held his teacup with precisely poised fingers. 'And I fear scandalmongery. People would spread malicious tales and calumnies about me.'

'Why didn't you mention the carpet to Mrs Unger? Or to me?'

'Was there a carpet? I didn't get a proper look. I told you I was using my cell phone as a torch.'

'But the carpet was right there on the floor of your room.'

He put the cup down. He said, 'When you see a dead person, you don't see anything else. I was transfixed.'

That at least made sense.

'Was there any blood?'

'Had I seen blood, it would have obtained a lodgement in my memory,' he said. When he was nervous he spoke this way. 'But I didn't touch the body. I simply bolted.'

'Your big mistake. It makes you look responsible for the death.'

'What would you have done?' He picked up his cup, though seemed merely to use it as a prop; he didn't drink.

I thought hard before I answered because I had been in the Ananda and I now knew what a spooky place it was – the hot, stifling rooms, the menacing corridors, the angry Mr Biswas with his crow-like face.

'I don't know. But I would have put my trust in Mrs Unger to get to the bottom of it.'

'That's what I have done,' he said, his voice breaking. 'I don't think she wholly believed me, or else why did she charge you with looking into the case?'

He had not counted on Mrs Unger getting in touch with me. And though I had hoped for a lucky break, I had not counted on Mina Jagtap's giving me all this timely help – the dead hand, the fragment of carpet – had not counted on Chitra's recognizing the carpet. All this because of my earlier visit and Mr Biswas's slapping Mina's face and firing her.

'I'm sure everything will be fine,' I said. Only when I spoke did I hear the doubt in my voice. I didn't believe this at all.

'I have to go. I'm supposed to meet Charlie at the Lodge. Thank you for the tea.'

He had put sugar in the tea the waiter had poured. He had stirred it. He had even lifted the cup to his lips. But he hadn't drunk any of it. He had not touched the bowl of unsalted cashews. This both annoyed me and made me suspicious. I am uneasy at meals where guests pick at their food or don't eat. I think: *Why are they here?*

Rajat had not simply dropped in; he had planned this meeting. He was trying to find out what I knew.

'Why don't you come along?' His eyes glistened as his gaze became a kind of pleading.

He was smallish, mousy, with a softness to him; weak and

compliant, almost feminine, with large dark eyes – soft and fear-ful, deep-set, with girlish lashes. Yet he was stubbornly like a girl too, unforthcoming. Now and then I asked him a question and he wouldn't reply, just stared, and I thought of old girlfriends. He had slender hands and tiny breakable wrists. In his fragility he reminded me of Mrs Unger's lost children, the bat-eared boy Jyoti who had been so animated and whom I had looked for my last time at the Lodge. 'He has moved on,' Mrs Unger had said. 'We're so proud of him.'

'Is Mrs Unger there?'

'Oh, yes. She'd love to see you. I'd try her on my mobile, but the battery's flat.'

'Ma is not fond of surprises,' I said.

'This is a pleasant surprise.' He clawed his cuff from his wrist and looked at his watch. 'We really should go.'

Just the thought of her in her vault sensitized me, made me tremulous. And the Calcutta heat helped too. The day was stifling, the humidity like a cloak, but in the way it slowed me and made me breathless it was like a foretaste of desire, the same heaviness, the same pulse of blood in my head, a flush of eagerness that I could taste – as though right before a great risky leap – and a dampness on my skin and eyes.

As Rajat talked, more urgently than I'd seen him before, we ambled to the street, where I hailed a taxi. When one pulled up, we got in and Rajat gave directions. After that he fell silent. He began gnawing a finger in misery, his knuckle under his nose.

'Won't she mind this? Our arriving together?'

His eyes, set close, gave him the look of a rodent contem-plating cheese on a tray – eager yet hyper-alert, the same nibble and the twitching nostrils. Yet his tight smile made him the fidgety embodiment of contradiction.

'Not at all. She of course likes you immensely.'

'And she likes you too, Rajat.'

'I fear she finds me loquacious,' he said. 'Even if we arrive together she won't suspect us of plotting.'

This unexpected remark surprised me, because it seemed exactly what she might think: I had never arrived at the Lodge with him before. But that was at the periphery of my mind. I was concentrated on one thing, Mrs Unger's vault: the perfumes, the lamps, her hands, her body slipping against the silk of her sari.

Rajat spoke sharply to the taxi driver.

The man threw up his hands. 'Traffic. Too many traffic.'

'Are you telling him to hurry?' I asked.

'Don't you want to see Ma?' he said.

I said nothing because I didn't want to be quoted; he seemed to be provoking me. He seemed odder, fussier in the taxi than he had seemed in the Hastings, not drinking his tea.

'Ah.' He sighed with relief as the traffic began to move. I knew the feeling. I was relieved too as the taxi coursed through Alipore. I watched for the wall, the gateway, the fountain. Mrs Unger, at the front door, turned abruptly at the sound of the taxi on the gravel driveway.

'Dear, dear boy,' she said to Rajat, and to me, 'I've been meaning to call you. You absolutely read my mind.'

She embraced him and at first he stiffened at her touch. Then she patted him and stroked his arms, and as she did so he relaxed and sighed and surrendered.

'What have you boys been doing?' she asked, and when Rajat didn't answer, she said teasingly to him, 'Madam has gone all silent.'

Rajat seemed uneasy yet watchful, as he had in the taxi, glancing around, smiling in apprehension. We were standing at the top of the outer staircase, on the carved porch, with its plump balusters, the cracked and ornate entry, chunks of plaster missing from the stair treads, revealing old red brick beneath, like a deep gash, the same raw red, the whiteness surrounding it like flesh, the Lodge like a noble wounded body.

'I didn't realize you had guests.' This was spoken by a woman exiting the Lodge, who took me by surprise. She left the front entrance, taking a gingerly step that made her seem old, the *chowkidar* holding the door open, Balraj saluting. Now she approached Mrs Unger.

'These are friends,' Mrs Unger said. 'They're family.'

The woman – thin, middle-aged, auntyish – was obviously American. She looked like a big insect, bug-eyed in large sunglasses, in an expensive, fitted summer dress. She frowned in the heat from beneath a wide-brimmed straw hat, dabbing her face with a hanky. Over her shoulder was slung a woven bag, not Indian but designer-stylish. She had thin, pale, bony arms and was brisk, in a hurry, in contrast to the child plodding next to her.

She held the hand of this dazed-looking girl in a starched dress and white ankle socks and black shoes – a classier version of the school uniform of the children at the Lodge. I smiled at her and, looking closer, I thought I recognized the child. But all Mrs Unger's children seemed memorable. They were unlike Indian children with parents; they were street children in a house, always seeming somewhat pent-up, trapped and a little reckless, with searching eyes, tidy in simple uniforms.

This child was almost certainly the little girl who had ridden back to the house with us the day we'd visited the Kali temple and what Rajat had called 'the monthly intake'.

'I know your name,' I said to the little girl. 'I just can't think of it at the moment.'

The woman said sharply, 'We haven't got all day for you to think of it.'

I smiled at her rudeness, then turned away. 'What's your name, sweetie?' I asked the little girl. But she stepped sideways as though I was menacing her.

'Any more questions?' the woman said, her clumsy sarcasm snarling her delivery. She kept her mouth open, showing me her teeth.

Taken aback, I stared at her, wondering if I should give her a rude answer.

It was a hot afternoon. The woman appeared irritable and hurried. There was a look of confusion and distress that short-timers and foreigners had in Calcutta: a posture, a scowl of discomfort, of actual suffering. She had that look. I said nothing because Mrs Unger was there, as always a calming presence.

But it was an odd scene: staring Rajat with somewhat triumphant glistening eyes, Mrs Unger in a gorgeous sari, the cracked
porch, the tense, offhand American woman in her big sunglasses
with the spittle of 'Any more questions?' on her lips, the stunned-
looking child who I'd almost recognized and the brittle echo of
'Madam has gone all silent' directed at Rajat. And I was standing
uneasily because I'd come unannounced. All of us on the broken
stairs of the grand Lodge, and the noise of traffic outside the gate,
the yelling children inside the house, the great strangling banyan
tree with its roots showing everywhere, in some places seeming
to tear the house apart and in other places holding the bricks
together with the fingers and claws of its tangled roots.

'I'll be in touch,' the woman said. She continued down the
stairs and into a waiting car, one of those shiny new hotel cars with
a logo on the door and curtained windows and an obsequious
driver. The little girl, bewildered, glanced back at Mrs Unger with
a puzzled face.

'I know that kid,' I said.

Mrs Unger smiled. She didn't help me. She hadn't explained the
woman or introduced us. Instead, as the car drew away, she sidled
next to me and squeezed my arm.

'Charlie's in the office,' Mrs Unger said to Rajat. 'He'll be thrilled
to see you.' After he left she said to me, 'I'm glad you came. I want
to get my hands on you.' She spoke in a low voice, her cheek on
my shoulder. I got a whiff of her perfume, which was heavy, like a
secretion of bodily warmth.

It was what I wanted to hear. I resisted kissing her. She seldom
kissed, but I wanted badly to kiss her, to throw my arms around
her for making me happy. *I want to get my hands on you* was a
male fantasy – my fantasy, anyway. It was what I needed, the
mothering that had got me back to work on 'A Dead Hand', a
thinly fictionalized portrait of Mrs Unger in Calcutta.

Children were playing in the outer rooms and some were
singing nearby. The odours of cooking food, the slap of bare feet
on the wooden floor, the high-pitched laughter. And then, as
she shut the doors behind us, Mrs Unger led me deeper into the

house and down to the spa level, which smelled of incense, petals floating in the fountain and, in the damp leafy garden just outside, elephant-eared plants and the trailing, gripping roots of the big banyan tree.

'I came to the house while you were away,' I said. 'I couldn't resist.'

Although Mrs Unger was the model of coolness and poise, I detected disapproval, a shrinking of her being.

'When you were in Mirzapur.'

She laughed very hard at that. 'I was nowhere near Mirzapur.'

'It doesn't matter. I don't even know where it is.'

'Neither do I,' she said.

'I had a breakthrough with the Rajat mystery,' I said. But the only reason I said that was to cover my surprise and somehow (so I thought) save her from embarrassment. I suspected, for the first time since I'd met her, that she was not telling me the truth. Yet she had spoken without any hesitation.

In her aromatic vault, on the table, she worked on me, but something in me refused to cooperate. I felt like clay. Doubt, misgiving, made my flesh inert. I wanted to give my whole being to her, yet a wariness kept me back, all the little hints, her not introducing me to the woman with the child, the woman's sharp retort, my recognizing the child and not remembering her name, Mrs Unger not reminding me. She had been holding back.

I had never noticed this before, but then I had never visited unannounced. The suddenness produced this disharmony and it probably hadn't helped that I'd arrived with Rajat. He had seemed to know something I didn't know. I had doubted him and now I began to doubt myself.

Mrs Unger's hands swept over me, pressing, smoothing, finding my muscles and the spaces between them. I mentioned earlier that Mrs Unger's tantric massage was not a sexual act but rather the drawn-out promise of one, foreplay as an end, always trembling on the brink. This produced a tremulous ecstasy that I could compare only to a rapture of strangulation: I was suffocated in a delirious choking as she ran her magic fingers over me.

But today it wasn't working. I could not pretend that it was. Instead of being relaxed by her touch, or aroused, I ached with apprehension.

'You're resisting.'

'No – I like it.' But I knew I sounded insincere.

'I can tell by the position of your toes.'

'Maybe it's my stomach. I ate some odd-tasting bhajis for lunch.'

'Blame the bhajis,' she said. 'You need to taste something sweeter.' She let go of me. 'Get up, slowly. You'll be a little dizzy, so be careful.'

She helped me off the table and steered me to the shower. The light was on in the shower and it must have been bright because when I was done and I re-entered the massage room I could barely see. The taper burning in the dish of oil gave no light. I could not see Mrs Unger anywhere.

I felt my way to the table and touched her foot, then traced my hand up her naked leg. She was lying face-up on the table and now I could see that her head was tilted, her back arched, her body upraised in offering, a posture of surrender.

'Ma,' I said.

'Baby.' She took my head in both hands and guided it downward, between her fragrant thighs. '*Yoni* puja – pray, pray at my portal.'

She was holding my head, murmuring 'Pray,' and I did so, beseeching her with my mouth and tongue, my licking a primitive form of language in a simple prayer. It had always worked before, a language she had taught me herself, the warm muffled tongue. But today she sensed a difference, my diminished will. Bodies revealed much more than words ever could.

'Next time, call me first or wait for me to call you,' she said, releasing me and turning on her side. 'You said you had a breakthrough in Rajat's problem. I want you to bring me good news.'

'I have some solid leads.'

'We can't let that poor boy suffer an injustice,' she said. When I didn't reply, she said, 'You told me you'd gone to the hotel. Is there something you should tell me?'

I could have told her about the fierce manager, about Mina, about the dead hand and the piece of carpet. But who would I be telling? She was someone else. I was sensing a different, darker side – or if not darker, then evasive. I did not know this woman. I couldn't make love to her. I couldn't tell her what I knew. She was not the same woman I had known.

And I thought, *She's American!* I could have imagined being bewildered by an Indian, by her indirection or secrecy. But I knew Americans. Or thought I did. *I'm black* didn't explain anything.

Rajat had said, 'This is a pleasant surprise.' She had pretended so, but I was not convinced. It was nothing she had said. My doubt arose from the air around her, the vibration, most of all from her hands and fingers – the truth was apparent in her flesh; mine too, probably. The truth was a throbbing in the blood, nothing to do with words or protestations. It was a quality of pressure in her fingertips that told me that part of her was absent, something untrue in the touch.

'I have to go,' I said.

'So soon? You just got here. We've only begun.'

I slipped off the table, which I always thought of as an altar but which now seemed like a sacrificial table. I began to dress as she stood over me. I was careful not to say anything because she was as shrewd an interpreter of the spoken word as she was of flesh and blood.

At the door, she touched me, saying, 'There's something you're not telling me.'

I kissed her, thinking to reassure her, and in kissing her I felt that I was revealing to her everything I wanted to keep to myself.

## 16

Now I was as irritable and bent as everyone else in Calcutta, this deranged city of trapped air and fallen grandeur where in the hot, pre-monsoon month of May it was as stuffy in the streets as it was in any room. Sooner than I expected, within an hour or so of having left with Rajat, I was back at the Hastings, wondering, *What just happened?*

Rajat had suggested that I go with him to the Lodge and I'd been tempted, as always, by the anticipation of Mrs Unger's vault: luxuriating in the thought of her healing hands, her penetrating fingers. I'd been roused by the very idea of seeing her. And then, unexpectedly, I'd seen the American woman tugging the small girl away from the Lodge and Mrs Unger insisting she was glad to see me. Yet the woman's rudeness ('Any more questions?') and the pressure of Mrs Unger's touch disturbed me. I'd felt almost a hostility in her hands and, having experienced this odd side of Mrs Unger, I was confused. It had been a mistake to go. Who was that American woman? Who was that child? Who was Mrs Unger now? Her hands had been hard and cold, holding me in an almost strangulatory way.

And it had been an interruption of my work. I resented Rajat's intrusion, his urging me, his reassurances; and I was angry with myself for having allowed myself to be tempted. I should have known he was insincere from his having ordered tea and not drunk any of it.

I needed to write, to compose myself. In the seclusion of my room, hiding from the harsh late-afternoon light and the hubbub rising from the street, I sat half dressed under the quacking dust-covered ceiling fan. For the first time, doubting her – and so doubting myself – I had time on my hands. And in this solitude I saw the little girl's vacant face and hesitant posture, her skinny legs stiffened in reluctance. I had once seen her in Mrs Unger's lap. *I am her mother.*

Rather than continue 'A Dead Hand', this appreciation of Mrs Unger, I broke off the narrative and wrote *Who is she?* and began to describe this new experience of Mrs Unger's vault – not a refuge but a kind of trap, where I felt like an imprisoned stranger.

What made writing this all the weirder was that I felt uncomfortable in my own hotel room. I didn't usually write here. I was unused to sitting in semi-darkness, facing a dirty window pane, hearing the quack and croak of the fan above my head. Usually I sat on the top-floor verandah, above the familiar stink of traffic, the noise of horns and bicycle bells and people calling to each other – the muffled screeches of Calcutta that thickened the air.

My room disturbed me and it was more than the scummy spookiness I felt in most hotel rooms, a heaviness of old dust and dead echoes, of the sediment of bare feet and bad breath, the nerves of all the previous occupants. The smell amounted almost to a sound, a sort of humming high-pitched whine of spectral presences – much worse in Calcutta than in other places – the layers of chipped paint, the crusted rugs and sticky varnish, the windows opaque from scabs of dirt on the glass.

Adding to this itch, as I sat at my little table I noticed a dresser drawer pulled out an inch. That was annoying because I was careful about shutting doors and pushing in drawers. The thought of rats or mice kept me scrupulous: I'd once jerked open a drawer in an Indian hotel and seen a rat sniffing and scuttling across my socks.

This discomfort and unease slowed my writing. Yet writing was the only way I knew to puzzle out the feelings I had, about Mrs Unger and the small girl and the ambiguity of Rajat's mixed signals. I almost laughed at the thought that it was Mrs Unger who was the subject of this effort, and it was she, through her tantric massage, who had returned me to writing and given me a new vitality. Even so, I had to force myself to write, jamming my ballpoint on to my notebook pages.

I broke off around eight thirty to order tea and a cheese

sandwich, the safest meal at this time of night. I was following Mrs Unger's usual advice. The ghee butter was rancid and the fish was rotten and the vegetables sodden and the rice stale at the end of the day, she said. And the water was undrinkable, having stagnated so long in the heat.

When Ramachandra came with his tray, I said, 'Just a friendly reminder. Remember to close the drawers. Like this.'

Exaggerating for effect, I shut the partly open drawer.

'Room boy leave open, sar.'

'It wasn't Jagdish.'

'Sweeper, sar,' he said, wagging his head.

The mission in this blame-shifting society was to win at any cost and to be blameless, and the simplest way was to rubbish the underlings. In multi-layered India there was always someone lower than you.

To make me small – to make me wrong – Ramachandra then gave me a formal lesson in shutting the drawer. Using the tips of his fingers, spreading his hands, he demonstrated how this ill-fitting and chunky drawer should properly be pushed closed. He acted as if he were manipulating a highly technical apparatus that required balance and acute tolerances – and of course it was a pitted wooden drawer lined with yellowed paper in a dresser that, when it wobbled at his touch, startled a cockroach into skidding across the floor.

I couldn't help laughing and, though Ramachandra was insulted by my laughter, he laughed too, with the humiliated force of a man who would never forgive it, awaiting his chance to laugh at me for some more serious error. Class and caste abuse had made the prideful Bengalis unusually vindictive and they liked nothing better than situations that would allow them to stand over a supine victim and crow, *I told you so* or *I've got you now.*

'Now let us examine other one,' he said, reaching for the bottom drawer.

'Don't bother,' I said and put my foot against it.

After Ramachandra left, I felt that this was perhaps my problem with Mrs Unger. I'd blundered by showing up unannounced, thanks to Rajat. Would she hold it against me? And maybe I had been manoeuvred into going by Rajat, who seemed very uneasy with what I might find in my investigations, this shabby business at the Ananda, his running away. What was he hiding?

I was now certain that he'd found himself in the Hotel Ananda room with a dead boy. I had all the evidence. But had the boy been alive on arrival at the hotel? If not, how had he died? And when? And would I ever find out the name of this small unlucky boy, whose withered hand I had in my possession?

The dead hand was now hidden in the space behind the bottom drawer that Ramachandra had reached for. It was safe. And the cut-off portion of carpet was with Dr Mooly Mukherjee at police headquarters.

I didn't write about any of this. I had a new and unexpected subject: Mrs Unger. I had gone to the Lodge this time as though to an assignation, tense with desire, that feeling in the pit of my stomach that was also a yearning in my mouth, an actual thirst, a slight headache, heat behind my eyeballs: desire was an acute form of hunger and I was seeking relief. I wanted to hold her, I wanted to be held. I was half consumed by anticipated lust.

And it had all gone wrong. First the agitated behaviour of Rajat in the taxi, then the sight of the small girl being led away by the cranky American and finally, in the darkness of the vault, being touched as if by a stranger. It was nothing Mrs Unger had said; in fact, she'd tried to reassure me. But something in her fingers told me that she was unwilling, that she hadn't wanted to see me. There was an element of violence in the pressure of her hands, something, as I said, strangulatory. But why? I had never felt this way before with her. In the beginning I'd known uneasiness, per-haps, but never fear. I had the idea that she was debating whether to caress me or throttle me with those powerful fingers.

Someone you know well says or does something unexpected and, no matter how slight, if it is entirely out of character it is as if you've had a glimpse of a stranger. You've learned something new, something you hadn't guessed – and something this person doesn't know about you. *Who is she?* I kept thinking. I thought I knew her so well and here I was, utterly baffled. The more she had touched me, the greater my sense that she didn't want me there, that she hadn't expected me, that the deadening pressure of her fingers was hostile, killing my desire and making me want to leave. I sensed a darkness I had never before felt in her vault and, in spite of the oil lamp and the incense, I was aware that Mrs Unger was giving off a bad smell.

She had lain and parted her legs and, as though asking a question or murmuring a prayer, I'd gone down on her. The taste was sour, a slipperiness, the negligent kiss of reluctant lips, an unyielding and impenetrable mouth bulging with teeth.

Now I had worked myself into such a state I couldn't eat the cheese sandwich Ramachandra had brought. I sipped the tea. I was stifled. The trapped air in the room tired me, but there was no point going outside, where the air would be even fouler. The bad light wearied me. I wrote, describing this new Mrs Unger, and in my description I saw the face of the small girl.

The lanterns and dim lights of evening, the fires and flares outside the Hastings, made a lurid pattern, as of disease, on the plaster walls of my room. I was too tired to sit in the glary light of the Hastings lobby; I couldn't bear the thought of seeing Ramachandra, who would be over-attentive as a way of bullying me. My ballpoint pen was heavy, unsteady in my fingers; my writing faltered.

I lay on my bed. I switched the bedside lamp off to rest my eyes. I dozed. The faces before me were ones I knew but couldn't name – children, not laughing any more; the small girl. And I slept, dreaming, the world becoming vivid and real, and in my dream were voices.

That was when I sat up and said aloud, 'Usha. Dawn.'

My face was damp from the heat. I blinked in the darkness. I didn't know how long I'd been asleep, but speaking the name startled me and seemed to pinch some part of my brain, quickening it, waking me up with the girl's name. This flash of insight was a needle-prick of sound that kept me wakeful. I tried to sleep, but remembering the name, connecting it to the child I'd seen in

Shibpur and in the taxi (*I am her mother*) created a stream of images I could not stop. The face became brighter when I shut my eyes. In one of the images I saw the sharp-faced American woman tugging Usha into the car and being rude to me as the small girl opened her mouth in soundless panic – her breath stopped – before being spirited away in an adoption that was more like an abduction. The skinny middle-aged woman did not look at all like a mother but more like a dog lover or a socialite.

My mouth was dry from having uttered the little girl's name. I lay on the hard mattress, in the dusty air, in the smell of the mildewed carpet, the chipped paint on the chairs, the scratched varnish of the desk, the accumulated fur on the wardrobe mirror, the threadbare curtains, the grime on the blue petals of the plastic flowers on the dresser, my cheese sandwich souring on its plate, the bread warping as it went stale. Even in the darkness the room was warm with decay, every item of furniture giving off its distinctive smell, and with all that there was the insistent stink of the street. The whole of Calcutta lay hot and ripe against my face.

The smells kept me awake and in this density of bad air there was the burned-toast hum of old cigarette smoke. Twisted on my bed, like a castaway, my nerves alight, I was hungry and yet disgusted by the thought of food. The furniture, picked out in its smells and its shadows, shimmered too from the sulphurous yellow of the street lamps at the corner of Sudder Street.

That was why, when I saw the door of the wardrobe flicker forth – the long narrow mirror on the door catching the light from the street – I took it to be just another nightmare effect of those yellow lamps. But no, the mirror was still moving in one direction, catching on its edge the reflection of my pale pop-eyed face. I didn't breathe, I didn't move. My body was convulsed with anxiety, tangled in the damp sheets. I was still fully clothed. The mirror glinted, seemed to wink at me, swung out wider, and then came the tuneless clang of the wire hangers inside the wardrobe, like cheap wind chimes stirred by a light breeze.

Swelling like blobby ectoplasm – the sight was unearthly – a crouching shadow bobbed and rippled towards the door of my room as I watched in horror. I'd double-locked the door after Ramachandra left so that I wouldn't be interrupted in my writing. That seemed so innocent now. The handle resisted with a click, the shadow grunted, then whined, frustrated air straining in its sinuses, another little whinny of regret. Something in those sounds spoke of weakness.

I sprang out of bed and rushed at the figure, which was half shadow, half substance, and easily knocked it down with a thump. I was prepared to push again, but the lumpy shadow began pleading in a shrieky girlish whisper.

'Please don't hurt me. Please.'

It was a male voice. My eyes were used to the dark; his were not. He lay tumbled to the floor like a small bundle.

'What are you doing here?'

He was still pleading through his fingers, his hands over his face. I pulled at his hands and his cell phone dropped to the floor. I knew it was a cell phone because it had opened when I snatched at him, and it was lit and lying at a convenient angle on the floor to illuminate Rajat, curled into a ball and whimpering.

'I'm hurt. I've broken something.'

But he wasn't hurt. He was cowering, afraid that, standing over him, I'd kick him, which was what I wanted to do.

'Please let me go.'

He spoke with an odd decorum and rather softly, because he did not want to rouse anyone in the hotel. He remained on the floor, obstinate, stupid in fear. I switched on the overhead light and under the shadows of the turning fan blades Rajat lay, so like a scrawny carcass that I was at once reminded of my mission: identifying the small body in the other hotel room.

'Tell me why you came here.'

He covered his face and whimpered into his fingers.

'Never mind. I know. You're looking for any incriminating evidence that I've found. You suspect I've got something on you.'

'No.' It was less a distinct word than a groan of misery, something like *Aw*.

'You invited me to visit the Lodge to see Mrs Unger so that you'd have time to come here and search my room.'

That *Aw* again, more anguished.

'But you didn't count on my coming back early –' I stopped myself before telling him that my session with Mrs Unger was a turn-off that left me so doubtful and suspicious I'd hurried back to my room. Now I had a whiff of mothballs rising from him.

'You must have been in that wardrobe a long time.'

'Please don't tell Ma.'

'That you came here?'

'Or that you found anything to implicate me. I know it looks bad, but –' he rolled over and groaned into the floor – 'I did not murder that child.'

'Who did?'

He began to speak, he choked up, then he squealed, 'I do not know. I had no hand in it.'

'Was it Mrs Unger?'

'Absolutely not,' he said, shaking off his tears. 'She is pure. She is steeped in nectar!'

Even in the heat, in this harsh light, with Rajat on the floor beneath me, I smiled at this statement and, in my reflex of disbelief, I kicked him in the arm.

'Sorry. I couldn't help it.'

'Ma helps these poor children,' he said, his voice strained from my kick. 'She is their mother.' He had become a little calmer – was it my kick? 'You saw the child when you arrived.'

'The little girl being taken away?' I said. 'Her name is Usha.'

'I don't know her name. I only know that she was being taken.'

Now I understood. I said, 'You wanted me to witness that. You wanted me to watch the American woman take her away from Mrs Unger.'

He didn't say no. He seemed to grow smaller on the floor. He was whimpering again. It seemed that every time I mentioned Mrs Unger's name he grew fearful.

'It happens all the time,' I said. 'Mrs Unger sells them. Doesn't she?'

'There are many,' he said. 'It is her greatness.'

Rajat, still contracting, now a tiny bundle with a head, began again to cry.

'You knew I'd see that and you knew I'd be so preoccupied with Mrs Unger that you'd be able to search my room. Who did you bribe to get in here?' But he didn't reply. He was still snivelling. 'I came back early. I surprised you and so you hid in the wardrobe. You're lucky I didn't hit you harder, you little shit.'

My bullying him made him cry more miserably and I began to feel sorry for him. He was murmuring, 'Please.'

'I want you to tell me everything you know about Mrs Unger.'

I stood over him. His murmuring had grown urgent, as though in a kind of panic he thought I was going to kick him again. This made me feel like a monster and, while it gave me a sense of power I had never felt before, it both embarrassed me and made me feel reckless.

'Ma is good. Ma is generous.'

'You're afraid of her, afraid she'll hear you.'

'Ma hears everything.'

The way he said that made him seem pitiful. I said, 'She can't hear you now.'

'It is Ma's power,' he said, turning his smeared face upwards to the light.

'So why did you come here?'

'I wanted –' he swallowed and started again – 'I only wanted to save Charlie.'

'From what? From whom?'

But he sniffed and turned his face to the floor.

'You wanted to save yourself. You're a sneak and a liar.'

'Yes, I am a sneak. I have taken advantage of you by invading your room. But, sir, I am not a liar.'

'Get up,' I said.

He struggled to his feet. His face shone with tears and saliva. His greasy hair was pushed sideways, giving him a look of insanity, and his clothes – he was always so neat – were rumpled and twisted.

225

'Empty your pockets.'

I was sorry I asked. What Indians carried in their pockets was so sad: an ID card showing his startled face, a torn bus ticket, a receipt ('From chemist shop, for my acne'), a tube of acne cream, some folded rupees, a few coins, a key chain holding three old keys, a small brass Ganesh on a loop, some grey pills of lint.

'Please don't report me.'

'All I care about is the truth,' I said. It was the echo of what I'd said to him in the lobby when we were having tea and it sounded even more pompous now. I was glad there was no one around to hear me.

'There is no god higher than truth,' Rajat said. I stared at him, smiling again, amazed that he'd managed to say something more pompous than what I'd just said. Even standing bedraggled and defeated in my room, almost clownish in a tragic way, he was capable of being superbly sententious. And he became more serious. 'But you will never find the truth here.'

'Then why did you break into my room?'

'I wasn't looking for the truth. I was trying to find all those lies that people are telling about me.'

'And what about that little girl Usha? Isn't it true that I saw her taken away?'

'I don't know what you saw.'

'I could call the police now.'

'I beg you not to,' he said and actually assumed the cringing posture of a *bhikhiri*, a beggar.

'Put that stuff back in your pockets,' I said and, as he picked it up, pinching at the lint, I added, 'Now get out.'

I unbolted and unlocked the door and, wincing, he slipped out. But he held on to the doorjamb with his skinny fingers, hesitating.

'Please, sir, come with me to the entrance or they will suspect that I broke in. It will make me look so disgraceful.'

Surprised by his sudden impudence, I laughed and followed him downstairs to the lobby and the front door, to make this little sneak look honest. The *chowkidar* was asleep, barefoot in his khakis, his truncheon like a pillow under his head. Rajat thanked me by bowing, making a *namashkar* with his prayerful hands and then fled into the yellow glare of the alley.

He hadn't found the dead hand that I had hidden in the space behind the bottom drawer – I checked this as soon as I got back to the room. He couldn't have found the carpet because it was in Dr Mooly Mukherjee's lab. But I knew that he had been looking to find any evidence I had of the corpse in his room and to destroy it; he knew that I was on to him.

He had also done me a favour – but why? Though he denied it, he obviously wanted me to see the small girl Usha being taken away. And his saying 'There are many', though spoken in praise, was really an implied indictment of Mrs Unger.

What impressed me most in all of this was that, in my every encounter with Rajat, he had never said a single negative thing about Mrs Unger. Not a word of criticism, out of respect or fear or both; only the most elaborate gratitude.

I slept badly and when I woke, gasping in the heat of early morning, I remembered one other drawer I hadn't checked – my desk drawer, where I kept my notes, letters and receipts in a folder. The letter from Mrs Unger that had started me on this quest – handmade paper, purple ink, *Dear Friend* – was gone. Somehow Rajat had thieved it.

In this uncertain time, a few days after that encounter with a darker Mrs Unger, the dramatic adoption of Usha and the intrusion of Rajat, I had a call from Howard at the consulate.

'Dr Mooly Mukherjee has been trying to reach you.'

'I'll give him a call.'

'I'm kind of curious about the result,' Howard said. 'That is, if you feel like sharing it.'

'I'll let you know.'

'I mean, the figure in the carpet.'

'Right.'

I called Dr Mukherjee. He said, 'It would be a lot easier if you came to HQ.'

'Can't you tell me over the phone?'

'I'd rather not.'

'Are there bloodstains?'

'As a policeman I have learned not to be too comfortable on the telephone,' he said. He pronounced it *tellyphone*. 'Telephones are leaky.'

We arranged a time to meet for the following morning. I did not report this to Howard. He called me – somehow he knew about the appointment. He said, 'Mind if I come along?' I couldn't refuse: he had helped me find Dr Mooly Mukherjee.

Dr Mukherjee welcomed us. 'Tea or coffee?' He remarked on the weather. The monsoon was due any day now. He spoke of his family, his daughter's wish to study in the United States, altogether chatty and inconsequential in the Bengali way. At one time I would have felt he was trying to distract us because he had nothing to report. But now I knew that he wanted to engage us because he had something important to say. He was chatting because he wanted our full attention.

The piece of carpet lay in a plastic pouch on his desk like a laboratory specimen, an inked-in label stuck to the outside.

'My youngest, Shona, wants so earnestly to go to America,' he was saying, stroking his moustache. 'Post-graduate study. Law-rence, in state of Kansas.' He said *estudy* and *estate*. 'I am hoping that Mr Howard will ask powers-that-be to look favourably on her visa application.'

'Dr Mukherjee has four brilliant daughters,' Howard said, avoid-ing a direct answer.

'With my good wife and my dear mother, that is six women in the household. Petticoat government, you could say.'

Bursting to ask, I said, 'What did you find on the piece of carpet?'

'Ah, yes, the material evidence,' he said, as though he'd for-gotten. But his delay was an attempt to be dramatic. He picked up the plastic pouch. He held it in two hands. He said, 'This is the curious incident of the dog that didn't bark in the night. You know the reference?'

'Sherlock Holmes.'

'"Hound of the Baskervilles"?' Howard said.

'No,' Dr Mukherjee said and looked delighted. '"Silver Blaze" story. Another clue is the curried mutton. About a racehorse.'

'I haven't read that one,' I said.

'Interesting not for what is there but for what is not there.'

'Bloodstains?'

'No blood. No substantial DNA. Traces of human hair, we think.'

'That's all?'

'Food. Oil. Bits of dirt and grit. Better ask' – he tugged at his moustache with his free hand – 'what is not there?'

Howard said, 'OK. What's missing?'

Dr Mukherjee manipulated the plastic pouch so that we could see the edge of the carpet, which was its true edge, with a design and a double-stitched seam. Because this was not the small fragment that Mina had sent me but the bigger stained piece I'd taken from the floor of the closet, it had a complete design and seemed altogether more identifiable.

I said, 'Do you mean you can make out the whole design of the carpet from this piece?'

'Of course, but so what?' he said. 'Carpets are standard designs. This is floral. Also vines. Maybe a bird on an arbour in the figure.' He twitched his moustache as if to reject the notion that the design was important. 'Maybe some curry gravy or ghee butter on top side.' He showed me the stain. 'Vegetable matter.'

I was smiling at the expression and Howard winked as Dr Mukherjee turned the carpet over.

'Observe seam.'

'I don't see anything.'

'Exactly. You see nothing.' He was triumphant. 'But look closely and you see double stitch and coupon stub.'

'Coupon stub?'

'Strip of cloth, where label has been torn off.'

'Ah, the label's missing,' Howard said. 'So what does that tell us?'

'That someone doesn't want carpet to be identified,' he said.

'But they were hasty. Large piece of label is missing. Coupon stub remains in stitching. This strip.'

Now he put the plastic pouch down and opened a large manila envelope. He took out a black-and-white photograph that showed a strip of pale cloth with a stitch running through it and smudges of ink beside it.

'What are those squiggles?'

'Squiggles are Devanagari script that has been cut in half by hasty removal of label from stitching.'

'But bigger.'

'Lab has enhanced script with photographic process. Basic forensic work, nothing special.'

'So it tells the manufacturer?'

'Not manufacturer, regrettably. But see' – he placed another piece of paper next to the bisected script and completed the word – 'it matches.'

'What does it say?'

'Place of origin.'

'And that would be?'

'Mirzapur. In UP.'

I frowned, as though in frustration, so as not to reveal the panic I felt.

'You are right to make such a face, sir,' Dr Mukherjee said. 'Very many carpets are made in Mirzapur. Mirzapur is carpet mecca.'

'So it's a wild goose chase.'

'I think otherwise. Useful chase. Some weeks ago you showed me a body part with no fingerprints – all prints abraded. I offered my opinion that this could have been the hand of a brickmaker or a worker in clay.'

'I remember.'

'It could also have been the hand of a carpet weaver. Making the knots all day, a person can lose his fingerprints. Perhaps the two are related?'

Afterwards, Howard said, 'You seem a little downcast by the news. He didn't find bloodstains. Isn't that a good thing?'

'He found something more important – to me, at least. The Mirzapur connection. And the link with that hand.'

'Tons of carpets are made there. You heard him.'

'News to me.'

'Mirzapur is full of sweatshops.'

'I need to go there.'

'Tell me why.' When I hesitated he said, 'You said you were doing a favour for a friend. Is this about the favour?'

'About the friend.'

## 17

We high-stepped past squatting groups of men who were bright-eyed with fatigue, clawing with skinny hands at their bowls of food, yellow gravy and blue, gluey-looking vegetables – Howrah station again, the Night Mail to Mugalsarai and Mirzapur. Howard led the way, excusing himself in chatty Bengali, past the men who were licking their fingers and lapping their palms with gummy tongues. Seeing us, perhaps hoping for a tip, the conductor showed us to our compartment. Howard was efficient in using the available space – the hooks, the shelves, the water-bottle holder. We sat facing each other across the little table and the coach jumped with a clang, shoving us against the cushions, then settled and slid clicking past the platform and into the suburbs.

'Ever read Nirad Chaudhuri?' Howard asked. 'He's great on Calcutta. He talks about how the land around the city looks "poisoned to death". And the countryside is like "a mangy bandicoot bitten by a snake".'

I was staring out of the window at the small battered tenements on the mudflats, wondering how to begin.

'What's wrong?' he asked, probably because I hadn't commented on the colourful Chaudhuri quotes.

'I have something to tell you.'

He sat back in his seat and cupped his hands in a hospitable gesture. 'Go on,' he said. 'We have plenty of time. Trains are great places for confessions.'

I said, 'A few weeks ago, I got a letter at my hotel . . .'

'It's an amazing story,' he said, an hour or so later, as we were stopped at Dhanbad.

I had told him everything – almost everything. I had left out the tantric massages and the caresses in the fragrant vault of the Lodge. I had left out my pleasuring her, avoiding any mention of the sacred spot on her lotus flower or my wand of light. That part was unexplainable and made me seem needy or obsessed, weak, easily manipulated, susceptible to Mrs Unger's attention – all true. I played up her philanthropy, the lost children, the goat sacrifice, the visit to Nagapatti in distant Silchar. I tried to describe the relationship between Charlie and Rajat, but I confessed that I didn't understand them at all. Howard found it all fascinating and didn't ask for more details. As for Mrs Unger's disclosure that she was black, what was the point? I was not capable of verifying this unexpected assertion.

The last straw was my witnessing the American woman taking the child Usha away, almost certainly adopting her, something that Mrs Unger had always said she deplored.

In telling him my story, I felt the growing humiliation that many people must feel when, in a quiet moment, they relate to a logical and contented soul the details of an irrational attachment. Only when I spoke to him (and remembered much more that I was too ashamed to tell) did I see the extent of my recklessness, and I wondered how big a fool I'd been.

Howard said, 'But it seems odd that she should ask you to investigate. I mean, why you?'

'She said she liked my writing,' I said. 'I know that sounds lame. But she also thinks I have influential friends.'

'Like who?'

'You.'

He laughed. 'That's us. Crime busters.'

'There was no crime that I could see. There was only a misunderstanding. When I started, I didn't think she really bought Rajat's story. I didn't buy it either. It sounded preposterous. A corpse turning up in a hotel room in the dead of night? Crazy.'

'This is Calcutta,' Howard said, 'where all things are possible.'

'Rajat seemed the excitable type. Looking for drama. Maybe it was a way of getting attention. So I thought. Then I met Mina.'

'The one who was slapped around and fired.'

'And the one who brought me the dead hand,' I said. 'She verified the story of the corpse. So Rajat must have been telling the truth.'

'Why didn't you tell that to Mrs Unger?'

'Because around the same time I got the piece of carpet. I needed to deal with that. I wanted something more. You know the rest.'

'About Mrs Unger denying she'd been to Mirzapur in UP, yes. But maybe the *chowkidar* got it wrong. There's a Mirzapur up in Murshidabad and another Mirzapur near Dacca. I checked. Maybe he was just guessing about where she'd gone.'

I liked his challenges. He was forcing me to think clearly. I said, 'Let's see if the answer's in this Mirzapur.'

But how could I tell him what I felt – that her touching me had told me something, that I didn't know how sincere she was until she put her hands on me that last time. The falsity was in her fingers and it had alarmed me; her power now seemed dangerous, even fatal. Howard was so rational I had no way of explaining my suspicions to him.

'Here's a printout of the factories,' he said, taking a sheet of paper from a file folder. 'We'll find more when we get there. We're meeting a Mr Ghosh there. He's said to be helpful – he's from the area.'

Howard was the perfect travelling companion. Calm, accepting, uncomplaining, and he spoke Bengali. He didn't judge me. He said he had been a Peace Corps volunteer long ago, and it showed: he was resourceful and curious. He was taking a professional interest in my problem, but he was also a friend.

Perhaps because we were two *ferringhis* travelling alone, the conductor didn't put any Indians in our compartment when the train stopped at Burdwan and Asansol and Dhanbad. Indians who boarded the train at those places filled the other compartments. And now I was used to the routine: the snack seller with his tray, the bookseller with his stack, the drink seller with his bucket of bottles, the man taking dinner orders. We had left Howrah at sunset. By eight we were eating from our food trays – 'Bird flu on a skewer,' Howard said of the kebab. Then he lay down and read the second volume of Doris Lessing's autobiography and I read my most recent pages of 'A Dead Hand', detailing my relationship with Mrs Unger up to our return from Assam, when she was still unambiguously a good person – not saintly but great-hearted, robust, always positive, the energetic soul of philanthropy and good works; a nurturer, the woman with healing hands. She was protective and sensual and vitalizing, 'Ma' in every sense.

I wanted to write more, but everything I'd discovered about Mrs Unger, everything I'd seen, I now understood was an idealized portrait of a woman protecting her son's friend. Where I'd seen light I now saw shadow; where I'd seen generosity I now saw self-interest; and the contradictions jarred me. These new details made her more human but harder to understand. I had loved being with Mrs Unger. I'd felt safe, even adored. I'd been able to count on her. Now I was doubtful. I didn't want her to touch me and, when she had, I'd recoiled and wasn't sure why.

I couldn't tell any of this to Howard. Anyway, this inner history of my relationship had very little to do with identifying the source of the carpet in Mirzapur.

Returning from the toilet – always a dose of reality on an Indian train – I remarked on how full the coach was, many of the passengers squatting in the vestibule outside the toilet, on the wet floor.

'Most of them are *yatris*, pilgrims, going to Varanasi. They'll be getting off at Mugalsarai – it's not far from there to the holy city. They'll be doing pujas and cremations and immersing themselves in Mother Ganga.'

'It's a nice thought, purifying yourself in a holy river.'

'But when you see the river you think only of disease. It's full of half-burned body parts and ashes and cow shit. Sludge and dead flowers. The Indian paradox. It doesn't matter that the river is muddy and putrid, it's still sacred.'

'It makes them feel better.'

'Right. And the goddess that wrecks and destroys is also the goddess of creation – Kali, the inaccessible.' He had stopped reading the Lessing book but still held it, his finger in the pages. 'You know the line from *Out of Africa*? "Africa, amongst the continents, will teach it to you: that God and the Devil are one, the majesty co-eternal, not two uncreated but one uncreated." A very Indian way of looking at the world.'

'But in India we're on the outside looking in.'

'So true. What was that expression you used in one of your pieces? "Romantic voyeur."'

I liked his quoting me after quoting Karen Blixen, not for the aptness of what I said but for the reassurance that if he remembered what I had once written, he was on my side. I needed a friend because we were strangers here, walking through this populous country, on this crowded train, in the bazaars and at the temples and borne along by the mob, never able to penetrate, never belong, always kept apart as spectators. He was a consular officer; he actually dated his ex-wife, who was at the embassy in Delhi; and he took an interest in Calcutta. But what excuse did I have? Really, I had no business here.

Never in my life had I been in a place that I found at once so worthy of study, so dense, so superficially exotic, with people so likeable and talkative, that was at the same time so impenetrable, even repellent. The more I tried to engage, the more I was excluded. Every activity in India, every Indian, every scene, said *You don't belong here* and *You will never understand*, but never explicitly said *Go home*. For a foreigner, living in India required complete surrender. We were not rejected, we were mildly tolerated, because foreigners in India always had a use.

'I could watch this for a year and still not understand,' I'd said to Mrs Unger at the Kali temple in Gauhati.

'There is nothing to be understood in India,' she said. 'Only to be accepted.'

That had been something else that attracted me to her. Of all the foreigners I met in India, she was the one who was most at home. It was not her sari or her hennaed feet, not even her pieties, though they stuck in my mind: 'Ida and Pingala must come into balance to allow the *kundalini* to rise in the Sushumna channel,' or 'The skills and benefits of White Tantra practices increase one's ability to master Red Tantra.' Nor was it her ability to live among the people and flourish. It was her certainty and her calmness, almost a way of breathing (*pranayama* she would have said) that made her brave.

'Anyone who has not learned to hate India has not spent enough time here. You can never love India – you will be destroyed,' she'd said.

'What then?'

'Respect India as you would a tiger. If not, you'll be eaten alive.' Another time, 'India is elephantine.'

She did not fear anyone in India. Yet most foreigners – Howard and I, for example – were so careful as to seem timid. Mrs Unger was bold, another of her maternal qualities. She was a protector.

Or so I had thought. I was headed to Mirzapur to find out if any of this was true.

We rocked through the night and at dawn most of the passengers got out at Mugalsarai, as Howard had predicted. The *chai* seller ladled milky tea into plastic cups for us and, two hours later, we arrived in Mirzapur.

Mr Ghosh had found our coach and stood outside as we descended to the platform.

'Welcome, welcome.'

He carried a briefcase and an umbrella and seemed, for our purposes, to be overdressed – a suit jacket, a tie, heavy shoes; burdened by the clothes, but it was a uniform. He was defining himself in the Indian way, to impress us with his seriousness, the important weight of his clutter, and he wore two lapel pins. A smudge of yellow dust glittered on his forehead. Emblems of power.

'Good journey?'

Howard said, 'Excellent. And we are honoured to be here.'

'Honour is mine. I am honoured to be your guide.'

He made no move to take our bags – that was the job of the porter. It would not have occurred to him even to offer. He fluttered his hands at a ragged man, who dived at us and snatched the bags.

'We must have a cup of tea,' he said. 'Tearoom is adjacent on station platform. We can discuss programme.'

He unbuckled his briefcase in the tearoom and brought out a map of Mirzapur. This he flattened on the splashed tablecloth while explaining that it was already out of date.

'We're looking for a particular carpet factory,' I said.

'So many are there. Big are there. Small are there.' He snapped his fingers at a waiter. 'What about cakes? What about eatables? Have you breakfasted?'

'Nothing for me,' I said and Howard signalled by raising his hands that he was content.

'What is factory name?'

'I don't know the name, but here's a piece of carpet from it. At least I think it is.'

Mr Ghosh handled it casually, as something valueless, and hardly looked at it. He smiled the smile of the Indian pedant I'd met many times, who enjoyed telling me a thing was impossible or had no meaning or could not be properly understood by a non-Indian. Mrs Unger always had a prompt reply for such people, but I was at a loss.

'No, no, no, no,' he was saying.

An Indian man of this sort got more pleasure out of saying that something was impossible than offering to be helpful. Here we had just arrived after fourteen hours on the train and he was telling us we were wasting our time. Being obstructive inflated his importance.

'Many factories make this carpet. It is standard design.'

'But we suspect this factory exports goods to America,' Howard said.

Seeming to gloat over our naivety, Mr Ghosh said, 'All factories export to America.'

'Maybe we should go back to Calcutta,' I said, to see what he would say.

'I can initiate suitable enquiries.' He shrugged and looked again at the piece of carpet. 'I can chalk it in.'

It would have ruined his pleasure to see us depart early and he could only be compensated if we stayed. If a thing seemed too easy, Mr Ghosh was of negligible importance. The idea was for him to strike a balance between the impossible and the negotiable.

Howard knew how to handle him. He thanked Mr Ghosh for meeting us. He expressed the hope that we would find what we were looking for. He said that we were delighted to be in Mirzapur, famous for its textiles, a legend in the carpet industry.

This elaborate politeness had the effect of arousing Mr Ghosh's civic pride and helping him relax, even if he was not disarmed. Howard was being properly appreciative, but I could see that Mr Ghosh viewed me (accurately) as impulsive.

I said, 'We think there might be child labour involved.'

'Child labour is so common.' Mr Ghosh looked defiant.

'One of these children might be dead.'

'Who lives forever?' he said and smiled, pleased with his reply.

'But he was a child.'

'Even children die.'

'This child might have died in the factory.'

He grinned his pedantic grin and rested on the handle of his umbrella. 'It is not nursery. It is factory.'

'Backbreaking work.'

'Excuse me, good sir. Not at all. Weaving work is done with fingers only. Children tie knots. As a Mirzapurian, I am familiar with this work.'

'Many children?'

'*Lakhs*, sir.'

Then we drank our tea in silence. Mr Ghosh had gained the advantage. Instead of guiding us, he was elaborating the difficulties.

But Howard was unfazed. He was attentive, sympathetic, deferential.

'We are ignorant visitors,' Howard said. 'You're the expert. What shall we do?'

Mr Ghosh took a sip of tea, sloshed it behind his teeth like mouthwash and swallowed.

'Familiarization is best,' he said.

'How do we accomplish that?'

'Windscreen tour.'

'Looking out the window?' I asked.

'Of hired motor vehicle.'

'How well do you know these factories?'

'From the ground up. Thorough knowledge,' he said, 'of ins and outs.'

'Exactly how many carpet factories are there?'

He became professorial again, leaning on his umbrella. 'Are you meaning carpet factories or factories that create weavings?'

It took me a moment to translate *vee-vings*. I showed him the piece of carpet again. 'This sort of thing.'

He handled it and removed his eyeglasses. He put on a different pair of glasses and studied the fragment of carpet he had dismissed as worthless some minutes before.

'This is like calling card,' he said. 'This is like signature.'

While he frowned over it, Howard glanced at me. I rolled my eyes. He smiled. I envied Howard his equanimity.

'We are in your capable hands,' Howard said.

'It is of some little interest.' He nodded at it and turned it in his hands.

'The design?'

'Not at all,' he said. 'Design says nothing.'

'What then?'

'Underside. Backing and stitching. Label has been removed.'

'So we were told.' I wanted to snatch the piece of carpet away from him and slap it against his head until he howled in pain.

'Made in Mirzapur,' Howard said.

'I could have informed you of this fact, sir.' He examined his fingernails and took an interest in one thumbnail.

'Would it help if we said we were looking for a carpet factory owned and operated by an American?'

'Several are American-owned.' He plucked at the cuffs of his shirt, straightening them in the sleeves of his jacket.

'I mean, an American woman.'

Mr Ghosh looked disappointed. He put the piece of carpet on to the table and tucked it into the plastic pouch. His shoulders went slack; he lost his smirk of superiority.

'American Goddess,' he said.

# 18

Where were the trees? Where were the parks? The place was dense and darkish and arterial. In this hot, shadowy city of jumbled shops and blatting traffic I had the feeling I sometimes got in Calcutta, that I was passing through the entrails of a huge unhealthy body. Not just the look of the place but a brimming odour of muddy water, a prickle of stagnation; it was the river.

'Formerly this was Cotton Exchange and banking street.'

Mr Ghosh sat beside the driver, nodding and narrating.

'See, house of British merchant.'

But it was all a failing semi-ruin mobbed by hurrying people. Our car was jostled by auto-rickshaws and cycle-rickshaws, by big, dusty buses with *Horn Please* painted on the rear and by the inevitable skinny cows. We travelled into the crowd of accumulating pedestrians, down side streets, and it really was like circulating inside an enormous, bloated, sprawling organism. Past sewers and sludge, the fruit sellers, old men hawking religious relics, pictures of bright-coloured gods with green and blue faces, children selling packets of aspirin. Everyone was selling, no one buying. In this flat city I could see only twenty feet ahead.

The human activity, all the shrieks, the car horns, the hawkers' cries, masked the background, the Mirzapur of crumbling shops and broken pavements. The frenzy obscured the reality, that the city was poisonous and falling apart. But this was the feeling I had in most parts of Calcutta, because I was a visitor with the luxury of making snap judgements, able to move on.

'Look at that balcony,' Howard said. 'So beautifully carved. And that venerable old man.'

His appreciation shamed me. He could see beauty in a peeling green porch, a wicker chair, an old coot in a nappy-like dhoti. What

I noticed was that none of the children was playing; they all looked like little old men.

But I had come here for a practical reason: to find the source of this carpet, to get to the bottom of Mrs Unger's mystery. I was hot and uncomfortable, groggy from the rattling night on the train. I now resented Mrs Unger for setting me on this path. I wasn't cut out for investigative reporting. But that shamed me too, for wasn't she a woman who devoted her life to good works? I now remembered what Mr Ghosh had said.

'Why do you call her the Goddess?'

He didn't answer. He was talking to the driver. I noticed that we were on a slight incline, a sloping road lined with shops and the usual monsoon drain, dry in this season but filled with heaps of paper and plastic rubbish. Beyond the shops the light was brighter, the sky higher, as though there was a valley on the other side.

I saw distant houses and a brown, deeply scored, stony embankment like a hillside.

'Ganga,' Mr Ghosh said.

This excited Howard, who said, 'Where are the ghats?'

'Ghats are there. Pujas are there. See garlands in river.'

I saw thick stone piers, pitted with age, porous as bone, worn by the sloshing of the river, and beneath in the slow slip of the water a scum of garbage and orange peels, sodden cast-off marigolds and festering lilies.

'Where are the factories?' I said.

'Temple first. Vindhyachal. Presiding deity Vindhyavasini Devi.'

'I don't want to see the temple,' I said.

Howard said, 'Why don't we let Mr Ghosh . . . ?'

'I want to see the American factory.'

'Two American factories,' he said. 'Obeetee is major exporter. Long history. Handlooms. Dhurries. Woollen druggets. You are wanting druggets?'

'I am not wanting druggets,' I said and, hearing a shriek in my voice, tried to calm myself. 'I want to see the other one.'

'They are abundant,' Mr Ghosh said.

'The Goddess. Why do you call her the Goddess?'

'She is making puja at Kali Khoh temple.'

'That's the only reason?'

'And when the business was cracked down, she prevailed over adversity.'

'Why the crackdown?'

'Hullabaloo,' Mr Ghosh said. 'We go later. In meantime we will visit handloom shop at Obeetee.'

Of course, for a visit to one of these shops he got *baksheesh* and when we bought something he would find out what we paid and would get a commission.

Howard began to say something, but I interrupted.

'We have very little time,' I said. 'I want to see the American woman's factory. I want to see the carpets. Maybe I'll buy something there and you'll get some rupees.'

'They are not proffering commission,' he said. 'See temple.'

'No temple.'

Howard said, 'How far is the temple?'

'Factory,' I said.

'Hotel Janhavi is adjacent. You can book in, bathe body, take some few breakfast eatables.'

'Factory,' I said.

'You are chiding, sir.'

'I am not chiding.'

Mr Ghosh sighed and, with great reluctance, he gave the driver a whispered order.

'What my friend means, Mr Ghosh, is that we'd like to see the factory first and then we'll look at the temple,' Howard said.

'Temple is treasure of Mirzapur. Many *yatris* come to see Vindhyachal. Then to Astabhuja for goddess Mahasaraswati puja. Then to Kali Khoh for Maa Kali puja. This is holy place! Not merely weavings and carpets and floor coverings and whatnot. It is historical. Thousands of years.'

He spoke resentfully, as if he did not want to take us where we wanted to go – my only reason for being in Mirzapur. And, thwarted in doing what he wanted to do, which was be in charge, he sulked and said nothing while we crawled through traffic. As in

Calcutta, traffic was also cows, pushcarts, wagons drawn by oxen and buffalo, auto-rickshaws and old men on bikes, too maddening to be picturesque.

'Where are we?' Howard asked.

'Station road. Embankment. As requested.'

Mr Ghosh made it clear that he was taking us under protest. The car turned into a side road and now the river was near enough to bulk in the air as a strong sewer smell. The light was gauzy in this openness. The city fell away at the littered and weedy bank of trampled mud. Beyond the stretch of water was another bank, low houses at the edge of it. Mr Ghosh groaned and nodded as the car laboured in the ruts and the wheels thumped into the potholes.

He said something to the driver. Then, as the car slowed down, 'Better we pass on foot.'

'How far?'

Instead of answering, he gestured vaguely with the back of his hand. He gathered his umbrella and briefcase and sighed as he got out of the car.

Ahead was a stucco wall about eight feet high with shards of glass embedded in the top, bristling like crude spikes. The gate was a pair of high steel doors, painted green and stencilled with a number. As I kicked along the dusty path, stumbling on tussocks and loose rocks, I thought: *Mrs Unger comes here?*

A man in a heavy suit of fuzzy brown wool like an old-fashioned army uniform stood at the gate. He wore a black beret and carried a shiny black club that he brandished like a truncheon. He had a brass plate pinned to his shirt, official-looking, like the *chowkidar* at the Lodge.

Mr Ghosh spoke to him in what I supposed was Hindi, first a greeting, then what sounded like a hectoring explanation.

'Not possible,' the guard said in English.

Mr Ghosh rested on his umbrella, using it as a cane. He spoke again.

The guard made an ambiguous head-bob and repeated, 'Not possible.'

Mr Ghosh turned to us and said, 'Not open to public.'

'Wait a minute,' Howard said, becoming decisive. He briskly approached the guard and looked him in the eye. He took out his passport and, nudging Mr Ghosh aside, held it open the way a policeman shows his badge. He said, 'I am from the United States consulate general in Calcutta. Do you see this? We are here on official business. Please open the gate and let us in.'

The guard looked at Howard's diplomatic passport. He muttered and then withdrew. After a few minutes another man appeared, this one in shirt-sleeves, and he examined the passport.

Satisfied that it was genuine, he backed away, and the next sound I heard was the hasp being lifted and the steel bolt shot. The door swung open.

'Coffee, tea?' the man said.

I said no. Howard said yes. We had tea in the man's office. Howard whispered to me that since we were lucky to have gained entry, we had to observe the courtesies.

The man said his name was Joshi. Born in Ahmedabad, he had come to Mirzapur to learn the weaving trade. He was about forty or so, potbellied, with thin arms and a string around his wrist. 'I am plant manager. Supervise, yes, I can do. Imitate I cannot. Weaving is very demanding,' he said, wagging his head to indicate the depth of his seriousness.

'I suppose it's very technical,' Howard said.

'So technical,' Mr Joshi said. 'First, design is made. Then master plan, each knot specified. We are having rooms where designers toil. They are pukka artists, no doubt. The weavers read designs. We have yarn, hand-spun. Dyeing vats. All facilities.'

'Do any of your carpets look like this?'

I showed him the patch of carpet.

'It seems one of ours,' Mr Joshi said. 'We have specific *naksha* for this. That is, master plan. This pile I recognize, too.'

'It is like signature, I tell you,' Mr Ghosh said, not to be outdone. 'I have informed the American gentlemen of this.'

Mr Joshi worked his thumbnail into the pile. He said, 'Not first quality,' and smiled. 'Not valuable. Not collectible. Third quality. Parlour unit.'

'How would this carpet be sold?'

'As export item. Machine-spun yarn. Not vegetable colour. Chemical dye. Standard *naksha*.' He flipped it over. He dug his nail into it again, as though determining whether it was edible. 'This piece is export only. You found in America?'

'Calcutta,' I said.

He stared at the fragment in his hands, then he smiled. 'Not possible.'

'What if it was taken without your notice, or stolen by an employee?'

'Our employees are living on site. On premises thieving is minimal.'

'By some miracle, this carpet ended up in Calcutta. It found its way to a hotel, where it was cut into pieces. That's where I came across it.'

'I have no knowledge of this unauthorized usage,' Mr Joshi said.

Howard said, 'We'd like to see your workshop.'

'Not possible,' Mr Joshi said.

'We'd like to meet your employees.'

'Not available.' He pretended to be impassive but I could see he was adamant.

Even Howard, the soul of politeness, hated to be rebuffed. He said, 'You are the supervisor, Mr Joshi?'

'Yes, sir. Plant manager.'

'Who is your boss?'

'The sahib, sir.'

'We want to meet the sahib.'

Mr Joshi's face became waxen and he swallowed hard as he seemed to make a rapid calculation that showed in his glistening eyes.

'Sahib very busy, sir.'

'Give him this card.' Howard handed Mr Joshi his business card from the consulate, with the American eagle embossed in gold on it. 'Please tell him we want a word with him.'

Mr Joshi fingered the card, studied it with his lips.

'*Chowkidar* has passed me this card already,' he said and then wagged his head, the wobble that meant yes.

After Mr Joshi left the room, Mr Ghosh said, 'Chap is doing level best.'

Howard simply shrugged. 'We've come all this way. Why not give it a shot?'

We sat in the tiny office, tired from the long night in the train, weary from the rebuffs. It was hotter here than in Calcutta, the slimy heat of the river thickening the air. We had not washed. We had hardly eaten.

'Better we go to Hotel Janhavi and make telephonic enquiries from there,' Mr Ghosh said.

We did not reply. I was not sure what to do, though what Mr Joshi had said reassured me. The carpet was definitely from this factory. It had arrived at the Hotel Ananda rolled around a dead child and had turned up in Rajat's room. So, some of the pieces fitted in some larger scheme, but the scheme itself was a mystery. Who was the boy? Where had he come from? Why had he been brought to the Ananda and why did the poor boy have no fingerprints? Perhaps the loss of fingerprints was associated with his weaving, as Dr Mooly Mukherjee had suggested.

All these disjointed speculations should have prepared me for anything, yet I was not prepared for what happened next.

A series of bangs, each one louder than the one before, seemed more jarring in the heat. A door slammed in the hallway, then Mr Joshi's door was flung open. Charlie Unger stood before us, very red in the face, his white kurta spotless.

'What are you doing here? What do you want?'

A person reveals his true personality in a show of temper. Charlie had never been more than a smirking shadow before, seeming to resent my being with his mother; or he had sulked and been oblique, but always enigmatic. All his talk of liking my writing had not convinced me. Now he was fussed and furious, hands on hips, defying us – defying me, his hating eyes dancing in anger, his lips twisted in disdain, the real Charlie.

'We'd like to look at your factory.' It was just an assumption that it was his, but he didn't deny it.

'Does Mother know you're here?'

'In a way, she sent us here.'

'That's crap. She would have called.' He turned to Howard. 'Who are you?'

'You have my card,' Howard said. 'I'm from the consulate.'

'You have no business here.'

'As Mr Joshi probably told you, we want to look around.'

'Listen, doll, take your friends and leave. Go back to wherever you belong. You don't belong here.'

Howard visibly stiffened at this, yet when he spoke he was calm and exceedingly polite. 'Please have another look at my card. You'll see I'm public affairs officer at the consulate. I am answerable to the State Department for the activities of all Americans in my area. Mirzapur is in it and so is Calcutta. That would include you.'

'I have news for you, doll,' Charlie said, trying to interrupt.

But Howard continued: 'If you want to go on doing business here, you'll show us your factory, your workshops and your employees. We're not leaving until we see them.'

'We're proud of what we're doing. My mother created this whole business from nothing.'

'That's admirable.'

'We're not breaking any laws.'

'Good. Now would you mind showing us around?'

'We're one of the biggest carpet exporters in Mirzapur. We're supporting a lot of families.'

He flounced out of Mr Joshi's office and we followed. Hurrying beside him, Mr Joshi opened doors and stood aside as Charlie said, 'Design room – colour plates are made here,' and on a low platform a dozen men worked over large sheets of paper tacked to boards, inking patterns in bright colours.

In the next room, men were transferring the coloured patterns on to a large piece of graph paper, one square at a time.

'Each square represents one knot,' Mr Joshi said.

248

The men smiled hello from their workstations, waving shyly as we left, hands on hearts.

'Why is this door locked?' I asked as we walked farther down the narrow corridor.

'Looms,' Mr Joshi said. 'The weaving room.' And he opened the padlock on the tongue of the hasp. He eased the bolt and opened the door.

'I don't care what you think. We're not ashamed of this,' Charlie said.

The door gave on to a large, high-ceilinged room. It could have been a school. I sensed a sudden hush, even over the rattle of the wooden looms. My first thought was that it was a schoolroom, the children small and attentive, all of them barefoot, climbing on benches, clinging to the big looms, some of them knotting yarn or stringing the vertical warps, others crouching, fastening knots, still more hammering, beating the interlocking strings and knots.

That was my first impression, little scholars, silenced by the entrance of the headmaster. But I quickly saw their solemnity, their fear, the intensity of their concentration – they were cowed and compact, like prisoners. It was a prison, a labour camp, filled with wooden frames and clattering; it was a mass of loose ends; it was a confusion of small souls toiling with tiny hands.

'Children,' I said. 'They're all kids.'

I walked over to a loom and when I approached a boy of ten or twelve he left off plucking at a knot and held up his hands to cover his face, as though he expected me to hit him.

I smiled and stepped back. I said softly, 'I know your name.'

'Yes, uncle.'

'I've forgotten what it is.'

'Jyoti, uncle.'

The self-possessed boy I had met at the Lodge, mouse face, bat ears, tiny head, narrow shoulders, the little soldier, broken now. *Ma is our mainstay.* I reached to shake his hand. He extended his hand and I held it softly and turned it so that I could see his fingers. His hand was claw-like, his fingers reddened, the fingertips rubbed raw.

'He has no fingerprints.'

But Charlie was smirking, standing next to Howard at the doorway.

'Go away or else I'll call security. Then I'll have you screaming the place down.'

'I'm reporting you,' Howard said.

'I told you, doll. It's all within the law.'

'No, it's not,' Howard said.

Charlie said, 'Then tell us the names of anyone in this country who's been convicted of using kids. Ha! Get out, doll.'

# 19

From the beginning, my first visit more than six weeks earlier, I had regarded the Lodge of Mrs Unger in Alipore as a refuge, a place of safety, of health and joy, where she was the protector, the guiding light, the mother of it all – Ma, great soft bosom in this itchy city of sharp edges and contending voices.

Now I saw the Lodge as a dangerous and unhappy place, and Mrs Unger as the sinister force that tyrannized over it. The smell of it was the smell of the sacred river, in India an odour of sanctity, which was also a whiff of stagnation, an odour of life and of death.

I had come to the Lodge unannounced, but she was waiting for me on the stone porch behind the cracked balusters, flanked by the worn, rain-pitted, almost featureless lions. I tried to imagine what this great neo-classical mansion might have looked like in its heyday, but I could not see it, could not recreate it from this cracked façade and exposed brick, from the burrs and bruises on its fluted columns. It was both monumental and ruinous, like Calcutta, with the same human face, gaping windows, cheeks of fissured stucco, a mouth-like door, open in a hungry appeal like the beggars at car windows at street corners.

'I've been expecting you,' Mrs Unger said. 'I thought you'd be here yesterday.'

'I had some business to attend to.'

Whenever I was away from her, I forgot how lovely she was, her feline features, the cast of her face, her high cheekbones, her full lips, made fuller by her slightly protruding teeth. She was beautiful, stately as a priestess. She had a broad forehead, a tipped-up nose and greeny-grey eyes (depending on the light) and her hair was going prematurely silver in places. Though she was younger than me, she seemed much older. Her body, so slender in her silken sari, her narrow, bony feet stippled with henna.

But this beauty today looked devilish, her smile – her teeth – frightening. Her two side teeth – eye-teeth, I suppose – bulged against her lips when she frowned and glistened, looking even more sinister, when she smiled. She was not tall, but she stood erect and gave the impression of height, and so she seemed dominant.

'I take it you've been successful,' she said. 'Come inside.'

In the Lodge the sounds of children's laughter unnerved me, as if they were at play, scampering at the edge of a precipice.

'I'd rather sit in the garden,' I said.

'But I owe you a treatment.'

The word struck fear into me now. How easily everything was reversed. Her beauty repelled me; the promise of a treatment was like a threat.

'I look forward to it,' I said, hoping she'd believe me.

'Bijoy, bring some tea,' she said to an apprehensive servant I had never seen before.

We walked together down the staircase to the side of the house where the garden was luxuriant. The pale trunks of the banyan trees twisted into the brick wall, the insinuating fingers of the long roots, the knuckles of the fatter wrinkled ones, the mossy stones, the gurgle of the fountain – the garden had seemed fertile before, a source of life. Now it was sinister, all of it, the sound of the falling water like a repeated warning.

'Sit,' she said, patting a bench.

This moss-covered statuary I had seen from the downstairs lobby, the damp bricks, the paved path, the fountain at the pool, a marble cow's head at its centre, spewing water through its rounded mouth. Mrs Unger smiled, drawing her lips back, showing her teeth, letting her tongue loll hungrily.

'Tell me what you've found. Put my mind at rest.'

Instead of sitting where she had beckoned me with her hand, I took a seat at the far end of the bench so I could look at her. My face was damp from the humid heat of the garden.

'I guess you know I've been to Mirzapur. Charlie must have told you.'

'I've heard a number of versions. Charlie's. Mr Joshi's. Even the redoubtable Mr Ghosh.'

'You're resourceful.'

'Not half as resourceful as you,' she said. 'Ah, here's our tea.'

She spoke in her actressy voice, her lines like lines in a play, as when I'd first met her at the Oberoi Grand. And because she seemed so well rehearsed, I was especially on guard.

The waiter in the white uniform spread a cloth over a stone tabletop and set out the tea things. Even those cups and saucers seemed worryingly like props.

'You can go, Bijoy.' Mrs Unger poured the tea into the two cups. 'So, was Rajat fantasizing or was there really a dead body?'

'There was a body.'

'In that squalid little room? As he said?'

I wondered if she was putting me on. She was speaking in that same actressy way, as though performing. Even her manner of pouring the tea was a sort of acting, her making a business of it as she spoke.

'Just as he said.'

'But surely they must have found the body.'

'The body seems to have disappeared.'

The other thing I noticed was that this Mrs Unger was almost a stranger to me. I thought I knew her, but this was someone new, or at least a woman pretending to be someone else and doing a good job of it.

'Disappeared? The poor thing.'

'Yes, it was a small boy.'

'I meant poor Rajat,' she said and giggled a little. 'So it's true. I wasn't sure whether to believe him. He can be such a fantasist. He was always dancing around me, telling tales.' She looked closely at me. 'I'm grateful to you for finding out the truth.'

She was peering at me from over the rim of her teacup. I stared back at her. She swallowed and put the cup down.

'Now you must report what you found.'

'To whom?'

'To the police. To the authorities. To the consulate – you have friends there, I know.'

'And what would be the point of that?'

'To hold him responsible. I had thought he was such a little charmer. As I told you, he had fairy energy. I didn't think you'd find anything, but now it seems he's involved in something sinister.' She slid closer to me and said, 'I knew you'd find out what really happened. You're a wonderful writer. That's why I trusted you, because you know that the aim of all art is to tell the truth.'

I was so transfixed by her performance that I did not respond at once. I did not know this woman. But she was half smiling at me with indignant certainty. I saw that she was waiting for an answer.

'I feel I *have* found out the truth.'

'Rajat was lying. Indians do lie all the time, you know. They are forced to lie because their culture is so strict. You never get the truth from them. "Yes, I'll take care of it." But they don't. That's why I went to you.'

'Rajat wasn't lying,' I said.

'The corpse was in his room. He must be exposed. And he said he had nothing to do with the boy's death. Please have some tea.'

'It's too hot for tea,' I said. What was she raving about? I was hot, sticky in this humid garden, among stifling big-leaved plants and tangled roots, its paths of wet mossy paving stones, the whir of gnats over the standing water, the biting flies and spiders. I did not know where to begin and I had the idea that she seemed like a different person because she was insane, especially crazy in this precious pose as an actress in a darkly comic drama.

'I'll go with you to the police,' she said. 'I was a fool to believe his reassurances. I always suspected that he was a malign influence on Charlie.'

'Malign' influence, not 'bad' influence – that was the sort of pretension you'd hear in a melodrama.

I said, 'You told me you didn't trust the police.'

'That was to induce you to take the assignment.'

I said, 'Why do you want me to tell the consulate what I found?'

'It seems to me that they should be told. It should be easy enough to let them know – after all, they're your friends. They should know, as the police should know. Rajat registered under an assumed name at the Ananda. This is very suspicious. He may have had a hand in the death of a child. He must be exposed.'

'And if I do it, if I prove that he's connected with the dead boy, the anonymous corpse, he could be charged with murder.'

'I don't know,' she said, but unconvincingly. 'He'd certainly have some explaining to do. But it would be all circumstantial.'

'Why do you say that?'

'Because the body is gone, presumably.'

'Not entirely.'

'What does that mean?' If she was disturbed, she did not show it. She went on sipping tea.

I took a plastic bag out of my briefcase, the bag yellow with formalin, and I pressed it to show her the pickled hand.

She squinted at it with deep curiosity, as though it might be something to eat, and she said without any emotion, 'That's disgusting. Is it human? Please put it away.'

'Not before I show you a detail.'

She winced, wrinkling her nose as I held it close. I said, 'See? No fingerprints. That's not unusual in certain trades. Masonry. Bricklaying. Cement work. And weaving. The fingerprints are worn smooth and are just about unreadable. So I've been told by someone who knows.'

All this time she had held her teacup at the level of her chin, as if to defend herself from me. Now she put the cup down.

'What are you saying?'

'This is the hand of a ten-year-old boy. The DNA tells a lot, though doesn't tell his name. He was wrapped in a carpet – one of your carpets. Very likely one of your workers.'

'Impossible.'

'Almost certainly. Mr Joshi told me that whenever someone dies at your factory, you personally take them to Varanasi to be cremated. I presume that's where this child was headed, until you wrapped him in one of your generic carpets, tore the label off and sent him to the Ananda, to Rajat's room.'

'You can't prove that,' she said.

'Maybe not, because you're like all the other foreigners in India – like Indians too. You delegate your jobs. Someone got this gruesome job. My guess is that not even Charlie knew.'

She had begun to laugh, but mirthlessly, a stage laugh. She said, 'Why would I have asked you to investigate this business if I'd known you could implicate me?'

'Because you hadn't counted on their keeping the carpet, it was such a cheap one. But we're in hard-up Calcutta. They dumped the body, not the carpet. And you hadn't imagined that a suspicious clerk who'd helped dispose of the child – another flunkey – would take pity and keep one of the hands.'

'You're wrong. Hindus never do that. They would immediately burn a body part.'

'Hindus, no. But this was a Christian. And a Naga. They have rather a fetish about body parts.'

'I had nothing to do with this. It's preposterous.'

'You knew all along what I just found out today at the consulate, that Rajat had applied for a work visa to the US. He was intending to emigrate. Had he got the visa, he'd be living with Charlie. That is something that seriously bothers you – his competition for Charlie's affection.'

She looked at me with a sour expression and said, 'Rajat is a kink. I suspect gender identity disorder. He probably wants gender reassignment. You have no idea what these people are like.'

I laughed at the terminology. I said, 'You concocted a plan to implicate Rajat in a crime. You had a corpse – that was convenient. When Rajat ran away instead of being caught by the hotel, the whole scheme came apart. So you put me on to it, another job delegated, so that you could compromise him. You assumed I'd be able to pin it on Rajat. If he was discredited, his visa application would be turned down. But I was lucky. I found out more than you thought I would.'

'I loved little Rajat, until you told me this.'

'You hated him. You wanted Charlie for yourself. And now you'll have him, because I'm sure that Rajat will be terrified when he finds out what you've done.'

She sat straight, her chin up, looking haughty. 'It's beneath me to argue with you. I've done nothing wrong. I haven't broken the law.'

She was impenetrable. Even when presented with the evidence of this obvious set-up, she was unmoved.

'Possibly true. But I'd like to know how this child died.'

She sipped a little tea, batting a fly away as she drank, and didn't reply.

'Worked to death, probably,' I said. 'I saw your factory. It's Dickensian. Little children imprisoned in a factory sweatshop, working on carpets. I saw Jyoti.'

She had begun to smile. 'This is India,' she said.

'Employing children is against the law,' I said.

'The law is never enforced because the children need work.'

'You're killing them.'

'I am saving them!' It was the only time in this conversation that she raised her voice, and this was a shriek of protest.

'And now I know where you get your labour force.' As I spoke I could hear the children laughing inside the Lodge. 'You take them off the streets. You buy them from villages. Poor places like Nagapatti. You get them healthy, you make them dependent on you and then you put them to work.'

'You don't know anything,' she said.

'I'm sure you sell some of them to adoptive parents. When I saw that woman last week, I knew.'

'I am saving them,' she hissed through her teeth, and I thought how her being slightly bucktoothed was an advantage in her saying something like that, to give it force. 'They would die otherwise.'

Now she frightened me, because she was without a shred of doubt. Her certainty gave her, if not power, then a demonic energy.

'I thought you had some intelligence, some subtlety,' she said. 'I had confidence in you. That's why I trusted you with this. But no, you're really hopeless. And you're ungrateful. You have no idea of the good I have done, the things I've accomplished. And not just this Lodge. Many things. Great things.'

She spoke with such conviction I almost believed her, but I also knew that a criminal's most useful gift was the ability to lie. It was one of the clearest signs of criminality that such a person had no use for the truth. Yet Mrs Unger was passionate.

'You think that by making up this preposterous story you've hurt me.' She leaned closer. 'You can't hurt me. But I could seriously harm you.'

*I won't give you a chance*, I thought, looking her straight in the eye.

She said, 'I'm going to do you an enormous favour.'

'Really.'

'Yes. I'm not going to destroy you. I could do it very easily.'

She was calm again; she had regained her composure. She saw that, though I knew the truth of the body in the hotel room, and Rajat would soon know, there was not much that I could do to hurt her. She was right: this was India. Child labour was common. The factories were everywhere. And children died.

'You're shocked,' she said. 'I despise people who come to India and say they're shocked. Especially Americans. What hypocrisy.'

If I had been enchanted before by her, I was now disenchanted. Yet having seen her dark side, I was even more astounded by her audacity. She now seemed to me as cruel as she had once seemed kind and I could not believe that both could exist in the same person, this American woman who affected saris and ran a home for lost children.

I didn't doubt that much of her work was unselfish, that she had (as she said) saved some children. But she saved them only to send them to work in her factory or sell them in adoptions. She wasn't wrong about there being child labour in India. Everyone knew it. But no one suspected her personal involvement. She was a motherly presence in Calcutta, famous because she never asked for donations. And she was persuasive. I could testify to the healing hands, the magic fingers. Gazing at her on this hot afternoon in the deep-green shade of her damp and tangled garden, I trembled to think how she had touched me, how I had touched her. How we had lain in each other's arms, knotted in the tantric postures. I had been bewitched.

Her beauty was distinct, but because it frightened me it seemed indistinguishable from ugliness. I thought: *There is no such thing as beauty.* There is desire and there is fear, and if desire can make a person luminous, fear can make that same person ugly. A lie in a lovely woman's mouth can give her fangs and make her a monster. The very features I had seen as benign and beautiful – the same cast of her face, the lips, the teeth, the breasts, the fingers – I now saw as fierce and deadly.

All this time we'd been talking I kept seeing the hard bone beneath her lovely skin, the hinges of her jaw, the seams of her cranium, the loops of her eye sockets. It was not a face but a skull. I saw her as bones.

'You've failed me,' she said. 'And I was such a fan. I had such plans for you.' She touched my thigh with her outstretched hands, her sharp finger bones on my leg. 'That's all right. I'm never surprised to find that people are stupid or wicked. I'm more surprised when they're kind.'

I didn't know what to say. I could not deny that she was kind – I'd seen enough examples of her charity. I'd been half in love with her. I was more ashamed of myself, more angry at myself than I was with her, because I saw my weakness reflected in her. Out of vanity and need I had yearned to please her. I was no better than she was.

'I still wonder why you chose me to look into this crime. Was it just because I'm a writer?'

'Not really.'

'What then?'

'Because you're not a writer. You're a hack. No matter what you write, no one will believe you.'

She obviously thought that by insulting me I would be hurt, but I was strengthened by my self-disgust. She could not have had a lower opinion of me than I had of myself. At that moment I wanted to kill her, and not just do away with her but stab her repeatedly in the face.

She smiled at me, as if reading my thoughts. Her face lit up – the glow I'd always found irresistible, of pleasure, of love.

'Darling.'

I almost responded. But she was looking past me, towards the far end of the garden, where Charlie was standing. I wondered how much of this he'd heard. He twinkled, the way someone does when he's eroticized. As I had once, giddily.

She beckoned to him. He obeyed, walking closer, and when she beckoned again it seemed like her way of dismissing me.

# 20

The burning ghat on the Hooghly was about a mile downstream from the Vidyasagar Bridge, which I had crossed with Mrs Unger on the day we'd visited the Kali temple, when she had taken me to the compound. I had been shocked by the goat sacrifice at the temple. I had been impressed by the intake of orphans at the compound. How was I to know the children, too, would be sacrificed, that they'd end up in her factory or be sold to visiting Americans? Rajat had remarked on the blood that had streaked her sari: *Bloodstained kind of suits her.*

I thought of that blood today as we turned off the bridge and made our way along the west bank of the river in Howard's consular car, a uniformed driver at the wheel, Howard beside him. I could see the ghat ahead, piled against the embankment like a rotting pier.

'I will talk to the priests,' Parvati said. She sat in the middle of the back seat, Rajat on her other side.

Parvati's decencies shamed me and so did her gifts. She was a pretty girl who lived with her parents; she could dance, play tabla, write poetry, do martial arts – could twist my arms off with a flourish of *kalaripayatu*. Parvati the beauty was awaiting a suitable match, which her parents would arrange. She was helpful, able and decorative. I had to admit I hardly knew her, but in any case I was unworthy: she was unattainable. But she was the perfect person for this ritual, a vestal virgin. She wasn't prim today. She knew exactly what to do and Rajat was a suitable acolyte.

Howard said, 'Your friend Mrs Unger was supposed to be getting an award tonight from the chief minister.'

'Don't know anything about it,' I said. 'What's the award?'

'Humanitarian achievement. She refused it.'

Rajat said, 'She hates publicity.'

Howard said, 'Her modesty was much praised. She got more publicity refusing it than she would have gotten by accepting.'

'She never asks for money,' Rajat said.

'I think we know why,' I said.

'We'll be watching her,' Howard said. 'Someone from the commercial section. After all, she's one of ours.'

'She deserves a prize for cleverly avoiding a murder charge. I can't think of anywhere but India where she'd be possible.'

The driver pulled off the road and parked by a drooping cow. He opened our doors and then stood by the car, guarding it. We walked slowly, gasping in the humid heat, through the weeds and low shrubs along a narrow path to the ghat. Three holy men sat cross-legged on the platform at the entrance, under an archway draped with fresh flowers. The men were gaunt and nearly naked, their faces set at us, their foreheads smeared with yellow paste. They did not blink at the flies darting around their long, matted and tangled hair.

Bowing low, Parvati stuffed some rupees into their brass jars. I did the same as she spoke to one of them.

'He asks if you have the body part.'

'The hand. It's here.'

I had wrapped it in a white cloth and tied it like a bundle, a makeshift shroud. Only I knew that it was stiff, claw-like, yellow, sealed in a plastic bag. A pickled hand.

The saddhu Parvati had been speaking to gathered himself and picked up a brass tray. He had loose, wrinkled skin, like seasoned leather, a loincloth like a nappy and necklace strings of heavy amber beads. He offered the tray to me. I put the cloth bundle on it.

With solemn grace, he brought this to one of the other old men and presented it reverently while the man muttered over it. Then he walked on to the ghat, holding the tray like a waiter serving dessert. Raising his arms, he tipped the tray, allowing the little bundle to slide on to the top of the pile of dry sticks, which were arranged as though for a campfire.

We watched from the embankment as the three saddhus began

chanting, deep and clear, almost melodious, a kind of droning with intermittent grunts that repeated and increased in speed and volume.

'I've never been this close to a cremation before,' Howard said.

Rajat snapped pictures. Parvati prayed, her head down – she seemed to be weeping softly. One of the holy men, still chanting, brought a flaming torch from a smouldering fire at the bank near where we stood. He whirled the ember, intensifying the flame, then poked it under the firewood until some of the smaller kindling caught and crackled. Then he added the torch to the noisy blaze.

The small white bundle lay on the uprushing fire. The licks of flame were like silk on this grey day. Then the thing seemed to tremble and to blacken without burning, and finally it lit, becoming thicker, fattened with flames. It glowed red like a large coal, keeping its shape but growing gauzy and insubstantial, withering like a tangle of whitened thread.

Maybe I imagined it – maybe it was the crack of the dry wood – but I thought I heard the dead hand itself speak, as if in the cooking it was given life by the blaze. I saw the hand outlined clearly as the cloth burned away. It was the last image I saw in the heat, the shadow of a hand that moved, jerked and clutched its fingers in the flames before it was consumed in a fizz of fire.

We all stared at it as it swelled to a light and cobwebby puffball of ash, bobbing lightly on the charred wood, emptied by the heat.

'Gone,' Howard said.

'No. Only changed form,' Parvati said – the Indian comeback, the sort of tease that kept Hindus faithful. She was still praying, still weeping softly. Rajat crept near her, his eyes glistening in sympathy as though sharing her grief.

'She gave you a lot of trouble,' Howard said.

I knew who he was talking about.

'She did me a huge favour,' I said.

'I've heard about her favours.'

'I'll tell you some time.'

He was smiling. His smile full of teeth was asking *what?* But he looked up and seemed to forget his question, because from the low, woolly-dark sky came the first drops of the monsoon.

Stinging drops of rain: I had never thought that rain could hurt so much.

Back at the Hastings, fresh from the burning ghat, I was relieved, knowing it was over. Time to leave.

'Post, sir,' Ramesh Datta said. 'A runner has brought it just now.'

An envelope. I recognized the handwriting, the ink, the dense handmade paper, like cloth. I brought it to my room and meditated on it. The handwriting was self-regarding. I hated seeing my name written in purple ink. I did not want to think what was in it – money, a miracle, praise or blame. I didn't need her any more.

I borrowed an umbrella from Ramachandra and walked to the Hooghly. Down Sudder, up Nehru, left on Ochterlony to the esplanade and then along Eden Garden Road to the river and Babu Ghat. It was the route of one of my old walks in the city, when I'd felt lost, waiting to be summoned by Mrs Unger. I paused in the downpour and flung the envelope into the river, setting it adrift in the greasy current with the flotsam of old fruit, rotting coconuts, curls of plastic and, sliding like scum from the ghats upriver, the buoyant ashes of human remains.

That ending, though true to the facts, now seems a little conventional. Other stories about India close with a cremation and the rain coming down hard – and you're left to imagine the finality of the downpour, the sweep of water like a curtain on the last act.

The real torrent didn't hit Calcutta until a week later and by then I was somewhere else, writing this book. Mrs Unger inspired it. She inspired much more, gave me the vitality to write it and taught me tantra – gave me the hands, the fingers, the energy.

I mentioned at the beginning that I had disappointed two women in my life and I suggested that I'd stopped looking for anyone else. But in the course of writing this book I met another woman, someone nearer my age. She'd had her share of disappointments too and at first she was wary of me. We became friends, partners and, at last, lovers. I knew how to please her, in ways she'd never known, and my pleasing her was a kind of teaching too. She returned the favour. I spent more time in the States and grew to like it more. Almost a whole year passed. We travelled, this woman and I. We bought a house together. I had learned to give myself, which is the beginning of love.

I look down at my hand, my fingers wrapped on the pen, poking at this last page, and I think of Mrs Unger, like an old flame, who gave me everything. But I didn't have to thank her for it, didn't have to be grateful. She was the illness and the cure, like a force of nature; life and death, the rain that gave hope, that flooded and drowned too; the pleasure and the pain.